DECEIVED

OTHER BOOKS AND AUDIO BOOKS
BY KATHI ORAM PETERSON

The Forgotten Warrior

An Angel on Main Street

The Stone Traveler

River Whispers

Cold Justice

Wanted

DECEIVED

=== A NOVEL ===

KATHI ORAM PETERSON

Covenant Communications, Inc.

Cover Image: *Cowgirl High Mountain Sunset* © Kent Fortie. For more information please call 801-205-3150.

Cover design copyright © 2014 by Covenant Communications, Inc.

Published by Covenant Communications, Inc.
American Fork, Utah

Printed in the United States of America
First Printing: November 2014

20 19 18 17 16 15 14   10 9 8 7 6 5 4 3 2 1

ISBN: 978-1-62108-853-0

To those who feel lost and alone in this world
Please know a loving Heavenly Father is always beside you.

ACKNOWLEDGMENTS

YEARS AGO MY SISTER, JO, took me on a cattle drive for research. She taught me how to saddle a horse, ride it, and herd cattle. I learned what it feels like to sit in the saddle all day, hear a rattlesnake, and run from a charging bull. Because of these experiences, I have been able to give more depth to the main characters in this book. Thank you, sis.

I have also been fortunate to travel to Ireland with my daughter Patrizia. We were there on St. Patrick's Day and found the country alive with celebration. I saw the dolmen at Poulnabrone, strolled on the Burren's limestone hills, and rode on a haunted bus tour of Dublin (I'm still a little scared). This story is filled with Irish touches. Thank you, Trizia.

I'd like to thank author Gregg Luke. Though he is a great writer, I leaned on his expertise as a pharmacist to help me find just the right drug I needed in this story. Thanks, Gregg.

I must thank my writing cohorts: Dorothy Canada, Ann Chamberlin, Terri Ferran, Tina Foster, Elizabeth Lane, Charlene Raddon, Maureen Mills, Linda White, and Roseann Woodward. Thank you, dear friends, for listening, reading, and critiquing parts of this book.

I am also extremely grateful to my fellow writers who went above and beyond by reading the entire manuscript: Brenda Bensch, Kathleen Dougherty, Kerri Leroy, Amanda Sowards, and Nikki Trionfo. I owe them my heartfelt appreciation.

I'd like to thank my publisher, Covenant Communications, Inc., and especially my wonderful and patient editor, Samantha Millburn. I also appreciate the many people at Covenant Communications for how they diligently strive to make each book a success.

I must thank my family: my husband for his constant belief in me and my children for their unswerving support. I could not write without them.

And finally, I am deeply grateful to my Heavenly Father for giving me the gift of writing. Because of this gift, I meet the most wonderful people and learn something new every day. I feel truly humbled and blessed.

CHAPTER ONE
REALITY BECOMES UNREAL

MUFFLED, QUARRELSOME VOICES, LIKE ARGUING ghosts, threaded through Tara Kelly's half-awakened mind. Murmurs echoed and reverberated, repeating patterns of sound. She struggled to reach full consciousness.

Thunder rattled the windows, finally jarring her numbed senses. She opened her eyes, but only smothering darkness met her gaze.

Must be a bad storm. Has to be the middle of the night.

She rolled onto one elbow in an effort to catch her breath. The pulse of her heart pounded in her ears. Tara pulled up to a sitting position. Gravity seemed to triple. She gasped for breath. What was wrong with her?

Perspiration soaked her nightgown. The hot room simmered in the silent blackness. Where was she? Had she really heard voices, or had she dreamed them? Perhaps the thunder mingled with sleep had conjured the sounds.

Just then, thunder echoed far away, and Tara swore she caught stealthy, closer voices beneath the rumble. She listened desperately.

Nothing.

But something was wrong.

She shook her head to clear it; her brain felt unmoored; her temples pounded. A dizziness, as if she'd risen too fast, clouded her vision. She had to get a grip.

A flash of lightning illuminated the antique armoire and settee near the foot of the bed. Tara's mind registered two of everything, but the brief double vision was enough.

Aunt Rosalie's house. Of course!

She'd been staying with her aunt for the last week. Even though Tara was more alert now, an unsettling weakness hung on her like a dark curtain. Her mind felt wrapped with gauze, reminding her of years ago when her grandfather had died and her life had spun out of control. All she needed was her aunt to see her in this state and she'd think Tara was having another breakdown and admit her to Twin Pines Psychiatric Hospital again.

That had been ten years ago. Tara had changed from that fragile nineteen-year-old and was now a successful twenty-nine-year-old bestselling children's book author and illustrator. Her doctor had taken her off depression meds long ago, and the only pill she was taking now was to help her sleep. She didn't take them very often; in fact, until she'd ended her relationship with Garrett, she hadn't taken one in months. Since their breakup and her moving in with Aunt Rosalie, she'd taken one every night.

Her aunt's house fell eerily quiet.

Wait.

Voices sounded in the living room.

Frenzied tones.

The voices are real and not a dream. Was Aunt Rosalie home? She was supposed to work late tonight. An officer in the Los Angeles police force, her aunt had a double shift and wasn't due home until morning.

Determined to find out what was going on, Tara swung her feet to the floor and fought a moment of vertigo. She felt her way to the door and panicked at the sudden amnesia she experienced. From the living room, she heard someone shout, "Get out!" and Tara suddenly remembered the thunder and the voices.

What is the matter with me?

She shook off her fear and opened the door a crack.

The living room was dark. From the dim porch light shining through slits in the curtain, Tara made out two blurry figures in the room: one tall and hefty like a man, one short and more slender like a woman. Another surge of dizziness made her grip hard on the door.

Struggling with a sense of sliding backward, she heard a muffled voice say, "You can't keep her from me." The man sounded like Garrett, yet she wasn't sure. He raised something shaped like a baton club above the woman's head.

This can't be happening.

Tara's stomach lurched with nausea. She forced herself to step into the corridor, leaning against the wall to stay upright.

As though watching a damaged flickering film, she saw the woman swing a hard right cross into her attacker's stomach. He doubled over. The woman pulled a gun. Taking aim on him, she yelled, "Get out!"

The man dropped the club and lunged, tackling her. The floor shuddered from the impact. A hard object slid against Tara's foot. She tried to focus on the swaying floor. Then she saw it.

Rosalie's 45 mm Glock.

A pained grunt came from her aunt, followed by the solid sound of knuckles meeting flesh. The man was going to kill her aunt. Tara had to help.

She slid down the wall and grasped the gun. The cold steel felt heavy and strange in her hand . . . but real.

I can do this. Just one clear shot.

With her last threads of strength, Tara willed herself to stand on unsteady legs. The man now straddled Rosalie, his hands around her neck.

Tara gripped the gun, her finger on the trigger, sweat stinging her eyes. Rosalie managed to hit her assailant in the face. He reeled backward.

The gun wavered in Tara's trembling hands. Her eyesight faded; spongy black dots began to blot away what little she could see.

She tried to keep the weapon pointed at the man as he and her aunt rolled across the floor, knocking over a lamp and an end table. The man's fist smashed against Rosalie's head, and Tara thought he'd killed her.

She had to do something. Now!

A loud, deafening blast ripped the room. Tara's vision went from charcoal gray to inky black. Fighting for the last strands of consciousness, the smell of burnt cordite filled her senses like poisonous gas, destroying love . . . destroying memory . . . destroying life.

* * *

Joseph White Eagle hated meeting strangers. But mostly, he hated coming to town when he was so badly needed at the ranch. May was the worst time to be called away even for one day. He should be riding the range, helping his men prepare for the spring cattle drive. Instead, he was here waiting by the baggage claim, eyeing passengers who disembarked from the LA flight.

He leaned his tired back against the cold wall of the Idaho Falls Airport concourse and shoved his hands deep inside the pockets of his worn denim jacket.

Joseph's cousin Mac had called late last night. He'd been there for Joseph through some mighty rough times; so of course Joseph said he'd do whatever he could to help. Mac's girlfriend had been murdered, and he needed a place to hide her niece, Tara Kelly, who had witnessed the crime. He didn't want to use the federal protection program because most of those people the authorities were hiding were criminals. Tara Kelly wasn't a criminal. She was a victim who needed special care. Besides, this was personal to Mac, and he wanted to make certain Tara was with someone he knew, someone he trusted.

In fact, Mac had asked Joseph to curtail Internet usage because the murder suspect, who was also a cop, was a computer genius. If anyone Googled names connected to this case, the killer would find them. Staying off the Internet wasn't a problem. Joseph was the only person on the ranch who used it, but to be on the safe side, he locked his laptop in his gun safe.

Mac had even taken Tara's cell phone so she couldn't be traced through her GPS. Even though cell phone service was sketchy at best in the remote regions of Idaho, a cell phone's GPS could still give her location to someone who knew what they were doing.

Joseph had Tara's name and the flight number, but that was about it. Mac's description of her was sparse: long brown hair and green eyes. That should be enough. Besides, she would look like she was grieving.

Grief was familiar to Joseph. His heart skipped as memories of his late wife, Jenny, threatened to surface. He owed so much to the Lord.

Shortly after his wife died, two Mormon missionaries knocked on his door. They taught him this life was only a step in our eternal progression and families could be together forever. This knowledge had awakened him from grief and made him realize Jenny would always be with him. She was probably the one who'd guided the missionaries to his door. She was expecting him to take care of their little girl, and to do that, Joseph had decided to move back home to his father's ranch in Little Lost River, Idaho.

He watched luggage appear on the conveyor belt. People jammed together, trying to claim their suitcases. Scanning the crowd, he couldn't see a lone woman.

Frustration bubbled up inside him. He had to get going. This was taking too much time. Time he didn't have to spare thanks to other troubles they'd had on the ranch.

All had been well until this last year. First the barn had caught fire, and rebuilding had cost three times what the contractor had estimated. They now had a heavy mortgage to pay off. Then a strange epidemic of hoof fungus had infected over a hundred head of his prime Herefords, which he'd had to put down. Last fall he could only send three-quarters of what he needed to market. He hoped a summer in the mountains on acreage he leased from the Bureau of Land Management would help the remaining cattle grow strong and healthy so by this fall he could recoup some of his losses. At least the Appaloosas were untouched. His herd of prime horses was his pride and joy, though he'd had to sell quite a few to keep the ranch going.

A tickling panic was continually growing inside Joseph that he might lose his ranch, his late father's ranch. In the midst of all this trouble, why was the Lord sending a woman in jeopardy his way?

Staying near the baggage claim area and the exit/entrance, Joseph watched as a trio of giggling girls, a businessman carrying a briefcase, and a matronly woman wheeling a suitcase walked past, all staring at him. Had they only seen a Native American in western movies? Good grief! He wasn't dressed in Nimi'ipuu buckskins or wearing a feathered headdress, just normal ranching clothes.

Nearing the exit, one of the straggling passengers lit up a cigarillo on his way out to the smoking area. Tailings of the aromatic smoke drifted to Joseph. He breathed deeply as he savored the scent. Joseph had quit smoking when he'd converted to the Church. The long, thin, brown cigar had been his favorite. His lungs craved one more sniff. Too quickly, the cedarwood scent disappeared.

As Joseph pined for one last whiff, two men passed him on their way to the ticket counter. One was dressed in an Armani suit, the other in designer jeans and a T-shirt. An odd-looking pair, but both spoke of money. After Suit Man got his ticket and said good-bye, his friend turned to leave. Joseph recognized the tanned and goatee-faced man.

Denver Harris saw Joseph at the same time. He had been a pain in Joseph's side for the last couple of years. Joseph had no desire to speak with him, but the man walked straight toward him. Not a person to back down, Joseph stood his ground. "Harris."

The lean egotist stopped a few feet from him. "Want to know who I just put on a plane?"

Joseph didn't answer.

"I'll tell you anyway. My good friend and lawyer, Winston Phillips. Ever heard of him?"

Again Joseph didn't say anything.

Harris went on. "He is famous for never losing a case. He's going to stop you from grazing your cattle on federal land."

"I lease the land where my cattle graze. My money helps pay for the upkeep of the rivers and streams you say you hold so dear."

"But your cattle are polluting the streams and killing off the bull trout. I intend to put a stop to it."

His tone and stare rankled Joseph. "It's not my cattle that's polluting. The BLM built miles and miles of enclosures to keep the cattle out of the streams. What you don't seem to grasp is that there are other animals that do the damage—moose, bear, elk, to name a few. Are you going to take them to court as well?"

"I might not be able to stop them, but I can stop you." The pencil-thin man turned and walked away.

Joseph pulled a cinnamon toothpick from his shirt pocket and stuck it in his mouth. The taste of cinnamon was a poor substitute for nicotine, but chewing the toothpick calmed his nerves. Harris was as irritating as a mosquito. In the last couple of years, he had sent Joseph a pile of threatening letters. This incident was yet another drop in the bucket of Harris's threats. And Joseph didn't have time to deal with him. Not now.

Finally, the last passenger exited the gate: a slender woman, around five foot six. Her eyes were hidden behind mirrored sunglasses. A black scarf covered her hair. She wore a navy blue suit that hung too big on her slight frame. With great trepidation, she neared him, skittish as a colt during a lightning storm.

This had to be Ms. Kelly.

She reached up and tugged off the scarf. Thick mahogany hair fell in giant curls to her elbows. Pulling the sunglasses from her face, her cautious eyes—green as watercress under clear creek water—blinked up at him. A timid smile pulled at her lips, and for a second, Joseph's heart stopped, then drum rolled. A prickling hit his lips and went down his throat.

He swore standing before him was his late wife, Jenny.

CHAPTER TWO
BITING WORDS

BLINKING BACK TEARS, TARA STARED at the man in front of her. His bronzed face could have been sculpted from metal, including the scar that arced over one high cheekbone. A black Stetson dipped low over his forehead. Contemplating eyes shaded by dark brows framed the gaze that probed over her like he thought he knew her. His temples flexed as he stepped back. Staring warily at her, he chewed on the toothpick clenched between his teeth.

Mac had said his cousin was part Native American, but he hadn't said he was broodingly good-looking or that he was withdrawn and suspicious of strangers. The last thing she needed was to be around someone who didn't trust her. She was tempted to make an about-face and return to the airplane. But with her aunt dead, Tara had no safe place to go. She swallowed hard, remembering her promise to stay in Idaho until Mac arrested Garrett.

She needed to stay put.

The man's hand trembled as he tilted his Stetson, and Tara realized he was visibly shaken. She'd misjudged the look in his gaze as suspicion when it wasn't that at all. What could it be? He finally managed to say, "Ms. Kelly?" His rich baritone voice vibrated from deep within his chest.

"Yes. Are you Joseph White Eagle?"

He slowly inclined his head. His eyes were as dark as black onyx, with tiny flecks of chocolate melting into them.

"Luggage?" He seemed to avoid her gaze, looking at the people clustered around the baggage claim area.

"No. There wasn't enough time. Mac grabbed these clothes and my purse." Tara was grateful her makeup and pills were inside.

He bit on the toothpick in his mouth and nodded like he understood.

"I have a little cash, but Mac told me not to withdraw money from my bank or use my credit cards. He even took my cell phone from me." Her voice faltered.

"Where we're going, you won't need one." His dark eyes locked onto hers. "Don't worry. We have a landline at the house. My cell phone is in my glove box most of the time. I rarely use it. As far as not having a change of clothes, I'm sure Bear will find you some at the ranch." Again he studied her, and just as Tara wanted to ask who Bear was, the man said, "Sorry 'bout your aunt. Truck's out front." He headed for the exit.

Tara trailed him outside. He walked toward an old Ford, and she caught up and went to the passenger door. Taking hold of the handle, she pulled it open. A snarl of white teeth and a throaty growl mere inches from her face caught her off guard.

Startled, Tara whirled around and reached for Joseph, who stood behind her. He was rigid, unyielding. She was embarrassed by her knee-jerk reaction of reaching out for help, especially since this stranger clearly wanted nothing to do with her. But Tara felt justified. The dog had been about to attack her.

"Scrap," Joseph scolded. "Knock it off." The dog, a brown-and-white border collie mix, melted into puppy tail and body wags. Looking at Tara, Joseph said, "He's protective of me and my friends." With a wave of his hand, he motioned the dog toward the driver's side of the blanketed bench seat. The animal immediately obeyed.

Joseph gestured for Tara to get in. Cautiously, she climbed inside the cab. Scrap cocked his head, one brown-spotted ear erect, the other flopping down. The dog seemed to smile. Tara had a strong feeling Scrap thought she was his master's friend, which meant she was now under Scrap's protection.

Tara could use all the friends she could get, even if one was a dog. She thought of Joannie, her best friend in LA. She worked for the LAPD with Rosalie and had a passion for drawing. When she learned Tara Kelly, the national bestseller of children's picture books, was Rosalie's niece, she had to meet her. They became instant friends. However, since Tara had broken up with Garrett, she and Joannie had spoken only a couple of times. And last night Mac had warned Tara against contacting anyone in LA until Rosalie's murder was solved. Joannie would be worried sick learning Rosalie was dead and Tara was gone too. Maybe later Tara could find a way to get a message to her.

As Joseph drove out of the airport parking lot, Scrap inched toward Tara, sniffing at her legs. Finally, the animal lay on the seat and rested his muzzle on Joseph's thigh.

The freeway headed north. In the distant landscape to the west and east were mountain ranges shaped like jagged saw blades. Along the freeway grew occasional clumps of what Tara assumed were weeds, though they had small, pretty blossoms, some yellow, some purple. Square plots of farmland with modest houses and looming shade trees flipped by. Small, leafy green plants dotted fields of brown, furrowed rows.

Idaho was a totally different world to Tara. Just yesterday she had been in LA and Rosalie had been alive. Now Tara's situation was unthinkable and confusing. Here she was with this cowboy—well, part Native American—in his beat-up truck, heading to the other side of nowhere. Tara had to find normalcy, had to make sense of something. The silence was smothering.

"Mac was so nice to think of my safety," she said. "He and my aunt worked on the police force but not together. Mac was in charge of his own department, which was probably just as well since Aunt Rosalie could get him to do most anything she wanted him to. He loved her so much."

A swell of emotion rose to her throat. She remembered how Rosalie had been so in love with Mac that she'd gone against Grandpa's wishes and moved some of her things into Mac's place without their being married. Gaining control of her emotions, Tara said, "Mac mentioned you were on the Los Angeles police force."

Joseph didn't reply, his attention focused on the road. Had he heard her? She tried again. "What made you decide to leave California and take up farming?"

He shot her a look she couldn't read. "I didn't."

"You obviously left California." She couldn't understand why he was upset.

"I didn't take up *farming*."

"Oh, but I thought—"

"I left California and took up *ranching*. My father's ranch. Appaloosa horses and Hereford cattle. If we *farmed*, it would be called a *farm*."

Tara exhaled an exasperated sigh. A farm? A ranch? Big deal. She decided to abandon her attempt to start up a conversation.

* * *

Inwardly Joseph kicked himself. He hadn't meant to sound sarcastic. She was from the city and didn't know the difference between a ranch and a farm. And she couldn't help that to Joseph she looked like the spitting image of his late wife. He was mixing what he wanted to see with reality.

Jenny had been gone for a long time. He hadn't even looked at her picture for several years. Seeing his wife's smiling face only reminded him of what he'd lost. Sure, there had been times they didn't get along. Jenny had resented the hours Joseph had spent at work, and she'd become suspicious and moody, but he chose not to remember that. Instead, he focused on the happy times. All that was gone now. He'd told himself not to look backward but forward. That's why seeing Ms. Kelly's timid smile, so like Jenny's, was painful and haunting. No wonder his patience was spent and his words were biting. Still, Ms. Kelly didn't deserve his rude behavior.

Joseph couldn't believe how sharp he'd been. True, he hated meeting strangers, but he was still usually easygoing and friendly toward them. Perhaps he'd snapped like he had because something had happened when she had grabbed on to him to get away from Scrap. Her touch had stirred emotions he'd thought were long gone. This poor woman was not responsible for the tangled feelings tying his insides into knots.

"I left the police force five years ago, after my wife was murdered," Joseph said to make amends and to at least try to be friendly.

Ms. Kelly took a shaky breath, and Joseph had to restrain himself from reaching over to comfort her.

"Does the pain of losing someone ever heal?" she asked after a moment.

She sounded lost and alone. Joseph knew exactly how she felt. "You never get over losing a loved one, especially to violence." His past life pounded on the door that shielded him from pain. Guilt shadowed him, nagged him. If he hadn't been so stubborn and insisted on going on that drive, if he'd followed Jenny's intuition and turned left instead of right, maybe the killer wouldn't have found them. If he hadn't swerved, the bullet would have hit him instead of Jenny. If he had stopped trying to track down the bad cop who had been feeding information to gangs and quit his job as Jenny had continually begged him to do, she would be alive today.

If . . . if . . . if . . .

But the cold hard facts were not ifs. Because of his bullheadedness, his wife had been killed instead of him.

Take a deep breath.

He stole a quick look at Ms. Kelly again. Her shoulders were slumped, her cheeks pale. When it came to females, Joseph was a disaster waiting for a catastrophe. For some reason, God wanted him to help Tara Kelly. Joseph might question why, but he'd do it. Somewhere, sometime, he knew the Lord would show him the reason.

In order to avoid saying the wrong thing again, Joseph decided he'd say nothing at all. Scrap's doggy snores played against the noise of the Ford's engine.

"What did Mac tell you when he called?" Ms. Kelly asked.

Joseph's intention not to talk dissolved. "That you saw your aunt"—he wanted a more gentle word than *murdered*—"die and that the alleged killer, Garrett Parker, was a cop and might be after you, so keeping your identity hidden was critical." He glanced at Ms. Kelly, whose entire demeanor shriveled. She needed to relax and think of something else. He continued. "Let's not talk about it. What do you do for a living?"

She appeared relieved and was breathing more easily. "I write and illustrate children's picture books. Most of them have to do with Irish folklore. My grandfather was from the old country. Not long after Aunt Rosalie was born, my grandmother was in and out of hospitals a lot. When she died, Ireland held too much sorrow for Grandfather, so he sold his family's estate and moved to America. But he always longed to return."

Joseph understood the sorrow and the need for a new start. He thought about what she'd said about picture books. "Wait a minute." Joseph took a hard look at her. "Are you *the* Tara Kelly who writes and draws those books my daughter reads?"

"Possibly. I wish I could have brought my art satchel. But everything happened so quickly, and by the time I thought of them, I was on the plane here." She seemed to be going through a mental checklist. "I missed my May first deadline. My editor is probably trying to find me." She grew quiet, as if a cold wave of gruesome reality had washed over her. "How can I think of work when my aunt has been killed?" She bit her pink, bottom lip. A tear slid down her cheek, and she swiped at it. "I was there! But I can't remember what happened."

Joseph let a calming silence ease between them. After a while, he said, "Don't punish yourself. Blips in memory have a way of protecting us from pain."

"But I remember taking my sleeping pill and going to bed, and then all of a sudden, I was in Mac's car. He was grilling me with questions I couldn't answer. He told me that as he'd pulled up to the house, Garrett had come out carrying a gun. He jumped in his car and took off. Mac found me stumbling around in Aunt Rosalie's flower garden. He said I was picking flowers." Ms. Kelly closed her eyes as if she felt the craziness of her words.

She pressed her palm against her forehead. "I remember blurry silhouettes and"—her eyes opened, squinted, and searched for more—"a loud blast and a smell like something had burned." She shuddered and looked at Joseph. "Why can't I remember?"

He couldn't stop himself. He reached over and patted her shoulder. "It will be all right. Give yourself time."

"I don't have time." Inhaling, she straightened in her seat. "I have to remember for Aunt Rosalie and for Mac." Her sad expression morphed into anger. "I want Garrett to suffer. I want him caught. And if I could, I'd be his executioner."

Surprised at the force of Ms. Kelly's words, Joseph understood why she felt so strongly. "Mac was upset when he called and didn't give me very many details. What does Garrett look like? Just in case he shows up."

"He's about your height, curly blond hair and blue eyes. He surfs a lot, so he has a dark tan."

"How long has Garrett worked for the department? Maybe I know him."

"He started three years ago, though Aunt Rosalie only introduced him to me last January. See, my grandfather left us some money, and she was always worried guys would date me for that reason. She thought Garrett was someone we could trust. We started dating, but he got so needy, called me three and four times a day, wanted to know where I was all the time. I started to feel smothered and broke up with him. He became so angry, he kicked a hole in my screen door. Aunt Rosalie offered to let me stay with her for a while." Exhaustion caught up with her, and her voice grew raspy. "Funny how you think you know people, and then find out they're not who you thought they were at all."

"Why do you think Garrett would kill your aunt?" The detective side of Joseph couldn't help but ask.

"That's just it. I can't think of a reason, unless she wouldn't let him see me and he blew up. He has a temper. Still . . ." Her voice trailed off.

"Well, people can be unpredictable and even downright deceptive." Joseph looked at Ms. Kelly and caught her in a yawn. Her eyes were sleep heavy. Turning his attention to the road before them, he knew he had to talk to her about what identity she wanted to use while staying at the ranch. He hadn't even thought about what he was going to tell his family and friends. Mac had called so late, and this morning Joseph had left before anyone else had stirred. "What should we tell everyone about you? Is there a name you'd like to go by?"

When she didn't answer, he glanced at her. Tara had fallen asleep. Poor thing had been living a nightmare for the last twenty-four hours. She'd been traveling on very little sleep and had to be completely exhausted. And even though they'd just been talking, riding in the truck with miles and miles of highway ahead of them must have lulled her to sleep.

That was all right. She needed to rest. He could ask her later.

* * *

When Tara awoke, to her surprise, Scrap was sitting in front of her on the floorboards of the truck. The animal's eyes were deceitfully innocent. Scrap sniffed one of Tara's bare legs. His cold, wet nose trailed up to her thigh, under her skirt.

Cautiously, she tried to push the animal away. "You have a very friendly pooch. Did you train him to do this?"

"Scrap!" As Joseph reached to push the dog away, his hand brushed Tara's arm.

Tara flinched.

Joseph's gaze locked onto hers as he seemed to gauge her overreaction to his touch. Breaking eye contact, he spat out, "*Scrap*, get up here."

The animal jumped onto the seat, blocking Tara's view. She was relieved because she didn't know if she could stand another moment of Joseph staring at her like he wished he could read her mind.

Ignoring the dog and Joseph, she peered out the window at miles and miles of silver-tinged sagebrush. She glanced at her watch. She'd slept nearly an hour. The truck turned northeast where a forest service sign pointed to Mill Canyon Road. A majestic snow-tipped mountain range rose before them. At the base of the mountains, cattle grazed. A small herd of antelope stood amongst them. Nearer to the road, a cluster of birds circled high in the sky.

"What are those birds called? And what are they doing?"

Keeping his hands on the steering wheel, he leaned close to her and peered out of the passenger window in the direction she had pointed.

He looked at her. Maybe it was his nearness or just the fact that his eyes reminded her of rich mocha, but Tara felt her insides clench as she held her breath. This man was darn attractive. Too attractive.

How could she think this way? She was running for her life, and her aunt had been murdered. Her feelings were all over the place. She had to stay on her guard and direct her thoughts to remembering what had happened last night, not stupidly thinking how good-looking the man protecting her was.

Joseph straightened in his seat and started to slow the truck. "Those are red-tailed hawks, and their circling is not a good sign. They usually eat mice, but a group of them means an animal is either dead or injured. Just hope it's not one of my cows. Since the turnoff, we've been on the ranch." He pulled to the side of the road and stopped. "I've got to see what they're fussing over." He got out, and Scrap jumped after him before Joseph shut the door, then they strode off through the sagebrush.

Tara was glad to be away from him and alone with her thoughts. But she didn't want to think of Rosalie's death or of Garrett being a murderer. No, she needed to find comfort. Tara turned her thoughts to her grandfather. He'd taken her in after her parents had died. Tara was only eight, and the Irish legends he had told her as she'd sat on his knee in front of the slow-burning fire opened a magical world to her that she drew into stories. Grandfather had loved to watch her draw and had told her if she learned all she could about drawing, her work could one day help others and make her famous.

Her grandfather had been a *shanachie*, a storyteller. With an expressive brow and a twinkle in his soulful eyes, he could weave a mystical tale of his Celtic homeland like nobody else. Some were happily-ever-after stories, but others were not. Like life, Tara supposed. Perhaps in his own way, Grandfather had been warning her of trouble yet to come because bad times had soon found them.

Aunt Rosalie had been too serious to be taken in by her father's storytelling. And even though Grandfather had tried his best not to quarrel with his daughter in front of Tara, sometimes Tara had overheard them. As Tara thought about the strain in their voices, she remembered how angry Rosalie had been.

Why was Tara thinking of that now?

With a shaky hand, she smoothed her hair away from her face, settling it behind her ear. *Odd how tragedy unearths buried thoughts and emotions.*

It would do no good to dwell on the past—it only made her realize how much she'd lost.

The fact was—Rosalie was dead.

And Tara had been a coward yet again by running away without giving her aunt a decent funeral. Mac had said the coroner needed to do an autopsy, but he would call her on Joseph's landline to let her know when they released the body. He claimed his cell phone was secure and the landline at Joseph's would make it hard for Garrett to trace.

How Tara wished she could call Joannie. She would have kept Tara updated without her having to bother Mac. Joannie might know how long Tara would have to wait before she could bury Aunt Rosalie. Tara didn't even know what kind of funeral to have. Should she call a priest or pastor? For a second, she wished she'd been as religious as her grandfather. After all the tragedy that had plagued her family, Tara didn't believe in God. What kind of God would take so many of her loved ones and leave her alone?

And I am alone.

She remembered how Grandfather used to say a person really wasn't a responsible adult until they turned thirty. Tara would be thirty in a couple of months, yet she didn't feel even close to being a responsible adult. She should have stayed in LA and taken care of things. Tara glanced out the window and watched Joseph's distant image disappear behind a sagebrush-covered rise.

* * *

Walking over a ridge, Joseph sidestepped Indian paintbrush and blooming cactus flowers, all the time listening for rattlesnakes. Ms. Kelly's concerned face was on his mind as she tried to remember what happened to her aunt. He understood what she was going through, how her emotions were whirling from shock. *Poor thing. And here I think she looks like Jenny. How stupid!*

He came upon the downed cow the hawks were circling over and a calf near her, bawling and looking at Joseph like he could make everything all right again.

Joseph squatted beside the Hereford's back and stroked her side. She wasn't breathing. The animal was still warm, but her round eyes were frozen open in a lifeless stare. He noticed thick blood saturating the ground.

Puzzled, Joseph walked to the other side for a better view. There was a wound through the chest near the cow's front leg. The bullet had hit her heart. She'd never had a chance.

Poachers would have taken the meat, not left it to rot in the sun. Who would have shot a cow for no reason? His mind went back to his confrontation with Harris at the airport. Was this what he'd meant by stopping Joseph? He wouldn't be stupid enough to think he could shoot cattle without getting caught. And if he were caught, it would damage his lawsuit. Harris was an egotistical jerk, but he wasn't stupid.

Joseph scanned the mountainside, where a shooter could hide. Could it have been Garrett Parker? Unlikely. The man hadn't had time to figure out where Tara was heading and get there before she did. Plus, why would he shoot a cow?

Nope, the shooter was sending Joseph a message. Long ago, his Nez Perce father had warned him about other people's prejudice and how sometimes, despite what they said to his face, they harbored resentment toward him because of his success and skin color.

But that was then . . . This was now. Most of his neighboring ranchers respected Joseph and his mother. Still, he wondered. Hard to believe, in this day and age, a man could hate you just because of the color of your skin. Of course, there were laws against it, but those laws had a hard time reaching the country. It was nearly impossible to legislate away long-held discrimination. He thought about the barn burning down and the strange siege of hoof fungus. Were they really misfortune? Joseph couldn't think of a single rancher who would stoop so low. Besides, they couldn't give his cattle hoof fungus.

Could the killer—the man who killed Jenny all those years ago—have finally found him? Was this some kind of vendetta? Definitely possible. The murderer had never been caught.

No! That would be too coincidental. Protecting Ms. Kelly had his imagination jumping all over the place.

Tugging his pocketknife from his jeans, Joseph cut the tags from the animal's ear. He would match the numbers with the calf's and note it in his books. Another dead cow. Would things ever start looking up?

Scrap yipped, drawing Joseph's attention. The dog stood by the calf that now lay on the ground. Immediately, Joseph went over to them.

"What's the matter, little guy?" As Joseph stroked the calf, he found blood. A bullet had pierced the animal's leg muscle. Whoever had shot the mama cow had meant to kill her. This wound was different. This wound was to maim and draw attention.

Joseph jerked his head up and scanned the mountain again, studying the boulders and thick stands of pine trees, trying to see the killer. Shooting harmless cows was little short of cold-blooded murder. Whoever had done this was making a statement.

But what was it?

And more importantly, why now?

CHAPTER THREE
ONE LONG BRONC RIDE

"GET THE BLANKET FROM BEHIND the seat!" Tara heard Joseph yell.

She jumped out of the truck, jerked the bench seat forward, and found a dusty army blanket. By the time she pulled it out, Joseph—followed closely by his dog—had reached her. He held a limp calf in his arms. Blood smeared the creature's hide. All at once, cloudy images came to Tara's mind.

Blood.

Red crimson blood on the wooden floor.

Aunt Rosalie's hair soaked in it.

The image was sharp. Vivid. Before she could make sense of the scene, it vanished. Closing her eyes, Tara strained to remember more, but nothing came. She wiped her brow with trembling hands and stared at the man before her, the injured animal in his arms. What must Joseph think of her standing here like an idiot? Well, she wasn't going to explain. Not right now. The calf was most important. "What can I do?" Tara asked, trying to act normal.

Perspiration trailed down the sides of Joseph's face. "Open the tailgate."

Tucking the blanket under her arm, she followed him to the rear of the truck and reached to pull the handle but found a rusty wire twisted around it.

"That's to tie a red flag on whenever I'm hauling." He readjusted his hold on the calf.

Dropping the blanket to use both hands, Tara ignored the wire and pulled up on the latch. She pushed and pushed on the stubborn tailgate. As it slowly opened, its hinges groaned. Suddenly, it gave way and dropped down. Tara bumped her forehead on the tailgate before falling to the ground. The sleeve of her jacket ripped on the wire, and she felt blood trickle down her arm. She'd been cut. Not wanting to make a fuss, she stood and tried to act like nothing had happened.

Joseph stared at her. "You okay?"

Tara tried to smile. "Just a little scrape."

"Lay the blanket inside the truck bed."

Despite her injury, Tara immediately did what Joseph asked. She noticed several huge, white blocks, each about the size of a desktop printer, in the truck bed and wondered what they were but didn't ask.

"You have a good goose egg coming on your forehead." Looking between Tara and the calf, Joseph eased the animal onto the wool material, then grabbed Tara's hand. He rolled up her sleeve and examined the gash. Pulling a large red bandana from his hip pocket, he wrapped her cut arm. "Can't do much for your forehead, but I'll take better care of this when we get to the ranch. When was the last time you had a tetanus shot?"

Her head throbbed, and her cut burned. "Don't know. Right now, this little one comes first. I'm fine."

"You're sure?"

She nodded.

Joseph reached out as if to hug her but stopped. Instead, he turned his attention back to the animal.

Watching him tuck the blanket beneath the unconscious calf's head, she asked, "What happened?"

"He's been shot." Joseph glanced at his watch. "It'll take us another fifteen minutes to reach the ranch."

The mere thought of gunfire chilled Tara to her core.

"We'd better get going." He started for the cab.

"But . . ." Tara gazed at the calf. "He can't ride back there by himself."

"You ever driven a stick?" Joseph asked.

"What?" Tara didn't understand what he was talking about: "driven a stick." Then it dawned on her. "You mean a stick shift?"

Joseph gave her a what-else-would-I-mean look.

"No. But I can stay with the calf." Tara grabbed hold of the side of the truck and tried to step up, but her skirt was too tight.

Joseph stopped her. "Look, I don't want to frighten you, but the calf's wound is fresh, which means whoever shot him could still be close by."

She scanned the mountain, worried the shooter could have been Garrett. For too long, Tara had let fear rule her life. She gazed at the helpless calf. This little creature needed help, and she couldn't bear for him to be left alone in the bed of the truck. "I'll be fine."

"If something happens to you, I . . ." Joseph stared at her, and he must have somehow understood how she felt. "Okay, but stay low. I'm going to be driving like a bat out of you-know-where."

Tara found it odd yet refreshing that a man would hesitate to swear. Again, she tried to step up on the bumper of the truck.

Joseph grabbed hold of her waist and boosted her onto the tailgate. His touch took her breath away. His eyes lingered on her forehead. "That's quite a goose egg. Are you sure you're all right?" He peered into her eyes, and Tara didn't know why, but she felt safe. This cowboy would take good care of her. For the first time since her world had been turned over and stepped on, a small bud of faith that everything would work out grew within her.

Ignoring her pain, she said, "I'm fine."

"I'll scoot the calf past the salt blocks, closer to the cab." Standing beside the pickup bed, he grabbed the blanket corner and tugged the animal nearer to the front.

Tara hurried to the animal and eased down on the floorboards. Feeling Joseph's worried gaze on her, she looked up.

He stood there with broody dark eyes staring back. The scar over his cheekbone twitched; his temples flexed, and once again, Tara had the feeling that Joseph White Eagle thought he knew her.

* * *

The road had been graded not too long ago. Still, a few ruts remained. Joseph skillfully drove around them. He worried about Tara. However, he truly felt that someone's shooting his cattle had been a personal grudge against *him*. For now, Ms. Kelly was safe in his truck and he needed only to worry about the knock she had suffered to her head and that nasty-looking cut on her arm. But something else bothered him about her.

Mental torment ignited in her eyes every now and again. She was fighting an inner battle—a battle that would be difficult to win unless she had help. He knew because to this day, he fought grief and the "what ifs" that haunted him.

He issued a silent prayer and pled for help from above. Something beyond his understanding was going on. Only God could guide him through it to help him keep her safe.

He passed under the log archway gate, where, burned in bold letters, were the words *White Eagle Appaloosa Ranch*. His father's people, the Nimi'ipuu, or Nez Perce, had been the first to breed quality Appaloosas, making the horse popular in America. A small part of him wished Ms. Kelly were in the cab instead of Scrap so he could point out the sign and direct her attention to something other than her loss.

* * *

A thick coat of dust covered Tara. As she wiped grit from her face, her eyes fell on a glimmering lake not more than two hundred feet away. It looked peaceful and calm, like it had nothing to hide, nothing to frighten her like the lake at her grandfather's. This was not that lake. No. Beautiful horses with colorful leopard-spotted coats on their hindquarters lazily grazed in the pasture near the water. Sunlight flickered over Tara and the calf as the road wound through pines and shade trees.

Turning her attention back to the animal beside her, she patted its white furry forehead marked with an unusual brown splotch shaped like a shamrock between his eyes. "Little calf, please don't die." She thought of an Irish blessing Grandpa Kelly had recited to her. The words tumbled through her mind, and she whispered, "Twice the blessing of God on you, little one." She stroked his forehead down to his pink nose. "Holy Michael Archangel, bless the beast. In the name of the Father, Son, and Holy Spirit."

The little prayer was meant to make people feel better, and amazingly, it did make her feel better. The animal's breath wafted over her hand. "You're going to make it, little Shamrock, not because of an old Irish blessing but because there's been too much dying."

As the road curved, a house came into view. She was surprised to see a modern cabin with picturesque windows looking out on the lake. A newer, mismatched wing protruded west toward the barn and another to the south. The beautiful lake shimmered beyond. Did this lake hide secrets? She couldn't help but wonder. The smell of freshly mown grass sprawling down the hill to the water's edge filled her senses. Had Tara arrived in some kind of heaven, or was this cover for some kind of hell?

* * *

Joseph jumped out of the truck with Scrap on his heels as his seven-year-old daughter, Katelen, ran out of the house, slamming the kitchen's screen door behind her.

"Daddy! She's here!"

His little girl took after his Nez Perce side more than her white mother's. Her round cheeks flushed, and her copper-colored eyes opened wide; then she rubbed her snubbed nose and tossed a black braid over her shoulder.

"Who?" Confused, Joseph tried to understand what she was talking about. He'd told no one he was going to Idaho Falls or that they were to have a guest.

"The mare from Wyoming." Katelen's sunshine smile now made sense. Joseph glanced toward the barn. Sure enough, a fancy metallic-gold horse trailer hooked to a gold GMC pickup was parked in front of the barn's double doors. He couldn't believe he'd missed the neon vehicle.

A man dressed in Wild Bill Hickok attire and looking like the typical wannabe cowboy dude leaned against the front fender of the GMC. This had to be Mr. Odell, who had called and set this up a few days ago. He held the lead rope to a buckskin Appaloosa mare that ignored the humans and nibbled on the grass.

Joseph heard trouble came in threes, but today it was a stampede. The most pressing issue right now was the calf. "Where's Allen?"

"Daddy," Katelen scoffed. "You sent him to check the line shacks two days ago."

Joseph had forgotten. Allen was the ranch foreman and Joseph's good friend. He'd been his partner on the police force until Jenny had died and Joseph had moved to Idaho. They'd kept in touch, and a few years later, Joseph talked his buddy into moving to Idaho and working for him. "Where's Wes?"

"He's in the barn with Irene and Digger. They're getting a stall ready for the horse." Katelen craned her head to look curiously into the pickup bed. She jumped up on the running board and smiled at Tara. "Who're you?"

"Katelen, don't bother the lady." Joseph tried to distract his daughter. He wished he'd been able to talk with Tara about the name she wanted to go by and the story they were going to tell his family. He couldn't do it now with Katelen standing here.

Joseph opened the tailgate and hefted the calf into his arms. Large spots of blood soiled the wool where the calf had lain. "We need to force fluids into this little fellah, or he'll die."

Tara hopped down and immediately placed a hand over her forehead. The jolt must have rattled her some. She motioned for him to go. "Take good care of Shamrock."

"Shamrock?" When Joseph had been a young boy, he'd named some of his favorite animals, but his father had warned him against naming cattle or horses because most of the cows went to market and the horses were sold. Names endeared the animals, making it near impossible to part with them. Yet, even to this day, Joseph named some—but only those they kept.

"His brown spot is shaped like a clover." Tara pointed to the marking on the animal's forehead.

Her hand was trembling, and he knew she must still be nervous. He looked into her eyes and knew for some reason, with everything she'd been through, this animal's survival was uppermost in her mind.

"The calf will be fine as soon as I see to him. Then I have to take care of this guy and his mare." He nodded in Mr. Odell's direction. "Will you be okay?"

Tara waved him on.

"All right, then. Feel free to take a look around the place." He glanced down at his daughter. "Come on, Katelen."

"Daddy, what's the matter with him? Let me see. Let me see."

"You can look once we get him in the barn." He trudged toward Odell and the horse. With his arms full, Joseph nodded for the man to follow him into the barn.

* * *

Tara let them go, certain she'd only be in the way. As she watched them pass the corral as they headed to the barn, a monstrous bull, horns shaped like large eagle talons, bellowed. Katelen jumped to the other side of her father as the menacing beast hooved the ground and lumbered to his watering trough, which he nudged with his horns before drinking. Tara was grateful for the sturdy-looking fence.

She nervously glanced at the blood-splotched bandana Joseph had placed on her wound. Her gaze trailed to the torn jacket sleeve. Wearing her aunt's suit made her feel as if Rosalie were with her, watching over her. Before the ride to the ranch, the material had been clean and Rosalie's perfume had clung to it. Now calf's blood smeared it, and it smelled of dirt and animal. Her aunt was meticulous about her appearance; she never would have let her suit get this dirty. *Oh, Aunt Rosalie, I wish you were here to scold me.*

Tara scanned her new surroundings again. Snow blanketed the mountains' jagged peaks, and a slight chill filled the breeze as if it blew straight off the glacier. The majesty of the scene cast a surprising spell of peace over her.

Gravel crunched beneath her now scuffed and dirty white high heels as she wandered to a rustic fence made out of poles that crossed, making an *X*. Three rails created the front side, and one supported the back. It trailed to the lake. Intent on the water, she walked close to the fence until something nudged her back.

Tara swung around and came face to face with a horse with huge dark eyes. Immediately, she stepped back. What did the animal want from her? She raised her hand to pet him, and the horse reared his head and walked away, swishing his tail as if he were pouting. He was black, except for his white rump, where dark spots artistically splattered his snowy hindquarters.

It stopped, and there was a gushing of water like a faucet had been turned on as the horse relieved himself.

"Oh, that's appealing."

"Miss, may I help you?" The voice was gruff.

Tara whirled around again, this time to an old woman whose Caucasian skin looked like a desert—taut, weather blown, and ancient. She stood with her arms akimbo. Fringed chaps covered her jeans to just below the knees; a Stetson, the brim as large as a rain gutter, rested on the old woman's gray head; and scarred cowboy boots arrayed her feet, which were planted hip width apart. From her nearly lipless mouth teetered a cigarette tipped with an inch of ash, and the woman stared down Tara's bruised forehead before trailing her eyes to the crude bandage on Tara's arm.

Tara nervously brushed her bangs over her goose egg and pulled the jacket sleeve over the bandana as she checked to see if the old lady packed a six-gun.

No sign of one. Finally, Tara said, "Uh, I, uh . . ." She clutched her hands together, trying to think of what she should say. The old woman's unflinching stare was none too friendly. Even without a six-gun, this Calamity Jane looked like she ate city slickers for lunch. Tara had to think of something and fast. "A calf has been injured. Joseph took him into the barn."

Voices drew near. Peering past the old woman, Tara spied Joseph and Katelen with several country-looking people following them.

One guy who looked like he'd stepped out of a western fashion magazine waved good-bye, jumped into his truck, and sped off. His empty horse trailer rumbled as he drove past, kicking up billows of dust Tara wished she could disappear into.

* * *

Joseph fanned away the haze as the truck and trailer disappeared. He was grateful Irene, his off-again, on-again girlfriend and a darn good veterinarian, had been in the barn on one of her weekly visits. She'd immediately taken over the animal's care and had even pulled Digger aside to help. This had freed Joseph so he could talk with Odell. He'd said nothing about the dead mama cow, not wanting his customer to worry about leaving his horse to breed with Joseph's prime stallion.

Joseph had reviewed his method of pasture breeding. He had already explained it over the phone, but he'd wanted to make sure the man understood. As they'd walked out of the barn, Odell had seemed satisfied. Joseph hadn't realized Katelen, Irene, and Wes had followed him out too.

As the dust settled, Joseph spotted trouble brewing. His mother had trapped Tara Kelly, and the poor woman looked as tiny and fragile as a butterfly caught in a black widow's web. He knew his mother could be harsh and direct at times. He remembered how upset she'd been when she'd learned Joseph had joined the LDS Church instead of following in his father's footsteps and worshiping God like the Nez Perce, and she had let him know how she felt about the matter. But with time, she'd mellowed and welcomed him home as a partner and co-owner. However, as she stared at Ms. Kelly, he knew she was not mellow now.

He glanced at his daughter, Katelen. Her eyes had widened as she watched the woman her grandmother was staring down. She knew what it felt like to be cornered by her grandma.

Joseph still hadn't thought of how to explain Tara's presence, especially to Irene. Though he didn't have strong feelings for her, he still didn't want to hurt her. Irene was a beautiful woman who dressed in halter tops, jeans, and chaps, but most of his attraction for her stemmed from the fact that she didn't remind him of Jenny and the life he'd lost with her.

But now what was he going to say? In Mac's phone call last night, he had told Joseph how crucial it was to keep Tara's identity a secret. Her life depended on it. If Joseph told the truth, he'd endanger not only Tara but his family and friends as well. He was grateful Digger was in the barn with the calf. That was one less pair of questioning eyes.

Maybe Joseph could say Tara was a new camp-jack he'd hired to help Digger . . . but a camp-jack had to lift fifty-pound dutch ovens out of a fire during roundup. Tara was bruised and bloody from just opening the tailgate. What would happen to her if fire was in the mix?

Praying something would come to him, Joseph walked up beside Tara. Mac had trusted him, and Joseph was honor bound to protect this woman.

His mother sucked a long drag on her cigarette. Everyone called her by her nickname, Bear. She was a proud woman, a woman who had seen, heard, and done it all. She'd taught Joseph life was one long bronc ride, and if you weren't careful, you'd end up with a mouthful of dust, picking cactus out of your rump.

He had to make his explanation good, or she'd see right through it. Clearing his throat, Joseph said, "Mother, Katelen, Wes, and Irene, I would like you to meet the future Mrs. Joseph White Eagle."

CHAPTER FOUR

CONVENIENCE

WHAT THE HECK? WHERE DID that come from? Joseph thought as he scrambled to fabricate the rest of his story. He shot Tara a work-with-me-here look. Surprise and alarm reflected in her pretty green eyes, but she remained silent. He peered over her head at his motley ranch crew.

Irene gave an audible gasp before she spat out, "Say what?" Tiny veins crossing her temples bulged. She reminded Joseph of a cornered cougar as she practically hissed.

Wes, his mother, and Katelen stood still, waiting for his earthshaking news to settle.

Yes, Joseph had some explaining to do. But first he'd address his mother. Bear's wiry eyebrows drew upward like an archer's bow as her leathery complexion gentled into an uneasy calm. She flipped her cigarette to the ground, and smoke shot out her nose. On the surface, she smiled, but her charcoal eyes fused on Joseph's like a mother grizzly concerned for her cub. His mother never questioned him in front of others. She would save her opinions for private. "Son, I assume your fiancée has a name."

Again, he regretted that he'd let Tara sleep on their drive home instead of talking to her. He couldn't very well take the time now to ask what she'd like her name to be while she lived here. "Mother, this is . . . Sarah Smith."

He stared at Tara, hoping she could endure the fake name he'd given her.

Without missing a beat, Tara offered a hand of friendship to his mother, all the while keeping a watchful gaze on the simmering Irene.

Bear stared at Joseph. Was she waiting for him to break out laughing and tell them it was a joke? He tried to appear sincere, forcing a smile to his lips and a look of love into his eyes as he gazed in Tara's direction.

His mother sighed, then turned on her Idaho country charm. "Call me Bear. Everyone else does. Welcome to our family, Sarah. Looks like you had a rough ride to the ranch."

"Thank you for welcoming me into the family." Tara smiled timidly. "I'm a bit of a klutz when it comes to opening a tailgate. I know Joseph has kept our relationship a secret. This must be somewhat of a shock."

Relieved Tara was going along with what he'd said, he wrapped his arm around her shoulders.

"Shock! Honey, you don't know the half of it." Irene jerked her stained deerskin gloves off her hands and slapped them against her bat-wing chaps. "I don't have time for polite, idle chitchat. That injured calf in the barn needs my tending, but believe me, Joseph, you and I are going to talk. That is, when and if you can pry yourself away from your *fiancée*." She snarled at him, made an about-face, and stomped to the barn, disappearing behind the double tongue-and-groove doors.

So much for not hurting Irene. Joseph figured he deserved her harsh words and more. It would be best to let Irene calm down before he tried to talk with her. Besides, right now, he didn't know what he would say. How could he explain that even though he and Irene had been dating, he was now engaged to someone else?

Katelen's pink bottom lip protruded as she kicked at a cobblestone in the hard ground, scuffing her cowboy boot over and over. Her small hands balled into tight, frustrated fists; her round face flushed. "Daddy, is this lady gonna be my mother?"

Joseph had not thought of the boomerang effect this would have on his daughter. Her eyes blinked hurt and confusion. He couldn't rescind his words. Somehow, when this was over, he would explain it to her. When that day came, he prayed Katelen would understand, but in the meantime, he had to patch things up the best he could.

He didn't know exactly what to say, but he forged ahead. "You'll always have the same mother." His daughter's blank stare told him he had to do better. He tried again. "We all have our own biological mothers."

Her brows pinched together, and Joseph realized a brazen lie was his only way out. "Someday she will be your stepmother."

Katelen turned to Tara. Cold accusation frosted her stare, and without saying a word, she stomped to the barn just as Irene had, except Katelen's black braids bounced about her small shoulders as she followed the woman she truly cared for.

"Katelen!" Joseph called after her. His news had been too much. His little girl's dream of his marrying Irene had been smashed to powder. He yearned to explain, to tell her his engagement was just make-believe, but he couldn't.

His mother patted Joseph's shoulder. "Leave the child be."

Tall and lanky Wes grabbed his battered hat and, holding it high overhead, let out a loud whoop. A grin as wide as the Continental Divide split his gaunt face. "Half of Little Lost River's gonna pass out over this one, and the other half—well, they're going to be spitless as a Siberian snake in the Sierra. I can't wait to see their faces when they clamp eyes on your future bride. Boss, this is the best darn news this ranch has heard since your homecoming five years ago." Wes slapped his hat back on his fuzzy head, then grabbed Joseph's hand and shook it like a pump handle. Once finished, he turned to Tara. Wiping his mouth with the frayed cuff of his grungy shirt sleeve, he leaned in as if to kiss her.

She stepped back.

Joseph shook his head at Wes. He didn't want him horrifying Tara any more than she already had been.

Wes stopped and grinned, pointing his finger at Joseph. "I got ya, Boss. I'll save the kiss for the bride till after the ceremony. When's the happy day?"

His mother stepped on the smoldering cigarette she'd dropped to the ground. "Yes, I was wondering that myself." She still studied Joseph like she was working on a jigsaw puzzle, searching for the right piece.

Joseph's mind spun in a whirlwind as he tried to think of a good answer that would sound genuine but not specific. Then it hit him. "Uh, that's why Sarah's here. We wanted everyone to help us decide." Joseph reached over and grabbed Tara's hand, trying to think of anything a man in love would do. Surprisingly, it felt natural, as if her hand belonged in his.

Tara nodded in agreement. "We definitely wanted your input, and there's no rush."

"Glad to hear you're using your heads." Bear's tone told Joseph she had dismissed the subject of the forthcoming nuptials. "While daylight's burning, we shouldn't stand around yammering. With the roundup and cattle drive breathing down our necks, we hardly have time to pick our noses, let alone plan a wedding. Sarah and Irene said something about an injured calf?"

"I'm glad Irene was here to start the IV on the little guy, and Digger's in there watching him. Between the two of them, I'm sure the calf will pull through." Joseph recounted the story of the dead Hereford and her calf for Bear's benefit.

They walked toward the barn door, and Wes pulled ahead, leaving them behind.

Bear stopped. "Joseph, why don't you go on in and see what else needs to be done. I'll take Sarah to the house and make sure she gets settled."

Joseph felt Tara's grip tighten. He knew better than to leave her alone with his mother. He still had to talk with Tara to get their story straight so there would be no slipups when they were apart. Plus, Tara had no luggage, so Joseph's mother would think that odd. Better if he did the honors of showing Tara the house while everyone was busy in the barn. "Thanks, but I wanted to be the first to show her our home."

Bear tipped her broad-brimmed cowboy hat. "Suit yourself."

Left to themselves yet wary of being watched, Joseph and Tara strolled in silence hand in hand to the house. He hated that he'd put both of them in this situation. Tara was grieving, and he felt like a traitor to his family, to Irene, and especially to Jenny.

Once shut behind the safety of the kitchen door, Tara jerked her hand free. "I don't know what you thought you were doing. I'm your fiancée? And Sarah Smith?"

Surprised by her burst of anger, he shot back, "You're under protective custody. My family's lives are at stake because you're here. The less they know, the better off they'll be, so you'd better act the part and act it well because I may be willing to protect your pretty little behind for Mac's sake but not at the expense of my family."

Her face paled like she'd never thought about the danger her presence was putting everyone else in. Joseph's words poured ice water over her rage. "I'm so sorry." Her hand reached to wipe her brow, and she flinched when she touched the goose egg on her forehead. "You're right. I'll try to not be a bother. Just point me to my room. I've barely slept in the last forty-eight hours. I know it's no excuse, but I am exhausted."

Joseph felt as low as a slug. He, at least, had his family. Tara had no one. On top of that, she had witnessed her aunt's murder, which she couldn't remember, and she had been uprooted from everything familiar. How could he have been so unfeeling—especially after she'd helped him with the calf and gone along with his story? He remembered her arm. "Let's take a look at your cut."

"No need. I can take care of it."

Ignoring her, Joseph went into the kitchen, collected the small first-aid kit from the closet, and returned. He set it on their huge, scarred banquet table. Popping open the box, he reached for her arm.

Tara pulled back. "Really, I can do this."

"To make our lie believable, you're going to have to help out on the ranch, so I want to know how serious this is." He guided her to a chair.

Tara's shoulders slumped. Joseph cautiously untied and pulled the bloodstained material away from the wound. She flinched. Along the cut, her skin was bright red. But the bleeding had stopped. He cleaned the wound, opened the Neosporin tube, and lightly wiped the cream over the tender flesh. "Again, I have to ask, when was the last time you had a tetanus shot?"

"I don't know. High school maybe. Ouch! Don't push so hard. What is that stuff?" She tried to pull away again, but Joseph held on tighter.

"Just Neosporin. This isn't as bad as iodine. Now, that stuff burns like the dickens on a scrape like this because of the exposed nerves, so take better care of yourself, or that's what I'll have to use next. I'll ask Irene to give you a tetanus shot while she's here. It would save us from losing another day driving to town." He kept working.

"Is Irene a doctor?"

"A vet. Living as far away from a doctor as we do, a veterinarian is the next best thing." He stopped tending her wound and looked up.

"Isn't there some law against a veterinarian giving a human a shot?" She stared at him.

"Probably. But in the country, you have to use common sense and get treatment from whoever is available at the time." He could see by the deep crease in her brow that she was still uneasy about it. Joseph had to say something to take her mind off the shot. "I'm sorry you were hurt opening the tailgate. But Shamrock needed your help." He used the name she had dubbed the animal, and it seemed to surprise her. The little smile he'd hoped for brightened her face.

"Is he going to be all right?" she asked.

Joseph focused on the wound on her forearm, studying the skin. "Think so. Right now, I'm more concerned about you."

* * *

The way Joseph's head leaned as he tended to her reminded Tara of Garrett on the night months ago when she'd cut her foot on the beach. Tara had taken her shoes off to run in the sand and had stepped on a small piece of glass. Garrett had studied her wound very much like Joseph had. Sometimes Garrett could be gentle.

The nice thought shifted to fighting silhouettes, a gun, and blood.

Blood everywhere.

She tried to force her brain to reach beyond to see more. The fleeting images faded.

Joseph glanced up from his work. "Tara? Are you okay?"

A little shaken, she swallowed the lump in her throat. She wondered if she should tell him what she remembered. She couldn't run to him every time a fragment of memory became clear. There wasn't much more to add to what she'd already told him on the way here. She would wait until the pieces fit together, and then maybe he could help. She answered in a hushed voice, "Yes, I'm fine. Really."

Concern furrowed his forehead. He studied her as he pulled out a pad of sterile gauze from the first-aid box. The scar over his cheekbone seemed to melt away as he gently placed the dressing over the wound and taped it down.

He closed the kit and stood. "Relax a minute while I put this back."

Joseph's talk of family and protecting them only reinforced the guilt of her aunt's death. People around Tara ended up dead: her parents, her grandfather, her aunt. Now her presence placed innocent strangers in danger. What was she going to do? Where else could she go?

She rubbed her pounding head as she glanced about her surroundings and waited for Joseph. Stark, mustard-colored walls enclosed the desolate room. A wooden rack nailed to the south wall waited for coats and hats. One dirt-smudged window bare of curtains allowed a meager portion of afternoon light to trickle in. A hutch stood in the corner.

Joseph returned. "Come on. I'll show you the way."

Pushing through café doors, he led her into a cluttered kitchen. A powerful smell of sour milk coiled in the air. The counters were stacked with emptied soup and vegetable cans, and houseflies circled around them. Plates with dried, crusted food sat on the counter, along with a bowl of blackened bananas and shriveled apples. The torturous ping of water dripping from the faucet onto dirty dishes echoed in her ears. Tara tried not to stare, but she'd never seen such a mess. Grandpa Kelly and Aunt Rosalie had always insisted on a clean, orderly house.

"Are you coming?" Joseph said. His look followed hers, and he appeared to be a bit embarrassed. "This time of year every pair of spare hands is expected to help with the cattle and horses."

As Tara walked beside him, he continued. "Digger has been the ranch cook, but since my father died six years ago, the old man tries to do too much. He's a stampede, leaving dirty dishes and empty cans in his wake."

Tara followed Joseph down the darkened hallway until he paused in front of a closed door. His hand caressed the doorknob. "I haven't been in this room for years. You'll need to do some cleaning."

He opened the door. Stale air greeted them. Tara cautiously stepped past Joseph. Dust motes drifted in filtered light rays peeking through cracks in the roller blinds.

Tara went straight to the window and pulled up the shades. Daylight hit a beautiful cherrywood, four-poster bed covered with a white satin comforter. Lace Priscilla curtains flanked not only the window but the french doors that opened onto a deck.

On a dusty dresser sat a tarnished silver mirror and a jewelry box made of cedar. A patina-stained antique frame held a picture of Joseph and a woman. Tara felt her heart miss a beat.

This was their room—Joseph and his late wife's.

Now Tara knew why Bear had been so concerned by the announcement of their engagement. Joseph's mother knew he was not over the loss of his wife. Tara looked at Joseph.

He stood stone still watching her appraisal of the situation. The silence between them crackled.

Because of Tara, this man had to push the memory of his late wife aside, pretend he had found love, and act like he was eager to begin a new life. It would be torture for him. How could she put him through this? "I can't stay here."

"I don't want you to." He glanced around and focused on the bed— *their* bed. His face paled as if memories of his wife swarmed him. He nervously patted his pockets, searching for something. Looking up at Tara, he said, "I haven't had a cigarette in years, but coming in here and seeing her things . . ." He fished a toothpick from his shirt pocket and bit down hard on the sliver of wood. "Anyway, my mother will never believe I've fallen in love again unless you stay here." His gaze turned to the photograph. "She's probably in shock to see how much you look like my wife."

Tara glanced at the picture again. True, she had the same color of hair and complexion, but the similarity ended there. His wife had a beautiful smile; her skin appeared flawless, and her eyes were brown not green. Tara could tell the woman was confident by the way her manicured hand rested on Joseph's shoulder, the tilt of her head, and her straight posture. Tara was many things, but confident wasn't one of them.

Wanting him to know she was sincere, Tara said, "Joseph, I feel awkward. I'll call Mac and see if something else can be arranged."

He moved toward the door. "No. I said I would do this, and I will. Jenny had a lot of clothes. You look the same size. Feel free to wear whatever you want. Get some rest. We'll talk later." He tipped his hat and walked into the hallway, shutting the door behind him.

* * *

Joseph leaned against the wall in an effort to compose himself. Looking at his wife's picture brought back too many memories, and the ache in his chest burned anew. The day that picture was taken they'd been visiting Bear on a week-long vacation. Jennifer had returned to her old self and was the vivacious young woman he'd married instead of the moody, suspicious wife she had become in LA. He had never felt so blissfully happy.

Shutting up the room had kept the memory of the times Jenny had been happy alive, as if she was still in there waiting for him. Now, like campfire smoke in the wind, she was gone. And she would never return. He scrubbed his palm over his face, walked down the hallway, and went out the kitchen door. Katelen was helping Digger with the garden. Joseph was glad she was with Digger and wouldn't hear the conversation he was about to have with the others. He needed to talk with Katelen, but he'd do it when they were alone and he could take his time to mend fences.

Irene, Bear, and Wes were carrying on a muffled conversation around the makeshift table the calf lay on, but when they saw him, they fell silent.

"Don't stop talking on my account." Joseph stared at the group. Wes's halfhearted smile and Bear's raised eyebrows told him he was the topic. "Unless you *were* talking on my account."

Wes muttered something about checking on Odell's horse and slipped away.

Bear patted Irene's shoulder and glanced at Joseph. The deep creases on her brow had softened. "Guess you two have some talking to do, and I need to go over the cattle drive menu with Digger. I don't want him to try to feed us a steady diet of snakebite kidney bean stew again this year. Makes for unpleasant evenings around the campfire."

She chuckled and pulled a pack of L&Ms out of her vest, shaking one free. Joseph immediately dug in his jeans pocket for the lighter he carried just for his mother. He hated that she smoked and had begged her to quit, but all he could get out of her was someday she would but not now.

As he flicked the tiny flame to life, his mother leaned on his arm and puffed a couple of times. She blew smoke out of the side of her mouth. Before leaving, she softly said, "Try to take the kick out of your words before you trample her." She didn't wait for him to reply before she walked away.

Joseph had dreaded this moment of being alone with Irene. He watched her adjusting the valve of the IV line. She checked the plug and stroked the animal's back.

"Digger said the calf's going to make it," she said, staring at him.

"You're the vet. What do you think?" Joseph stood across the table from her, arms folded, hoping he would say the right words. He was supposed to ask her something, but for the life of him, he couldn't remember what it was because when she looked at him, all he could see was the pain in her eyes. He hadn't intended to hurt her. As soon as Tara left, life could go back to normal. But he couldn't tell Irene that.

She flipped her long auburn ponytail over her shoulder and tilted her straw Stetson to the back of her head. "Actually, I'm beginning to doubt my judgment. Take us for instance."

"Irene, I'm sorry. See, when I had to fly to LA a couple of months ago, I ran into Sarah. She'd been a good friend of Jenny's. And one thing led to another." Joseph was surprised how easy he could fabricate a story. A lie. He was lying to keep Tara safe and to protect his family and friends, so why did he feel like such a jerk?

"Oh, that's supposed to make me feel better? Why didn't you tell me about her when you came home? Why keep her a secret all this time? I guess I should have known something was up since you haven't taken me out since you returned and since you've never pressed for more than a kiss when we went out before that. I thought you were grieving for your wife and that going to LA had put you in a funk." Hurt clouded her red-rimmed eyes.

He wanted to console her, but she deserved better than what she was getting from him. She deserved a man who loved her madly, and Joseph knew he never would. He'd tried. Their being a couple made sense, but he'd never been truly attracted to Irene.

Jenny had been his first love and his last. Maybe it was best that this was happening so he and Irene could part ways now. "I'm sorry."

"What is it, Joseph? Did you sleep with her and now that religion of yours has you thinking you have to marry her?"

"That's enough." Their heated stares merged. "Irene, I hope someday you'll understand why I had to do this."

"Understand! Oh, I understand all right. I've been the world's biggest idiot to have believed we had a future together."

"We had an unspoken agreement."

Irene blinked at him, confused. "Agreement?"

Joseph rubbed the back of his neck, wondering how he was going to say this. "Irene, you don't love me."

"So? How many married people do you know who love each other?" She didn't wait for an answer. "You even told me those last few years with Jenny were difficult. Love doesn't have anything to do with it. I fit in here. We both love Katelen, and our love for her should be enough to make us happy. Besides, I can care for your ailing cattle. And I can ride the range from dawn till dusk. That love thing between spouses is highly overrated."

Was she right? The last few years with Jenny had been tough. She'd begged Joseph to quit the force. And when he wouldn't do it, she'd started going out with friends, leaving Katelen with babysitters. Toward the end, his marriage had been in trouble. Joseph had to face it; he was rotten when it came to relationships with women. But despite that, he realized he still believed a couple had to be in love to get married. "You know I care for you. You're a good friend. There's a man out there who will make you a lot happier than I ever could." Joseph reached to pat her shoulder. She stepped away. He shrugged. "You know I'm right."

"Maybe . . . maybe I will take a look around." Irene started packing things into her medical bag. "The calf's going to be okay. He's pretty drugged up, so you'd better keep an eye on him for a while."

Joseph remembered what he needed to ask Irene. "Wait. Before you leave—I hate to ask this, but I don't have much of a choice . . ."

Irene folded her arms.

"Would you mind giving Sarah a tetanus shot?" Joseph didn't know what to expect.

Irene laughed. "You sure you want *me* to give it to her?"

"If you don't, I'm going to lose another day taking her to town."

Irene sighed. "As usual, I'm a convenience."

Joseph's gaze lowered to the barn floor. What a mess he'd made of things. Glancing up at Irene, he shrugged. "Sorry. But you know how life is out here."

"Yep. Better than most." She thought for a moment, shrugged, then said, "I'll give your *fiancée* a shot if that's what you want me to do. Need to call Dad first. He wanted me to check some of his cattle. I need to let him know I'll be late. See, Joseph, I'm nothing but helpful when it comes to you." She picked up her medical bag and headed toward the house, where she'd use the landline to call her father.

As he watched her go, Joseph couldn't help wondering if he'd done the right thing by sending Irene in while she was angry to give Tara a shot.

He could do nothing now to stop the inevitable clash that was about to happen.

CHAPTER FIVE

NORMAL PEOPLE

ANXIOUS TO GET OUT OF Aunt Rosalie's suit, Tara opened the closet. The top shelf held Stetson hatboxes. Her eyes trailed down to Joseph's late wife's clothes. Somehow, looking at and touching her things felt wrong. But what else could Tara do? In the rush to get her out of LA, Mac had only had time to grab Rosalie's suit. He hadn't wanted Tara to go back into the house and see the crime scene again.

Colorful blouses, shirts, dresses, and jeans hung before her. She would never choose to buy any of these, let alone wear them. Her clothes were muted colors, mainly blacks, browns, or dark greens, which was strange, now that she thought of it, since she had lived so much of her life in LA, where people dressed in lavish tones and were on the beach most of the time. She wasn't a sun-loving kind of girl, especially after her breakdown. She spent her days at her drawing table. Her art was her world of color, not her clothes.

She finally pulled out some jeans and a pale green, long-sleeved shirt. These were quiet tones and would do for now. She changed, being careful of her arm. Standing barefoot, she folded her aunt's suit, set it on the bed, and put the high heels on top. Her aunt's clothes were the only tangible evidence she had of her. Sorrow filled Tara's heart at the thought, threatening to overwhelm her.

She scooped up the clothes, holding them to her chest. Rosalie was dead. The reality of her passing seemed worlds away. Tears puddled in Tara's eyes. How she longed to see Rosalie and have her tell another on-the-job story. She'd loved giving Tara all the gory details even though Tara had begged her to share only the highlights, but right now, Tara would have taken any of it just to hear Rosalie's voice again.

If she could have, Tara would have curled up on the bed and cried and cried the way she had when Grandpa had died. But she was no longer a teenage girl plagued with depression, and even though the tendency to feel sorry for herself was overwhelming, she knew she couldn't indulge. No good would come of it.

Setting Rosalie's clothes on a chair, she made a mental note to clean and mend them. She turned back to the closet.

What was the likelihood Jenny had her same shoe size? Not good. Tara pushed the clothes aside and stared at several pairs of cowboy boots and sandals. Finally, she spied a pair of old sneakers. She grabbed them and read the size on the inside heel. Seven. Tara was a six. If she tied them tight, they'd work.

Next, socks. She'd have to look inside the dresser drawers for those. Even though Tara had Joseph's permission, this seemed even more personal than the rest of the clothes. Inside those drawers would be not only socks but under things too. Tara gazed at the picture on top of the dresser of Joseph and Jenny.

The woman smiling back appeared happy, yet a hint of strain lived in her eyes and wrinkled her brow. Something had been amiss. Tara picked up the picture to take a closer look.

A loud knock came at the bedroom door. The banging made Tara jump, and she nearly dropped the picture. Gathering her wits, she set the photo back in its honored place and padded over to the door. "Who is it?"

"Irene."

Tara couldn't handle Joseph's mother or his daughter or even Joseph himself right now. But Irene? Irene, she could manage.

Even though the woman was a bit upset that Joseph was engaged, she couldn't have had a serious relationship with him or he never would have fabricated an engagement for Tara's cover. Maybe Tara could find a friend in Irene. Maybe Irene could tell Tara more about Joseph's wife. Somewhat relieved, Tara opened the door.

Irene swooped into the room, carrying a medical bag, her chaps flapping about her legs. Her presence overpowered the frilly room. "Joseph said you needed a tetanus shot." She set her bag on the bed and tugged off her cowboy hat. Her auburn hair was smoothed back into a ponytail at the nape of her neck, and tiny flyaway hairs rose from the top of her head.

Joseph had said he was going to ask Irene about a shot. "Are you sure you want to do this? I mean, I don't want to get you in trouble."

Irene held her hat. "Doc George gave me some vials of tetanus antitoxin because his office is so far away and most people won't go to town for just a shot. Now, I'm not going to force you to have it, but have you actually ever seen anyone who's come down with tetanus?"

Tara worried that Irene thought she was questioning the woman's professionalism, and that wasn't it at all. She just didn't want Irene to risk losing her license by giving her an injection.

"Not a pretty sight," Irene said before Tara could respond. "Symptoms don't happen for a couple of days, but then the wound begins to redden. Red streaks crawl up your arm, and the end result is lockjaw. Actually"— Irene tapped her chin—"I've heard it go the other way too: lockjaw first. But it doesn't matter because, at that point, there's not much that can be done." She inhaled a deep breath and added, "But if you don't want it . . ." She reached for her medical bag on the bed.

Sorry she'd said anything and not wanting to be more of a problem than she already was, Tara said, "Okay, I'll have it."

As if all the fun had been taken away, Irene gazed about, not looking at Tara, more absorbed in her surroundings than the injection. "Can't believe he put you in here."

Spotting the photo on the dresser, Irene tossed her hat on the bed and scooped up the framed photograph. She stared at the image, not looking at Tara. "So, you were a friend of Jenny's?"

Tara didn't know what to say. Was that a statement or a question? Sounded like a question. How should Tara answer? Irene might have known Jenny; in fact, they could have been friends. Joseph had obviously told Irene something about Tara and his late wife, but what? Somehow Tara had to walk through this minefield. "Yeah, we were friends. Were you a friend of Jenny's too?"

Irene shrugged, still not looking at her. "I really didn't know her very well. Joseph met her in LA while he served on the force with his cousin, Mac. Joseph and Jenny came to visit every summer until she was killed and Joseph moved home with his little girl." She returned the picture with her back toward Tara. "Fortunately for everyone, Katelen looks more like Joseph than his late wife." Turning around to face Tara, Irene repeated, "So you and Jenny were friends. That's just peachy." She opened her medical bag on the bed and grabbed a syringe and a bottle of medicine. "Tell me more," Irene said, not looking at Tara as she stuck the needle into a small rubber top and pulled on the plunger, filling the syringe.

Why wouldn't the woman look at Tara as she spoke? Strange. And Tara didn't know how to answer her. If she said she worked with Jenny, that could backfire, especially if Jenny didn't work outside the home. But if she said she had been Jenny's neighbor, that might fly. "We were neighbors."

"I see." Irene studied the liquid in the syringe. "So you must have known Joseph too." Pulling the needle from the bottle, she put the medicine away in her bag and turned to Tara.

Irene's large hazel eyes gave nothing away and seemed to measure Tara's worth. "Well, you know. Neighbors see each other now and again." Tara's eyes were drawn to the syringe. She didn't like the looks of the needle. The thing looked big enough for a horse or even a bull.

"Must have been more than that for him to fall in love with you the last time he was in LA. Just how did it happen?" Irene turned away and peered in her bag. She pulled out a small, packaged alcohol swab.

Tara couldn't help but notice a shiny glint in Irene's eye. Was she angry? Why? What had Tara done to her? Then she knew. How stupid and blind had Tara been? Irene was more than a little upset that Joseph was engaged; she was downright jealous—jealous of Tara and her make-believe engagement.

Tara had to do something, say something. The woman held a very wicked-looking needle and was about to give Tara a shot. "Irene, I didn't realize you had feelings for Joseph."

Irene stared at her long and hard. "He's a good friend is all. I've known Joseph for many years. I just don't want to see him or his little girl hurt in any way."

"I don't plan to hurt anyone." Tara thought about the lecture Joseph had given her, that her just being here was putting his family in danger. Why had she let Mac talk her into this? She should be back in LA. She should be taking care of Rosalie's funeral, taking care of all the expenses, and going through Rosalie's papers, not cowering here on the other side of nowhere, afraid of her shadow and dealing with a jealous woman who was about to stab her with a very sharp and long and thick needle.

"See, I've watched him grieve over his wife for five years. Whatever happened in LA before he settled here with his little girl messed him up something awful. The last while, that haunted look he used to carry in his eyes had nearly disappeared until today when you showed up. Now, where do you want this?" Irene held the syringe up and flicked it with her finger before pushing the prong, allowing a drop of medicine to bubble from the needle tip.

Tara didn't know what to think. The woman claimed to be Joseph's friend, but she obviously wanted more from him. More than Joseph was willing to give. And now Tara was here, and Joseph was engaged to her, and Irene had no idea they were lying. And Tara couldn't tell her the truth. She was going to have to let this woman, who saw her as a threat, give her a shot. Reluctantly, she unbuttoned the cuff of her sleeve to roll it up.

"You'll never be able to get it high enough. I strongly recommend your rump, but I can put it in your upper arm. Just open your shirt enough that I can get at your shoulder." Irene stared at her with calculating eyes, her vengeful expression hard to miss.

Tara's fingers fumbled on the front buttons; her hands shook. She hated that she was letting this woman intimidate her. But Irene's eyes had declared war, and she was armed and dangerous. Tara could say or do nothing to make things better. She had to play along.

Pulling the shirt away from her shoulder so Irene could give her a shot, Tara watched as the woman holding the syringe with one hand tore the alcohol packet open using her teeth. Easing the moistened swab out with her free hand, Irene spit the empty wrapper on the bed. She rubbed Tara's upper arm with the swab. Tara didn't want to watch, but if she turned away, Irene might think she'd won this small battle of wills. Instead, Tara said, "Irene, I'm sorry Joseph hurt you. I had no idea he was in a serious relationship."

Irene maliciously smiled and jabbed the needle into Tara's arm. Tara ground her teeth, trying not to flinch. She'd had many shots at Twelve Pines. She wasn't afraid of a needle. She gazed at Irene.

"*He* wasn't." Irene stared straight into Tara's eyes.

* * *

The barn fell silent. Since Mac's call last night, Joseph had been thrown into the path of a twister blowing his guarded life to smithereens: his mother thought he'd gone off the deep end, his relationship with Irene was over, he'd hurt his daughter, and he'd thrown Tara into a tough situation.

Was this too much? A woman's fate lay at his feet, and he didn't know if he could keep her safe. He hadn't been able to shield Jenny. Because he'd been blind to the danger and had stubbornly insisted they go on a ride, his wife had died. But now things were different. With Tara, he knew of possible danger, and he'd stay vigilant no matter what.

A heavy sigh escaped him. Taking his mind off the mess he'd made of things, he examined Irene's work on the calf. The animal looked freshly bathed, and a bandage covered the wound. Irene was a darn good vet. Even though she was upset with him, he knew she would help with the roundup and cattle drive. It would be hard for both of them, but she would be there.

"Boss." Wes entered the barn. "Bear wanted me to tell you she's riding out to the north pasture to check the cattle. With some of our cows gettin' shot, she's worried."

Joseph looked at Wes before glancing back at the house once again, concerned about Tara. With Wes here, Joseph'd best go inside. "Okay. Can you keep an eye on the calf? I need to check something in the house."

Wes sucked air between his teeth. "I saw Irene go in there. Didn't look none too happy."

"No, she didn't, did she?" Joseph strode past Wes to the barn's open door. At that moment, Irene came out, slamming the screen door behind her. She steamrolled straight to her three-quarter-ton Chevy truck, jumped in, and took off, spinning the tires in the barnyard gravel and dirt and causing a cloud of dust. Whatever had happened between Irene and Tara couldn't have been good.

"Might be a wise idea if you steer clear of the house for a while, Boss." Wes had followed Joseph. "Cat fights can be ugly. Your new lady's probably licking her wounds."

With how tired Tara had been and all she'd been through, she was probably not in the best of moods. And who could blame her? Even though he didn't know Tara well, Joseph knew enough about women to realize it was best to let her calm down for a spell. "You're right. I'll take Katelen and catch up with Mom so Sarah can get some rest. If anyone stops by, don't let them go in the house. They can wait until I return, or they can come back later."

Wes chuckled. "Sure is nice to see you worrying about a woman again."

Worried was an understatement. Come tomorrow and the days following, he wouldn't let Tara out of his sight, but today he was pretty certain she was safe from her aunt's murderer. Besides, taking his daughter on a horse ride to find his mother should give him some much-needed father-daughter time.

* * *

They'd ridden for well over an hour, Katelen on her pinto, Joseph on his bay roan blanket Appaloosa. He was proud of his young daughter's riding abilities. Since she was old enough to walk, she'd had a love for riding horses. She had a way with them, like she could read their thoughts and they could read hers.

His mother had given Katelen her own pony, and many times Joseph had found his little girl in the barn telling her troubles to the black-and-white pony she'd named Oreo. Katelen loved to fuss over the small horse, currycombing her at least once a day; giving her apple treats; and training her to do tricks, such as fetching or counting by stomping a hoof. And, of course, Katelen rode the animal every chance she had. She was not allowed to ride out of sight of the ranch unless an adult was with her. To Joseph's knowledge, she'd never broken the rule, but she rode around the ranch tirelessly.

He'd hoped to talk with her about Tara, but Katelen rode ahead of him, a definite sign he was still in the doghouse. Fine. At least they were together. They'd ridden past the sweet-smelling hay field, past the north grazing pasture, and to the timberline on the mountain with no sign of his mother.

Katelen reined Oreo to a stop. Joseph rode up alongside her. "Maybe Wes heard her wrong."

"Maybe." Katelen leaned over and stroked her horse's neck. She wouldn't look at Joseph.

"I know I should have told you about Sarah before today. But don't take your anger with me out on her. She's really a nice person." Joseph didn't know if Tara was nice or not, but he had the impression she was. If only he could tell Katelen that Tara had written and drawn some of her favorite books, that would sway Katelen to at least give her a chance.

However, that information would only endanger Tara—and Katelen. He thought of a way around the problem. "She's an artist. I know you like to draw. I bet she could give you some pointers."

Katelen shrugged. "Drawing is for sissies. Can she rope a steer like Irene?" His little girl cocked her head quizzically at him.

"To be truthful, sweetheart, I don't even know if she can ride a horse. But we can teach her. All I'm asking is for you to give her a chance."

Katelen rolled her eyes at his impossible suggestion. At that moment, a horse nickered behind them. Turning in her saddle, Katelen yelled, "Grandma!"

Bear's large, white, leopard-spotted horse drew up beside them. She'd had the horse going on fifteen years and had ridden her over many mountain passes and through several deserts. They were a perfect match: sturdy, reliable, and didn't take much guff.

"Thought we'd missed you," Joseph said. "See anything out of the ordinary?"

Bear tipped her broad-brimmed cowboy hat back and took a long drag on her unfiltered cigarette before she blew the smoke out. "I herded most of the cattle near the tree line on the mountain, hopeful that would discourage poachers. Puzzles me to no end why someone would shoot the cow and calf the way they did."

"Daddy, can I head back home?" Katelen usually enjoyed talk about the cattle, but Joseph figured even though her grandmother was here, today she wanted to get away from him.

"Sure. Gran and I will follow."

Katelen gave her horse a giddyup and took off.

"She's given ya the cold shoulder, huh?" His mother shook her head as she watched her granddaughter leave.

Here was his opportunity to speak to his mother about making Tara feel more welcomed. "I'm sorry I didn't handle the situation better. It's just, during my trip to LA a couple of months ago, things got serious between Sarah and me. I wanted to tell you, tried to tell you, but every time I saw an opening, something came up. We've had our hands full with one thing after another."

Bear took the cigarette from her lips. "But, son, she's your future wife. How could you not tell your family about her? Doesn't make a lick of sense to me."

"For years I've been wallowing in grief over Jenny. Seeing Sarah made me realize I needed to move forward and take a chance on love again. I didn't know how to tell those closest to me." He sighed. "I'm hoping you'll help me out."

"Son, if you don't know by now that I'd move heaven and earth for you and that little gal of yours, then I've failed." She reached over and slugged his arm, her way of giving him a hug.

"Thanks. Katelen's getting too big of a lead on us. We'd better head back." Joseph turned his horse toward home. "The calf should be coming around. Wes is with it now."

"Hold up there." His mother pulled a rifle shell from her shirt pocket. "I found this over the ridge up in the trees. Figured if ol' Harlen shot those cows, he would have hidden next to that granite boulder at the bend. Looks like a thirty-aught-six Springfield cartridge. Not his usual ammo, but that old snaggletoothed hermit is probably trying to throw us off track. If the law could catch him, I'd have him arrested."

Joseph took the shell and examined it. "You could be right. I don't mind his shooting a cow to survive every now and then, but he didn't take the meat. Maybe I should ride up to his cabin and have a talk."

"Son, won't do no good." She shook her head. "Best to let it be. Sides, you sort of have your hands full right now with Sarah." She kneed her horse to move on.

Joseph looked at the cartridge again. It could be Harlen Cruger's, but then again, thirty-aught-six Springfield cartridges were fairly common and could be used in many rifles. Every rancher kept a rifle handy. They even had gun racks in their trucks.

At the last cattlemen's association meeting, almost every truck had one. Denver Harris had interrupted that meeting with another threat to make ranchers suffer if they didn't stop grazing their cattle near his favorite fishing creek.

Joseph wondered if Harris had a rifle. The man's main problem was with federally owned land, not private property. All the same, he could be brewing up trouble for the coming cattle drive. Joseph was glad he'd sent Allen up to their summer grazing to check on the line shacks and make sure the fences the government had built were in shape. Moose had a tendency to walk right through them, and then Joseph's cattle were blamed. Joseph doubted Harris was behind it. Harris found pleasure in making threats, not in doing something like this.

That left Harlen or the local ranchers. They used rifles with the same thirty-aught-caliber cartridges a lot, especially for hunting. In fact, Joseph had several at home. Could it be possible someone at the ranch had killed the cow and wounded the calf?

Joseph's cop training surfaced. When he had been on a case, everyone was suspect. He chided himself. He was not going back to being suspicious. His snooping around trying to find the truth was what led to Jenny's getting murdered—that and his stubborn pride. He was in a different place, a different time. No one at the ranch was a criminal; they were *normal*.

Normal people didn't go around killing innocent people . . . or cattle, for that matter.

He thought of Tara. With her arrival, LA had returned to his life whether he wanted it or not. The hairs on the back of his neck bristled. In his gut, he knew something was wrong.

Very wrong.

CHAPTER SIX

EYES WIDE OPEN

TARA SANK DOWN ONTO THE edge of the bed. The place on her arm where Irene had given her the injection burned and throbbed. Tara didn't know what to think about Irene. Tara hated that Irene believed they were enemies. The thought of someone not liking her always made her uncomfortable. If this were any other time, she'd go out of her way to make peace, but she couldn't risk slipping up and telling Irene something she shouldn't. If Grandpa Kelly were here, he'd say the Irish legend of the Evil Eye was at work.

He'd said everyone had felt the singular, malefic Evil Eye's glance in their lives. He firmly believed it had placed a curse on his wife's family because Grandma's father had won his vast Irish estate in a poker game and had cheated to get it. From that point on, the Evil Eye had cursed their firstborn daughters to either go insane or die at an early age. Grandfather put no store in the fable until his wife died shortly after Rosalie was born. Being the sole inheritor of the estate, he sold it and moved to America, thinking he'd broken the curse and saved his daughters. But then Tara's parents had died in a boating accident—Tara's mother was Grandpa Kelly's firstborn daughter. He believed Tara had been spared because of the countercharm he'd said over her nearly every day. Even now she could hear his thick Irish brogue tell her, "The blessing of God be upon you."

Oh, how she missed Grandfather. What would he tell her to do in this situation? His voice came back to her. "Child, get about the Lord's business. Make yourself useful, and the evil one will stay his distance."

The Lord's business.

Tara had no idea what that was, but it probably had something to do with not feeling sorry for herself and getting busy. Even though she was tired, she had to do something. She ignored her throbbing arm and rummaged through the dresser to find some socks. She pulled them on, stepped into the sneakers, and tied them. As she headed for the door, she knew exactly what she would do. One thing her grandfather had taught her, and taught her well, was how to clean. The sink filled with dirty dishes called to her.

As she neared the kitchen, a man's gravelly voice sang, "Rambling rose, pick your nose. How I want you without your clothes."

Tara chuckled under her breath and walked in to find a man stirring a pot in the cluttered kitchen. Joseph had mentioned the ranch cook, and if Tara remembered correctly, she believed his name was Digger. It looked like he had cleared away most of the emptied cans she'd seen earlier.

Upon spying her, he cleared his throat. "You must be Chief Joseph's newly intended?"

Tara was surprised he'd made the connection since he hadn't been with the rest of the group when Joseph had made the announcement, but she was the only stranger here, so it really wasn't a stretch to come to such a conclusion. She nodded.

"Well, it happens, I guess." His rawhide skin formed deep creases around his eyes and across his forehead. He wore a tattered and dirty baseball cap with lettering that read "Bart's Bait Shop" on the front.

He wiped his stubby, thick fingers on the soiled dish towel slung over his shoulder and held out the same hand to shake hers.

Smiling, Tara accepted his offer. "You must be Digger. Joseph has mentioned you."

He snorted, shrugged, and wiped his nose on his shoulder before clearing his throat. "Yeah, well, I knowed him since he was a pup. Been cookin' at the ranch now goin' on forever." He leaned closer and whispered, "Ya got to have some of my snakebite kidney bean stew. Have my own secret recipe, and no one in these here parts has been able to top it."

"I can't wait. Is that what you're fixing now?"

"Nah. I save it for the drive. Making spaghetti for tonight's supper." He checked the large pot of water on the back burner, which was boiling madly, so he grabbed a box of noodles and poured them into the water before adding a liberal helping of salt.

"Digger, I'm here to help. What can I do?" She rolled up her shirt sleeves. Glancing at the bandage covering the cut on her forearm, she realized it might be tough to keep it dry, but she would be careful and take her time.

"Well, tie me to a raccoon and set his tail afire! Never thought I'd see the day when a woman on the White Eagle Appaloosa would offer to help in the kitchen. Does Bear know about this?" He opened the complaining oven door to check on garlic bread warming inside.

"No. I thought I would surprise her." Tara set her sights on the pile of dirty dishes in the sink. Most were pots and pans. Sensing Digger's stare, she looked up. For a second, the good-ol'-boy expression was gone, replaced by . . . Tara wasn't sure. He must be a friend of Irene's and had expected Joseph to marry her. Tara wanted him to like her and not see her in a bad light. She pasted on a smile, trying to thaw the moment.

He continued as if nothing had happened. "Oh, she'll be surprised all right. In a few minutes, the family's gonna be in here searchin' for some grub. If you really want to help, you can lay out the table fixins."

Digger had accepted her but with some reservation. Shaking off her worry, Tara got busy.

* ***

When Joseph walked into the house for supper, he was surprised to find Tara in the dining room. She was dressed in Jenny's light green, long-sleeved shirt, jeans, and sneakers, and Joseph once again marveled at her likeness to his late wife.

Tara was in the middle of spreading a red-and-white-checkered tablecloth on the scarred dining table. The last time they'd eaten with a tablecloth beneath their plates was when Jenny had been alive. Joseph was going to have to learn more about Tara so he could keep them separate in his mind. Pulling off his hat and hanging it on a wooden rack next to Bear's ten-gallon Stetson, he said, "Someone special coming?"

"I don't know. Digger asked me to set the table, and I found this in the corner hutch." She went back to the task and pulled out red cloth napkins. "How many people do you usually have for dinner?"

Joseph did a quick head count. "Six, though Allen is setting up the line shacks. But with you here, we still have six."

Tara placed the napkins around the table, then returned to the hutch and grabbed the white ceramic dishes, more items that hadn't seen the light of day since Jenny's death. Joseph hadn't seen them for so long he'd forgotten they existed. "We usually eat on paper plates."

"For every meal?" Tara's fine brows bunched together like she'd never heard of such a thing.

"Yeah, it's no big deal." Why did he feel defensive? "Makes it easy for Digger and the rest of us. No one has much time to fuss with dishes."

Tara set a plate by each napkin. "But isn't that expensive?" She didn't wait for him to reply. "And bad for the environment? Even when just Grandpa Kelly and I shared a meal, we ate on stoneware. He said I needed to know how people in polite society behaved." She quickly looked up. "I'm sorry. I didn't mean to imply your family isn't polite or anything." The red heat of embarrassment crawled up her neck.

Joseph put his hand over his mouth to hide his smile. Here was the difference between Jenny and Tara. Jenny hadn't cared about the cost of things or about the environment, and she had never blushed.

Tara's forehead wrinkled with concern. "What I meant to say is while I'm here, I can do the dishes, so we might as well use them. Please don't be offended." She bit her bottom lip.

Joseph chuckled. "I'm not. It's been so long since we've had a woman in the house."

"And what does that make me?" Bear walked in. She'd changed into her sweats, her short hair still damp from her evening shower.

Joseph glanced to Tara for help. She shrugged and turned her back on him as she fetched drinking glasses. Joseph cleared his throat. "You're my mother. That doesn't count."

"If your father were alive, he'd have something to say about that." She pulled out her chair at the head of the table and sat.

"You know what I mean." Joseph smiled sheepishly, hoping she would understand.

Tara passed him as she placed the jar-like glasses above the plates, and she whispered, "Say you're sorry."

His mother must have heard because she added, "Your fiancée is very wise."

"It's just . . . well, Ma . . . You're like one of the guys."

She glared at him.

"I mean, you're taking care of the ranch, the cattle, the horses. I don't think of you as a woma—"

His mother folded her arms, cutting him off. "The way you're talking, it's plain amazing you were ever born."

Tara passed Joseph again. Tilting her head, she said softly, "You're making it worse."

Joseph knew she was right. "Sorry, Ma."

Digger rushed in with a huge bowl of spaghetti about the same time Katelen and Wes arrived. The three did double takes at the table setting. Wes pulled off his straw cowboy hat and smoothed his short, fuzzy hair. Katelen glared at Tara. She knew who was behind this change. The little girl pulled out her chair and plopped down, a pout on her lips.

Digger placed the spaghetti next to Bear, an expression of deep respect in his eyes for his boss. He obviously thought of her as a woman. Joseph had suspected for a long time that Digger had feelings for his mother, but Digger would never admit it—not unless he was caught off guard.

Digger winked at Tara. "Ya done good, kid. Be right back with the garlic bread."

"Let me." Tara motioned for him to take his seat and disappeared into the kitchen before he could stop her.

Digger's eyes grew wide. "Holy mackinaw. I finally have some mighty fine kitchen help."

"Don't get used to it," Bear stared at Joseph. She was obviously still concerned about the new woman in her son's life.

Joseph couldn't let his mother's statement go. "I don't know why not. Sarah told me she wanted to help all she could while she's here."

"And how long will that be, son?" His mother was not letting up.

"Once we're married, forever." His lie swirled around the room and came to rest on his shoulders.

Tara returned with the bread and sat on the chair beside Joseph. Though she seemed to take everything in stride, he could tell she was tired. She was running on pure adrenaline, and he hoped once she went to bed tonight, she could rest. If her mind was anything like his after a tragedy, she'd be in trouble. His mind always tripped back to the time right after Jenny died, and when that happened, no matter how tired he was, he couldn't sleep. His mind kept replaying what had happened. With luck, Tara wouldn't have to contend with such memories since she couldn't remember how her aunt had died.

Joseph caught his mother's eye. She maintained her determined stare. She was not going to let Joseph off the hook. Sometime, some way she was going to corner him and demand to know more about his fiancée.

But not here. Probably after supper. If he was lucky, he could grab Tara, slip out after everyone was finished eating, and play the part of a devoted man who wanted to spend time with the fiancée he loved, thus delaying the uncomfortable powwow with his mother.

* * *

After Joseph said a quick prayer over the food, mealtime dragged by with hardly anyone speaking except to say "Pass the bread" or "Pass the water." Tara was too tired to think of anything clever to say, so she didn't try. Every once in a while, she would catch Bear staring at her, and then the gruff woman would give a friendly smile. Katelen's attention lay fully on her plate. The men were too busy eating to notice anything other than food. Tara was glad when people started to leave. As she stood to help clear the table, Joseph took her hand and guided her out of the house.

She pulled back, trying to return. "I promised Digger I'd help him."

"He can handle the cleanup."

Tara had her doubts as she remembered what the kitchen had looked like when she'd arrived, though when she'd gone in to help him with supper, it had looked much better. Still . . . "I'm the one who used the dishes from the hutch. I can't leave those for him."

Joseph leaned close to her. "Everyone expects an engaged couple to spend time together. We're supposed to be in love."

He was right. They had to keep up the pretense of being engaged, at least for a little while. She followed Joseph to a small garden conveniently close to the kitchen at the back of the house.

He led her to a white wrought-iron bench where people could sit and gaze out over the garden with its new spring plants, the barnyard, and the lake beyond. It was past eight thirty, and the sun was just beginning to set.

Once seated, he let go of her hand. "You look awfully tired."

"I suppose that's a compliment from a rancher?" She smoothed her hair away from her face, worried about her appearance.

"Actually, yes." He smiled. "It means you've put in a full day's work. I didn't mean to worry you. You're still good-looking, but you have dark circles beneath your pretty green eyes." Joseph leaned forward, resting his elbows on his knees.

He'd said she was good-looking and her eyes were pretty. No one had complimented her since her grandfather had died. Not even Garrett. "Does that mean awfully tired is better than extremely tired?"

"Sure does." A smile tugged at his lips. "How'd it go with Irene? Did she give you a shot?"

"Oh yes." Tara rubbed her sore arm. "Still hurts. You do know she loves you, don't you?"

"Did she say that?"

"No, but I could tell by the way she talked about you and your family. I feel horrible that to protect me, you had to jeopardize your relationship with her."

"Well, don't. Irene and I—"

The back screen door slammed shut, and Wes headed to the barn. He waved at them.

Joseph sat up and slung his arm around Tara, pulling her against him before acknowledging Wes with the tilt of his head. Tara was tempted to lean back on his shoulder like a woman in love would do. Knowing she should put on a good act, she followed the inclination and cozied up to him. Joseph tensed, but he didn't push her away. Wes changed directions and started toward them.

"If he comes over, he'll ask a lot of questions." Joseph gently placed his hand under her chin and tilted her head up. His warm breath played over her face. They'd both eaten garlic, but she didn't smell it on him. Instead, she smelled a hint of cinnamon, probably from the toothpicks he was always sticking in his mouth. She looked into his eyes, but she couldn't tell what he was thinking.

And then he closed his eyes and kissed her.

Startled, she tried to keep up her end of the act, so she followed his lead and gave in to his embrace.

His lips were soft, coaxing, and tender, not demanding like Garrett's had always been. She had to remember this was a show for Wes. Joseph was only pretending. And she shouldn't like being kissed by this man, who was really no more than a stranger, but in the short time she'd been with him, she knew he was a good, honorable person who loved his family and had a strong sense of right and wrong. Beyond common-sense reasoning, Tara liked the feel of his lips on hers, so much so that she deepened the kiss, moving her lips slightly.

A tingling spiral of emotions wrapped around her heart, making it difficult for her to breathe. This kiss was more than she'd ever experienced. But it was something she hadn't been looking for and didn't want. What was she doing?

She had to break the spell. She was not an actor, and playing this game of an engaged couple would only make her life even more complicated, if that was possible.

She pulled back a little, breaking the kiss. Not wanting to be abrupt, she quietly asked, "Is he gone?"

Without moving, Joseph looked up, then back to her. "Yeah. Sorry about that." He straightened. "A kiss was the only thing that would have stopped him."

Joseph didn't seem fazed at all. The kiss had meant nothing to him. She had to pretend it meant nothing to her too. She could do it. She had to do it.

"Wes was going to feed Shamrock." Joseph stood. "I should see if I can help him. We're going to have to use a bottle, which sometimes doesn't go very well when a calf is missing his mother."

Tara stood. "Would you mind if I did a load of wash? My aunt's suit is dirty from the trip."

"Of course you can. The washer and dryer are at the end of the hall."

"Thanks. And I'll see if Digger needs help with the dishes."

"No." Joseph took her hand, walking her to the back door. "You've barely slept in the last forty-eight hours. I want you to go straight to bed. Or the 'awfully tired' compliment I gave you will change to 'extremely tired.' And you don't want that." He winked at her, turned, and went to the barn.

* * *

Suffocating darkness froze Tara. She strained to see, but inky blackness stared back. Her heart slammed against her ribs, warning her to flee.

Flee now!

Something . . . someone was after her. She had to move but didn't know which direction was safe.

And then she heard them.

Whisperings.

Faint.

Desperate.

"Whyyyyyy?" Raspy, breathless voices mingled together.

"Who's there?" Tara's skin goose fleshed.

"Spirits from the Hole of Sorrows," they hissed.

Gray, gauzy images appeared in the distance, floating above some type of small structure. Tara could barely make out a thin capstone perched on high portal stones. All at once, she recognized where she was: the dolmen at Poulnabrone in Ireland. Grandfather had taken her there but only in the stories he'd told of the homeland. This dolmen—set on the Burren's limestone—was a portal for spirits to pass into the dreaded abyss of the Land of the Dead.

One image broke apart from the others and came straight toward Tara. "Why did you do it?" As the spirit drew near, Rosalie's face appeared, her hair a wild matted mane; her eyes dark, sunken holes; her cheeks smeared with blood. She hovered above Tara and then, all at once, swooped down mere inches from her face. "Why?" she yelled. Her mouth gaped open. Her breath smelled of rank decay.

Tara shot up in bed, sucking in deep drafts of air. Sweat dampened her flannel nightgown, making it stick to her. Wisps of her hair clung to her neck and forehead. She glanced wide-eyed about the room. Soft rays of moonlight fell through the glass patio doors. Shadows of the dresser, the chair in the corner, and the door to the bathroom showed she was alone and still at Joseph's house. Yet she felt a presence she couldn't see.

"It's a bad dream, that's all." Trying to push past the eerie feeling of being watched, Tara slid her legs over the side of the bed.

Water. She needed a drink. Everything would clear up with a swallow or two of water. She managed to stand on shaky legs. Her head pounded. Her mouth and tongue were dry. And then she saw movement beyond the bathroom door. Wild fear streaked over her.

Rosalie was in the bathroom, waiting for her.

No! Rosalie's dead.

The voices came again. "Come . . ."

Aunt Rosalie wasn't alone. Someone was with her. Tara had to get away. Staggering to the french doors, she fumbled with the lock. Her fingers wouldn't do what her mind demanded. She tried and tried to grasp the lever. Finally, she caught hold and pushed it aside, unlocking the door.

Cold air washed over her. She had to get away.

* * *

Joseph looked at his watch and was surprised that it was nearly midnight. It had taken a while for Wes and him to teach Shamrock to latch on to the bottle's nipple, but once the little one had realized what came out of it, he'd had no problem. After they'd finished feeding the calf, it had settled down for the night. Wes had taken the opportunity to kid Joseph about smooching with his fiancée, and Joseph had good-naturedly shrugged it off. After Wes had headed for the bunkhouse, Joseph had decided to stay up a little longer, still trying to come to terms with the kiss.

What had he done? And then he realized that since the moment he'd met Tara and seen how much she looked like Jenny, in the back of his mind, he had wanted to kiss her. He craved kissing his wife, and he had to know if kissing this woman would be like kissing her. It hadn't been. He was such a fool. A sick fool! What kind of delusion was he living?

Leaving the calf safely in the stall, Joseph walked to the open barn door and gazed out at the still night. Silver moonlight glanced off towering pines, cottonwoods, and outbuildings. In the distance was the shimmering lake. Stillness crept from the water to the trees. Night prowled over the landscape. When Joseph had been a young boy, his father had stood here many times and told him Indian legends, how Mother Earth needed rest so Father Sky sent the moon to cast a spell over the land.

As a kid, Joseph had believed. But when he grew up, moved away, became a police officer, and married, he realized such sayings were a type of Indian religion. For quite a while, he'd shunned religion of any kind . . . until Jenny was murdered. During the dark days following her death, the light of the Church had miraculously entered his life.

Though he still revered the earth and sky, Joseph knew God had created the world. He wished his father had lived long enough that they could have discussed his new belief. By now his father knew, but Joseph would have liked to have discussed it with him. His dad had always been spiritual.

Joseph noticed a movement in the shadows of the house. Who was out this late? The figure dashed across the lighted barnyard, heading for the road. By the silhouette, he could tell it was a woman.

Bear wasn't that tall.

Irene was gone.

Katelen was in bed.

That left Tara Kelly.

CHAPTER SEVEN
VOICES

Sharp rocks cut Tara's bare feet. Fear made her numb to the pain. She pressed on, running, running, running. The outdoors seemed surreal, hazy, ghostlike. The mantra *Get away* played over and over in her mind, fueling her steps. Panicked that the voices would catch up, she raced through the darkness down the road lined with towering trees.

Movement to the right drew her attention. They'd found her! At any moment, they would be on her.

Hide!

Taking shelter behind a large cottonwood, she stood mannequin still, straining to listen. She watched for spirits, for Rosalie, for Garrett, for movement of any kind. Her full concentration zeroed in on the ghostly shadows.

She barely heard the footfalls from behind, but they were there. She ducked and started to run as iron arms wrapped around her middle. She screamed and turned, kicking and flailing at the man who held her.

"Knock it off. It's only me."

That was not a spirit or Rosalie and definitely not Garrett.

Tara stopped struggling and stared at the face only inches above hers. Moonlight shone on Joseph White Eagle's chiseled features, the scar over his high cheekbone and his Roman nose. Here stood her fake fiancé.

Relief washed over her as she melted into the safe haven of his arms. Light-headedness followed. Her rubbery knees barely kept her upright. Trying to keep from collapsing, she clung to him. "I thought you were a spirit. No, I mean . . . Garrett. I thought you were him."

Joseph cradled her against his chest, giving her extra ballast. "He couldn't find you that fast."

She shook uncontrollably, not really knowing if it was from nerves or from the cold. It didn't matter because she was safe now. Safe in Joseph's arms.

"You're freezing. Let's get you to the house." He turned her around. With his arm about her shoulders, he led her back.

Trying to keep up, she winced as she stepped on the jagged gravel, the pain from her raw feet finally catching up to her. Joseph immediately scooped her into his arms and held her close. "If you thought Garrett was after you, why didn't you come get me?"

To hold on, Tara put her arms around his neck. "I didn't know where you were." Her chin trembled.

"You didn't look, did you?"

"I feel foolish now. Do we have to talk about it?"

"Yeah, I think so. I can't keep you safe if you don't tell me everything." His voice was calm as he kept walking.

She stared at the shadows hiding his features. Would he understand—even more than she did—what was going on with her?

"What sent you running out of the house barefoot and in only a nightgown? I'm surprised you were able to run on the gravel, though you were pretty scared and probably didn't feel a thing."

"A bad dream mixed with my own fears." She wished she could look into his eyes to see if he thought she was losing her mind.

"Were you sleepwalking?"

"No. I've never done that."

"But you told me Mac found you in your aunt's garden, and that was the first thing you remembered, right?"

"Yes, but . . ." She couldn't tell him tonight's dream was mixed with reality *and voices*. She'd confided such fears to Aunt Rosalie, and she'd admitted her to Twin Pines. Tara couldn't risk Joseph doing the same thing.

"What seemed so real in the dream?" Joseph coaxed her for more information.

She had to answer, had to pretend she had nothing to hide. She'd choose her words wisely. "In the dream, Aunt Rosalie was covered with blood. Lots of blood." She buried her face in his chest, fighting another swell of fear and a touch of nausea.

"Believe it or not, this is a good thing." He sounded relieved, but he didn't know everything. She couldn't completely trust his reaction.

"You don't understand," she said as she tried to think of a way to tell him. "Rosalie had blood matted in her hair, smeared on her face. She was angry with me. Wanted to know why I did . . . something. She was screaming and screaming and screaming."

"Your subconscious mixed with your raw emotions is stirring reality with nightmares and coming to the surface." Joseph cleared his throat. "Whenever something horrific happens to a person, this is expected."

Maybe he was right. Joseph had been a cop and had probably helped a lot of people through trauma similar to this. Plus, he had been through the grief of losing a loved one. "Did you have bad dreams after your wife was murdered?"

He stopped. She could feel his eyes on her. "Yes. And I won't lie to you. I still do. Though, I can tell you this: as time goes by, the dreams happen less often. They say it is part of the grieving process."

"It was so real. I thought I was awake, but I wasn't sure. And I believed Rosalie was after me. That she wanted me . . . dead." Tara bit her lips, worried she had said too much.

"That's just guilt." Joseph had a calm answer for everything.

"Guilt?"

"Survivor's guilt. You feel like it's your fault your aunt died and you didn't." He started walking again. "That happened to me too when I lost Jenny. Took a long time to get over." They were nearly to the house. "I'm curious. Did Mac say if your aunt had an injury to her head?"

Mac had said very little about Rosalie's injuries, but in Tara's mind, a scene flashed of a man sitting on top of Rosalie, his club high in the air. A chill sliced through her, making her tremble even more. She had to hold on to the image. Dagger-sharp pain pierced her forehead and made her gasp. The image faded. "I . . . I'm not sure. When I think I remember something, it fades."

Joseph reached the grass and set her down. "What do you think you saw?"

"Some man—Garrett, I think—had Rosalie on the floor in her living room and was going to strike her with a baton club." Though her headache had subsided, the goose egg on her forehead throbbed.

"Nothing else?"

"No. It's so frustrating. You must think I'm crazy." She couldn't believe she'd said the word out loud.

"You're pretty hard on yourself. Give it time."

Time? Tara didn't have time. The longer she stayed here, the more danger could befall his family. She couldn't risk it. Her aunt Rosalie had died because Tara had been too afraid to be on her own. Tara didn't want to put more people in danger, not again. "Too many people have died because of me, and I'm not going to cause any more sorrow."

Out of nowhere, voices whispered, "Come to ussss . . ."

She looked around.

No one was there.

She glanced at Joseph to see if he'd heard them as well. He didn't seem bothered. All at once, she knew why—the voices were taunting only her.

She had to stay calm and be strong.

"Come . . . to . . . us." The voices came louder, echoing in surround sound.

Ignoring them the best she could, she said, "Look, you didn't sign up for this. I think it's best if I leave. I've disrupted your life. Your girlfriend is upset with you and so are your mother and daughter. Since you lied about our engagement, you can lie again and tell them I had second thoughts. I could be gone by morning." She headed for the house.

Joseph caught her elbow, whirling her around to face him. "Where would you go?"

She had no idea. But she had to leave. "Away from you and your family."

"Did I say something to offend you?"

She stared up at the man who towered over her. "Of course not. But . . . but for some reason, death follows me."

"What makes you think that?"

"My parents died when I was a child. My grandfather when I was in my teens. Now my aunt. Anyone who comes close is in mortal danger. I thought I could stay here. I didn't think about you and your family's safety. What if I am sleepwalking and I hurt someone?" She folded her arms to control a fresh onset of trembling.

"I can't imagine you hurting anyone. You're not aggressive. And besides, *I* found you. Tara"—his voice was soft and gentle—"people die. That's part of life."

Tara shook her head. "You don't understand the whole picture. If my parents hadn't been so desperate to get away from me and have some alone time, they'd still be alive."

Joseph shook his head. "Parents need time to themselves."

She'd heard the same argument before and countering this point would go nowhere. Shifting to someone else, Tara went on. "If I'd stopped my grandfather, he'd still be alive."

"Stopped your grandfather? How did he die?"

Tara didn't know quite how to explain. She'd repeated the story many times to her therapist. The words should be easy to say, but now they were stuck in her throat, unwilling to come to life one more time.

Joseph rubbed her arm. "Tell me."

"I was nineteen. There was a lake near Grandpa's house. He and Aunt Rosalie had a big fight. He stormed out and walked right by me. I could have stopped him. I knew he was going to the lake to think. He always did. I wanted to give him time to cool off. Later I went out and found him by the dock . . . dead in the water." She covered her mouth with her hand, trying to compose herself.

"That's a horrible thing for a nineteen-year-old kid to see." Joseph rubbed her shoulder.

"I could have stopped him. And if it weren't for me, Garrett Parker would not have killed Aunt Rosalie." She felt the weight of a gun. Confused by the sudden impression, she glanced at her hand. Empty.

Joseph smoothed a hair away from her face and shook his head.

"I know it sounds absurd, but I can't be responsible for one more person's death."

He shifted his weight from one leg to the other, folding his arms. "You really believe what you said, don't you?"

He sounded too much like a therapist. Instead of answering his question, she asked, "Do you think I could live with myself if something happened to your daughter?"

Joseph took her arm and folded it into the crook of his. "I'm not going to let anything happen to my daughter or my mother or anyone else on the ranch. I didn't mean to make you feel paranoid when I told you their lives were at stake here. My intention was to make you understand we need to work together to keep everyone safe. We can pull this off. I *was* a cop, you know. A darn good one."

"So was my aunt."

He stepped closer and placed his index finger on her lips. "Shhh." He took it away. "If it makes you feel better, you're not part of my family, nor is there any affection between us. If you believe people close to you end up dead, it won't affect anyone here. No one is close to you."

His words were like cold water shocking her to the stark reality that she was on her own with no one to turn to. The concept wasn't new, but every time she faced it, she felt more isolated.

Joseph seemed to sense the cruelness of his words. "Look, let me put it this way: what happened in your past has muddied your thinking. You are not responsible for your loved ones dying. Life isn't that simple. There's always a story behind a story. Illusions deceive us into dismissing facts. What you claim happened in the past does not change my mind about keeping you safe. Mac trusted me to watch over you. I can do that. And no one will die."

She hoped he was right.

Joseph opened the back door. "Get some rest. Tomorrow's going to be a big day. I'm sure Digger will put you to work."

Tara had a great deal to think over. Deep down, she had clung to the wish that he would make her stay. That somehow the kiss they had shared on the bench meant something more. That was an illusion, and like Joseph said, it was a story behind a story. He was clear and methodical in his thinking. Perhaps the kiss meant nothing to him, but that was okay. His levelheadedness meant a lot to her.

Maybe this could work.

The voices had stopped.

When Joseph was close, she felt safer than she had for quite some time. She'd wait a couple of days while she tried to remember exactly what had happened and how Rosalie had died, but after she faced the facts, she'd return to LA. No more running.

As she entered the house, Joseph started toward the barn. Quietly shutting the door behind her, she smelled cigarette smoke. The only person she had seen smoking was Joseph's mother. An ashtray sat on the granite countertop under the kitchen window, and tails of smoke rose from a smashed cigarette. The curtain fluttered in the opened window.

How much had Bear heard, and what, if anything, would she do?

CHAPTER EIGHT
THE DRIVING FORCE

TARA HAD BARELY SLEPT EVEN though the voices had stopped calling to her. She would have taken a sleeping pill, but she'd taken one when she'd first gone to bed, and two in one night would make her too groggy the next day. What kept her tossing and turning was thinking about what Joseph had said coupled with the terrifying thought that she was close to a breakdown.

She hated Twin Pines. Even though the doctors were attentive and the nurses kind, she never wanted to go there again. Not only had she been detached from the world, but the drugs had also made her feel like a boat drifting on waves of hopelessness. That was why she only took a sleeping pill on rare occasions. But when Tara had stayed with Rosalie, Rosalie had convinced her that getting her sleep was more important than worrying over the side effects of a pill. Rosalie had always known what was best. Tara missed her.

Once dawn broke, Tara dragged on jeans, a long-sleeved shirt, and socks. She wanted to call Mac before people started getting up. She remembered seeing a landline phone in the kitchen. If she hurried, she could use it before Digger came in to cook breakfast.

Tiptoeing in stocking feet, she made her way to the phone and dialed Mac's cell number. He'd told her his cell was secure and Garrett wouldn't be able to trace it.

After several rings, he answered with a groggy voice. "Yeah." He sounded angry.

"It's Tara." She didn't know quite where to start, but finally, words tumbled out. "How are things going? Have you found Garrett? Is the autopsy done? Do you need me to come home and help with the funeral?"

"Calm down." Mac's voice gentled. "You've only been gone one day. Do you honestly think I wouldn't call you if we'd captured Garrett?" He didn't wait for an answer. "And though Rosalie's death is a top priority"—his voice caught with emotion—"it takes time to get results from an autopsy."

"I'm sorry, Mac."

"Is everything all right there? Is Joseph treating you well?"

"Oh, yes, I just . . . Well, I had a bad dream, and I feel like I've abandoned you when you need me most." Tara felt foolish for bothering Mac. "I woke you up, didn't I?"

"It's four in the morning. I had to stay at a motel because my house is a crime scene, and I didn't get to bed until two, so yeah. But I needed to get up. We got a lead on Garrett's whereabouts. Doesn't look like he's heading your way. I put some guys on it, but I need to check on how it's progressing." He paused a moment. "Look, you've been through a lot in the last forty-eight hours. Are you taking your pills like you're supposed to? Rosalie always worried about you taking your medication. Those pills are meant to help you sleep and not give you nightmares."

"Yes, of course I am." Tara was touched that her aunt had discussed her well-being with Mac. In a strange way, she felt as if Rosalie was still watching over her. "I don't want you to worry about me. Just find Garrett as soon as you can so I can come home and help with the funeral."

"Rosalie would be proud of you." He paused a moment, as if he was trying to control his emotions. "Don't worry. We'll find him. Take care." Mac hung up.

Poor Mac. Tara knew he deeply loved Rosalie and would do anything for her, but now she was dead. Tara didn't know how he functioned, let alone did his job. She slowly placed the receiver on the hook and made her way down the hall; then the back door opened. Digger was probably coming in to start breakfast.

Once safely in her room, Tara tugged on a pair of Jenny's cowboy boots. They were a little big but not bad. Tara wanted to do everything she could to fit in. Mac was doing his best in LA, and she needed to do her best in Idaho.

She was nervous about facing Bear and Joseph after last night. She wondered again how much Bear had heard. As soon as she could, she'd have to tell Joseph his mother might know their engagement was a sham. What could Tara do in the meantime to take her mind off of it? The answer was obvious: help Digger with breakfast. She hurried from her room to the kitchen, where he was frying bacon. "What can I do?"

"Will wonders never cease?" Digger glanced at the clock on the stove: 5:30 a.m. "I have to tell ya, after you ducked out on helping with the dishes last night, I didn't expect to see you up and dressed until closer to noon." His whisker-stubbled face softened to a smile. Besides his usual ranch attire of jeans and a plaid shirt, he wore his baseball cap backward and had a dish-towel apron tied around his middle. "You can take care of those flapjacks on the back griddle if you've a mind to."

Grateful for the chore and a chance to act like last night had never happened, Tara grabbed the spatula.

* * *

Joseph had left the ranch before anyone was up and planned to be back before Digger had breakfast on the table. He drove up the dirt road to the lookout point on the mountain, kicking up dust clouds as he went. Almost every morning, he took Scrap with him as he surveyed his cattle and horses. After this last year and the trials they'd had at the ranch, he was more than a little cautious when it came to his animals. He pulled to a stop, put on the parking brake, and got out. Scrap trailed him to the mountain ridge where Joseph could see most of his five-thousand-acre ranch. On the east range, his cattle grazed near the tree line on the mountain. To the west, down in the valley near the lake, roamed his horses.

The horse herd had diminished to fifty head. In his father's glory days, there had always been at least a hundred. But his father hadn't had the economic burdens Joseph had. Even though his father was dead, Joseph wanted to make him proud and restore the ranch to what it once was, if not better. What would his father have done about someone shooting their cattle? He would have become more vigilant; that was a given.

Joseph scanned the mountain, looking for anything out of the ordinary. Was the shooter who had killed the cow and wounded the calf out there waiting? Who had Joseph offended? No matter how many times he asked those questions, he had no answers.

"Come on, Scrap."

As Joseph drove home, the dog lay its head on his leg. He stroked the soft fur beneath the bandana collar. Katelen had tied it on him last week. His mind wandered to last night and his daughter and his fake fiancée. How he loved his daughter and hated that she was upset with him because of Tara.

The thought shifted again. He would never forget the image of Tara standing next to the cottonwood tree, the moonlight catching her silhouette. He realized he hadn't thought of Jenny when he'd seen Tara. The kiss they had shared on the garden bench must have chased away the false image his mind had projected. Now he saw Tara as only a woman who needed help. His help. Last night in the darkness, he could tell she was terrified. Her nightmare must have been horrifying for her to be so scared. She'd struggled hard when he'd tried to keep her from running.

It might be a good idea to give Mac a call to find out a little more about this woman. Not that Joseph planned to send her back if he learned something shocking, but he wanted to know all the facts so he could help her. Plus, he needed to check in with Mac, find out how the investigation was going. While he had him on the phone, he'd ask him more about Tara's past.

Meanwhile, Joseph aimed to get closer to her to win her trust. For some reason, she was withholding information from him. It may take awhile, but he would get to the bottom of what was bothering her and maybe, in so doing, help solve the case.

It wouldn't be an easy job since the woman was terrified of almost everything. He couldn't blame her. She'd been through an emotional tidal wave when her aunt was murdered in front of her.

As he drove up the last hill, he admired the tree-lined road. The pines and aspens were thick through here. Topping the crest, he suddenly came upon a red Dodge truck parked across the middle of the road and a man standing in front of the vehicle, arms folded.

Joseph couldn't swerve to miss him or he'd crash into trees, so he slammed on his brakes instead. Scrap thumped to the floor. The truck's tires locked, and dirt flew high in the air, blinding Joseph for a millisecond. His vehicle came to a stop without touching the other vehicle. When the dust settled, he checked on Scrap. A little dazed, the animal still jumped onto the seat next to him and shook off the incident.

Joseph had stopped within a few inches of Lester Fimble, Irene's father. What was that donkey-faced old man up to? Whatever it was, he'd nearly gotten himself killed.

Joseph wrenched open his door and jumped out. "Not a good idea to park in the middle of the road. Got car trouble?"

Lester drew a Browning rifle from the bed of the Dodge. "Nope. Been waitin' for you."

"Hold on . . ." Joseph couldn't believe the man had pulled out a gun.

"We need an understanding." Lester used the weapon's barrel to tip back his work-stained cowboy hat, then pointed the gun at Joseph. "While you were courtin' my daughter, I couldn't very well tell you exactly what

I thought of you. She'd have gotten upset and all, but your little surprise yesterday changed things." Lester's tongue licked his bottom lip. "There's a name for two-timing skunks like you."

"Look, Irene and I were never serious. She doesn't love me. Ask her." Joseph couldn't blame the man for being upset. His daughter had been hurt. If someone hurt Katelen, Joseph would feel the same way. But Lester had taken it to the extreme.

"Don't need her opinion on this. This is between you and me. You used my little girl for your own selfish pleasure, and I won't be forgettin' it." The elderly man shoved the rifle into Joseph's gut, making him back up a few steps.

Scrap growled at Lester.

"You gonna sic your dog on me?" Though Lester's finger wasn't on the trigger, it was dangerously close.

"The dog's loyal."

"That's more than I can say for you." Keeping the weapon on Joseph, Lester's eyes narrowed as he stared him down.

"Look, Irene and I only dated. That was all. Your daughter is a wonderful woman, a good friend, and one heck of a vet." He hoped flattery might sway the man to be reasonable.

"I know," Lester scoffed. "It's beyond my reasoning why she wasted time with the likes of you."

Scrap's growls grew louder. The hackles on his neck stood on end.

"You want to be around for your daughter and watch her grow up, don't you?"

"Lester, would you think about what you're saying? You're threatening my life."

The old man chuckled. "No, just warning you. You hurt *my* little girl again, you and I are going to do more than just have some words." Lester shifted the gun and shot the rear tire of Joseph's truck.

The blast reverberated through the trees and echoed over the mountain. Air gushed out of the tire, and the wounded truck leaned to one side.

Lester stepped closer to Joseph. "Changing your tire will give you time to mull over what I said." The old man backed away, returned to his truck, and sped off.

Trying to regain his composure and take in what had happened, Joseph stared down the road. On the dirt and gravel lay the spent shell. Joseph picked it up, studying it. *A thirty-aught-six, just like the one Bear found.* Lester knew enough about cattle to know where a bullet would do the most damage, and because Joseph had broken up with Irene, the old man now had a grudge against him. But when the cattle had been shot, Lester hadn't known about Joseph's engagement. For that matter, Irene hadn't either.

Still, Lester jumped to the top of Joseph's list of people who had it in for him.

* * *

By the time Digger and Tara had breakfast ready, Wes was up and eager for something to eat. Katelen had stumbled to the table too, a pout curling her bottom lip at the sight of Tara. Bear was a no-show. Digger motioned for Tara to sit down when he did. For some reason, without Joseph there, no one said grace over the food. They just started eating. The clink of utensils on stoneware dishes made the only noise, and Tara noticed the lack of polite conversation this morning was much the same as the silence over the meal last night. She'd still been recovering from her flight yesterday and was trying to feel comfortable here, so she hadn't said anything. This morning she wanted to say something but didn't know what, so she kept her head down and ate.

Finally, Joseph came in covered in a film of dust. He gave her a hello nod, sat at the table, and piled food on his plate. Tara waited for someone to say something to him like, "Where have you been?" or "What are we supposed to do today?" but no one spoke as they ate.

Strange.

Tara thought of several things she wanted to say to him, but was it her place? After all, she was only a guest. However, she was a guest who was supposed to become part of this family, so it would be within her right to speak up. About to ask what everyone was going to do today, she stopped as Joseph stood and grabbed his hat. Wes and Katelen followed. Joseph's mind must have been too occupied with ranch work to bother with Tara this early in the morning.

As she rose from the table, Digger got up as well. "Mind taking over the cleanup? I need to see what's on the chief's mind for the day. He seems a mite upset."

"No problem. I'd be happy to take care of the dishes." She made a mental note that when Joseph was upset, he became quiet. But everyone else had been quiet too. Had they all been upset? If she stayed here long enough, she'd learn the nuances of mealtime and how to tell if someone was upset or not.

Tara donned rubber gloves she found under the sink. They came up to her elbows. Ready for battle, she busied herself washing dishes, wiping off counters, and scrubbing the tile floor. By the time she finished, the kitchen was transformed: the sink sparkled, the counters were cleared, and the floor had a Mr. Clean shine. She was in the process of filling a bowl with more bright, red, shiny apples she'd found in the pantry when someone came in.

Bear stood in the doorway, a coffee mug in hand. Tara had wanted to be alone with Joseph's mother so she could ask if she'd overheard them last night, but now that the opportunity presented itself, her courage disappeared. How could she ask the woman—her supposed future mother-in-law—if she had been eavesdropping? The words stuck in her throat. Tara continued to fill the bowl.

"Those store-bought apples are hard to hide among the others." Bear went to the sink, the chink of her spurs echoing off the tile floor. She rinsed her cup and set it on the counter, then took an apple from Tara's hand. "See here?" She pointed with her knobby-knuckled finger to a small area darker than the rest of the apple. "That's a slight bruise. No telling where it's been or what it's been through to get here."

Bear's assessing gaze never left Tara as she spoke. "Sometimes if you hide them among the homegrown ones, people don't even notice and never question where the fruit came from." She placed the Red Delicious in the bowl.

Tara saw through the hidden code and folded her arms. "You heard me talking with Joseph last night?"

Bear's left eyebrow drew upward. Her gaze trailed to the ashtray Tara had cleaned and put back on the counter in its usual spot beneath the kitchen window. Bear cleared her throat. "Smokin' makes it hard to sneak around. Plan to quit soon as I get a chance." Her pale blue topaz eyes settled on Tara.

Embarrassed, Tara sighed. Now not only Joseph knew her dark secrets, but so did Bear. To double-check, she asked, "You heard everything?"

Bear's complexion crinkled like cracked clay as she faintly smiled. "Enough to understand you need our help. I want you to know, Sarah— that's not your real name is it?"

She shook her head.

"Probably shouldn't tell me either."

Again, she shook her head.

"Well, Sarah Smith, or whoever you are, I want you to know my son's a darn good judge of character, and it sounds like he's agreed to help you out of a sorry fix. We stick together here on the White Eagle Appaloosa. There'll be no running out in the middle of the night or day." The woman's words were bossy, but the way she said them—with worry and concern—softened the delivery.

"I won't." Tara decided right then that she liked Bear.

The woman headed for the door, pulling a pack of cigarettes from her vest pocket. She tapped one out, then stopped. "I would like to know what the man you're running from looks like in case he shows up."

"He's as tall as Joseph, curly blond hair, and really tan."

"Anything else?"

"He's a cop and knows how to use a gun." Tara couldn't think of additional information. "I'm new to this; I'm not sure what to tell you. You might want to talk to Joseph. He can fill you in." She brushed her bangs away from her forehead. "I'll do everything I can to avoid being a bother."

A lopsided smile gentled Bear's face. "Good. With you here, we've got another hand to help us with the cattle drive."

Cattle drive?

A new fear washed over Tara.

* * *

As Joseph showed Katelen how to prepare the formula in the three-quart nursing bottle to feed Shamrock, Wes and Digger joined them.

"Chief, what would you like us to do today?" Digger watched him closely. The old man had to know something had happened.

Joseph made sure the nipple was secure, handed the bottle to Katelen, then turned to Digger and Wes. "Take the bull from the corral and put him with the herd. Check on the cattle too. After what happened yesterday, we need to check them more often than we have been."

Digger and Wes watched his every move, taking in his instructions, and waiting for more.

"And, uh . . . keep a lookout for Lester Fimble."

Wes and Digger looked at each other, perplexed. They obviously hadn't heard the rifle shot or seen the flat tire in Joseph's truck bed.

"I don't want to explain; just know I have my reasons."

They both left to saddle up and head out. Watching them go, Joseph wondered if he was doing the right thing by not telling them or even reporting Lester to the sheriff. And he should have called about his cattle being shot. Who would have killed an innocent cow for no reason? Lester? Harlen, the old hermit? Denver Harris? If it had been Harris, Joseph needed to warn the other cattlemen in the area because Harris's fanatical environmental views had him on the outs with most of the ranchers. But right now, with Tara needing to keep a low profile, he didn't want to draw attention to the ranch by getting the law involved, though if one more thing happened, he'd probably have to.

Katelen made her way through the stall gate. Shamrock saw the bottle in her hand and came right over, readily taking the nipple in his mouth and sucking. The calf remembered what to do from the night before. Even though they could keep the critter alive, bottle-feeding him was one more thing that had to be done at least twice a day but most likely three with a calf this young. Joseph wanted to see if one of the friendlier mama cows would let the baby nurse.

"Daddy, can we name him something else?" Katelen held the bottle with both hands as the calf sucked long and deep.

"Why? Shamrock fits him." He pointed to the brown clover marking on the calf's white forehead.

"You're always telling me we don't name cattle we're going to sell. Aren't we going to sell this one?" His daughter had him there.

"Sarah isn't used to ranch life. She'll learn, but for right now, why don't we let her call the calf what she wants?"

Katelen didn't answer, and Joseph knew his daughter wanted to change the animal's name because Tara had been the one who had called him that. His little girl still clung to the hope of him marrying Irene.

He gazed at Katelen, who seemed to have moved on and was now having fun trying to hold the bottle. He chuckled. "I'm going to bring in a mama cow—the one that lost its calf a few days ago—and see if she'll let him nurse."

"Do you have to? I promise I'll feed him." Katelen's little forehead wrinkled with hope.

"We have more cows than this one to take care of, plus the horses." He heard a vehicle pull into the barnyard, and then Irene got out.

Great.

Had she spoken to her father? Did she know he'd threatened Joseph and shot out his tire? Joseph decided to meet her before she came into the barn. He didn't want Katelen to overhear them discussing the matter.

He stepped out into the sunlight just as Bear left the house. *Good grief.* All he needed now was for Tara to join their ranks and he'd have a triple threat of women. He needed to talk with each one but not at the same time.

Irene waited for Bear to come to her before the two of them walked up to Joseph. Should he ask Irene about her father or wait?

Wait. He didn't want his mother dragged into this quarrel. "What brings you out here again?" he asked as friendly as he could.

"Wanted to check on the calf, if that's all right." She shielded her eyes from the sun with her hand to look at him. "And I wanted to see how your *fiancée* was feeling after the tetanus shot. Some people have bad reactions." The halter top Irene wore with jeans and chaps revealed more of her cleavage than usual. He studied her face, searching for a sign that she might know about her father's threats. If she knew, there would be a crack in her expression. She gave him a brilliant smile like yesterday had never happened.

"Besides," Bear chimed in, "if memory serves, you asked her to take a look at some of the horses out near the lake. Anyway, that's what you said a couple of days ago. If she's going to do it before the drive, today's a good day. I'll go with her."

"I want to go too." Katelen had walked up beside Joseph. He glanced down at her. In her hands was the empty bottle. He looked back at the stall to see she'd closed the gate so Shamrock wouldn't get out. Of course she had. He should have known his little rancher would have made sure the animal was safe before leaving it alone.

If Katelen went with Bear and Irene, she'd be away from Tara, which was a good thing, a win-win for everyone. "Why not?" He glanced toward the house. With them gone, he might have a chance to learn more about Tara.

* * *

Tara scrubbed Bear's scuff marks from the newly waxed floor. Her arm ached where Irene had given her the shot last night but not enough to stop her. She also washed Bear's cup, dried it, and was putting it away in the cupboard when she heard voices at the back door.

Irene and Katelen walked in laughing and smiling, but they halted midstep when they saw the kitchen.

"Holy Moses!" Irene turned in a circle. "It looks like *Better Homes and Gardens* threw up all over in here. Did Digger die? He don't like nobody fussin' in his kitchen."

"After breakfast he asked me to help out." Tara really didn't need to defend what she'd done, yet she felt she had to.

Katelen's expression held hatred as she glared at Tara. "I'm tellin'." She stomped to the door, deliberately scuffing her black-heeled cowboy boots across the tiles. The screen door banged behind her.

Irene bit her lips together and placed her arms akimbo on her hips. "So, Sarah Smith, thought I'd check on you before heading out to the horses. Sometimes a tetanus shot will give the patient a slight fever. How're you feeling?"

After the cruel and deliberate way Irene had given her the shot, Tara had very little reason to trust this woman even though at this moment she sounded like a caring professional. Tara grabbed a bottle of cleaner, squirted the scuff marks Katelen had left on the floor, and wiped them up. "I'm fine."

"Good." Irene rubbed her chin. "You know, something's been bothering me."

Tara put the cleaner and scrubbing cloth away. Not wanting to know but realizing there was no way this woman would leave until she said her piece, she asked, "What's that?"

Irene stared at her for a moment. "Why would a country boy like Joseph take up with a sickly looking city woman like you? Can't figure it out."

So Irene wasn't going to dance around Joseph and Tara's engagement like she had yesterday. This morning she'd taken her gloves off and was ready to fight. Trying to appear calm, even though she was irritated by the woman's dig regarding her appearance, Tara drew in a deep breath. Screwing up her courage, she put on the guise of a fiancée. "It's called love. Rather a foreign word to you, I suppose."

"You suppose wrong. Joseph loves me, but you're making it difficult for him to remember." Irene glared at Tara.

Tara knew by the woman's revealing top she was doing all she could to help his memory. "If he loves you, why is he marrying me?"

"Well, that's the mystery of it. And I intend to find out." She tipped her cowboy hat to Tara, pushed the screen door open, and left. Irene had laid down the gauntlet and plainly stated her intent.

What in this crazy, countryside world was that overbearing woman going to do? She'd blow Tara's cover if she nosed around too much. Tara had to think of a way to stop her, but she quickly realized she could do nothing on her own. She would have to tell Joseph what Irene had said.

But she couldn't at the moment because Irene and Katelen were outside with him. She was tempted to clean the rest of the house to ease her nerves, but after Katelen's reaction, she thought it best to wait and talk with Bear or Digger before cleaning more. Maybe she could wash her aunt's suit she'd worn yesterday. And then what? Jenny and Joseph's room? She could clean in there. Joseph had already given her permission.

After turning on the washing machine, she dragged the vacuum she'd found in the hall closet to her bedroom and started in. She vacuumed under the bed; dusted the dresser, night stand, and headboard; switched the clothes from the washer to the dryer; and decided to give her bathroom a good scrubbing. Coming out of the bathroom, she saw the picture of Joseph and Jenny. Joseph had told her to make herself at home, but she couldn't with them watching her every move, so she slipped the picture in a drawer. After grabbing her aunt's suit from the dryer and folding it neatly, she realized she was finished. She figured she might have a chance of finding Joseph alone, so she rolled down her sleeves and left the house.

Scanning the empty barnyard, she was disappointed not to see him. She'd been under the impression that Joseph would always stay near. He had to be here somewhere. A nagging worry about Garrett surfaced, but Mac had said he didn't think Garrett was headed her way, so she pushed the ugly thought aside and started for the barn, hoping she'd find Joseph caring for the calf.

She took a deep breath as she walked across the gravel, reveling in the sweet scent of grass and hay. The black Appaloosa stallion that had nudged her yesterday pranced around his corral. In the adjacent corral stood the tan-colored Appaloosa mare the man had left.

Spellbound by the power and grace of the horses, Tara stepped up on the lowest rung of the fence and marveled at the beautiful animals. She remembered what Bear had said about helping with the cattle drive. Tara had never ridden a horse in her life. Could she do it? Could she actually climb up in the saddle of one of those huge beasts and act like she wasn't scared? Her stomach cartwheeled.

Hearing a calf bawl, Tara whipped around. Joseph stood behind her with Shamrock. "Well, what do you think?" He motioned toward the calf. The animal's bright, brown eyes blinked.

Excited to see the calf doing so well, she hopped down and ran to it. She fell to her knees and hugged the animal's neck. Examining where the bullet had been, she said, "You can't even see the wound." She looked up. Joseph didn't say anything, just stood there quietly scanning the mountain and road. Worry tugged at his face, and Tara thought of something that might ease his mind. "I called Mac this morning."

"You did?"

"I needed to touch base with him. He said he had a lead and believed Garrett wasn't heading this way."

"That's good news." Still, he appeared worried.

"Has something happened?" Concern flashed through Tara.

Joseph shook his head like he was shaking off a trance. Focusing on her, he smiled warmly. "Since we gave Shamrock plenty of fluids with the IV and bottle-fed him, he's bouncing back really well, don't you think?"

He didn't answer her question, so she rephrased it. "Is something bothering you?"

"Sorry. I had a disagreement with Irene's father this morning."

Somewhat relieved this wasn't about her, she rose and wiped the dust from her pant legs. "Disagreement?"

"Nothing major—just him letting off steam." He clenched his jaw, which clued her in that there was more to the story.

Perhaps this *was* about her. Did she dare ask? Maybe in a roundabout way. "Was that why you didn't say anything at breakfast—because you were upset about Irene's father?"

Joseph tilted his head as his eyes widened in a puzzled expression. "Didn't *have* anything to say."

She wondered if that was true or if Joseph was trying to avoid telling her. Was Irene's father upset about her and Joseph's fake engagement? Trying to find out more, she tried again. "My offer still stands: I can leave, and you could make amends with everyone."

"No. Irene and I were passing time dating. Lester was being Lester."

This was her opportunity to tell Joseph about Irene's threat. "Irene said she was going to try to find out why you want to marry me. I think she could cause problems."

"She's just kicking up dust. Don't worry about her. Besides, the more she sees us together, the more she'll get used to the idea of us being a couple. It's kind of like the way you helped me convince Wes yesterday . . . with the kiss; I'm sure we can do the same with Irene. We simply need to convince her we're in love." He stared at her.

Heat crawled up her neck to her cheeks. "This keeps getting worse and worse."

"I know it's highly unlikely someone like you would fall in love with someone like me."

"Oh, I didn't mean it that way. You're a good-looking guy."

He gave her a teasing grin.

Who was she kidding? Eyes dark as flint, noble brow, chiseled features—he was darn handsome despite the scar on his cheekbone. But she couldn't let him think she was attracted to him. That would only further complicate an already messy situation. "I mean you have a cowboy ruggedness any woman would find irresistible."

His grin spread to a full-blown smile.

"I mean—" Totally flustered, Tara hid her face in her hands, feeling the heat from her cheeks on her palms.

Joseph put his arm around her shoulders. "I'm giving you a tough time. Don't worry, we'll pull this off. No one will know who you really are."

Though still embarrassed, she peered into his eyes. His gaze looked empathetic and caring, much the same as she'd seen in his mother's eyes. Then, thinking of mothers, she remembered her conversation with Bear. "Did you speak with your mother this morning?"

"A little. She went with Katelen and Irene to check on the Appaloosas."

"Did she tell you she overheard us talking last night?"

He shook his head, though he didn't appear surprised by the news.

"Well, she did. I think she heard a great deal because she wanted to know what Garrett looked like. I suggested she speak with you."

Joseph seemed a little concerned and yet relieved at the same time. "Good. I'm sure when we have some privacy, she'll bring it up." Shamrock nudged Joseph's leg. He let go of Tara and patted the side of the calf. "These little ones bounce back quickly. What he needs, though, is for one of our cows to adopt him so we can take him out on the range once he's strong enough. I need to bring one of the more gentle cows back to the ranch. If a cow is around the calf so she gets used to him, we'll have more success in coaxing her to let him nurse. Sometimes it works; sometimes it doesn't. If you're up to it, I'd like you to come with me to collect a mama. Can you ride?"

"I've never tried." Fear gripped her. "Really. Let me stay here and clean the house."

"Well, you need to learn to ride. The cattle drive is coming up, and you'll have to ride then. I'll put you on Shotgun."

"Don't you have a horse called Poke-A-Long or Turtle?"

Joseph pulled a toothpick from his shirt pocket and put it between his teeth. "The reason I named the horse Shotgun was because I traded my shotgun for her. The name has nothing to do with how fast she runs. I'll grant you she can be a little spirited, but she's smart, and that makes up for it. She'll be a good horse for you. If you're afraid, the only way to get over it is to ride."

Getting over fear had been a mighty obstacle in her life. Fear had led to her breakdown. Fear had brought her here. Fear had been the driving force dictating her actions most of her life. Maybe the time had come to face her fear. Riding a horse might be the medicine she needed to make her stronger.

Yet Tara's new determination did nothing to stop the nervous flutter in her stomach.

CHAPTER NINE
WILD FEAR

THE PICKUP CAB WAS HOT and stuffy with Scrap, once again, lodged between Tara and Joseph. Tara rubbed her sweaty palms over her jeans as she tried to avoid worrying about riding. "Katelen wasn't very happy when I cleaned the kitchen this morning."

"She'll get over it." Joseph kept his eyes on the road.

The little girl's dislike for her was going to be tough to solve, and there wasn't much Tara could do about it. She looked over at Joseph and noticed his black Stetson resting on his head. "I'm curious; why do you wear your hat when you're inside the truck?"

A teasing grin drew his dark eyebrows together. "What?"

Trying to entice him into a conversation, she continued. "Why don't you remove your hat when you're inside a truck or a building? I thought all cowboys took off their hats when they were inside."

"You want to know when I take off my hat?"

She gave him an I-wouldn't-have-asked-unless-I-wanted-to-know nod.

"I take this hat off for two reasons. One, when I bathe." He stopped, as if hoping she would fill in the other reason.

She could play this game. "The other reason is when you eat. You took your hat off last night for supper."

"That's just a country thing and doesn't count."

"Okay, how about for the 'Star-Spangled Banner'?"

"Okay, three reasons." He shrugged as if conceding the point.

Tara rapidly tried to think of events that men removed their hats for. "When you go to church?"

"All right, four. When I bathe, for the national anthem, church, and . . ." He tilted his head, widened his eyes, and raised eyebrows. A low chuckle rumbled from deep inside his chest as he added, "When I go to bed."

"That's so obvious." She couldn't believe she'd missed that one. "Sleeping shouldn't count."

He seemed pretty pleased with himself as he took his eyes off the road for a second to playfully glance at her.

Tara decided to use the jest as a way to learn more about his relationship with Irene. "So, has Irene seen you with your hat off . . . when you . . . sleep?"

As if playing poker, he zeroed in on her with an I'm-playing-your-bluff look. "Nope. Why?"

She deserved his question. She now wished she'd never started this conversation. This was diving into forbidden territory. Territory foreign to her. Her cheeks grew warm, and she knew she was blushing. She reminded herself that his flirting meant nothing. He was acting. That was all. Besides, so was she. She couldn't allow herself to get rattled and embarrassed over every little thing. If only her blushing wouldn't betray her emotions. The *only* thing Joseph White Eagle was serious about was keeping her safe until she could go home. They were strangers forced together out of necessity. She glanced at Scrap, who, like a tennis spectator, had been watching them volley their questions back and forth.

Joseph followed her gaze. "You know," he said to the animal as the dog's white-tipped tail thumped against the seat. "Some people ask the most disturbing questions just to get a rise out of others."

Scrap whined as if he sympathized.

Joseph glanced at Tara.

She put her hand over her mouth to conceal her smile. If she didn't watch out, this spark of attraction could easily turn into something more serious. She couldn't afford that. In fact, she couldn't afford to forget the reality of why she was here and that her very life was at stake. The frivolity of this situation abandoned her. With a more somber tone, she said, "No, not to get a rise out of people. Some are sincere and merely want to know more about those to whom they must trust their lives."

He slowed the truck, pulled from the main road, and stopped, then shut off the engine. He turned in his seat, his intense dark eyes looking straight at her. "Tara, my life is an open book. I'm a father, a son, and a rancher. Irene is a good friend, but that is all. I eat, breathe, and live for this ranch and the people I love. I believe in God and know He has a plan for each and every one of us. Right now, His plan has you staying here with me and my family. I'll do whatever it takes to keep you safe. But that doesn't mean I'm not going to tease you. Despite our phony engagement, despite the acting, we can be friends and have a good time, can't we?"

Tara was relieved he was being straightforward. "Of course."

"All right, then. Let's find that mama cow to take her back to Shamrock." He got out of the truck.

She climbed out as well and followed him to the rear of the old rusted horse trailer hitched to the pickup. He unlocked the gate latch and eased open the creaking door. It didn't take him long to unload the animals. Joseph tied his horse on one side of the trailer and Tara's on the other. "Get to know your horse while I saddle mine." He left her alone with the animal.

Tara raised a hand to pet the horse's neck as it turned its head to her. She reached for the animal's forehead and stroked where a white blaze trailed down its black nose. An ancient Irish legend her grandfather had told her came to mind.

The cave fairies. These fairies were known as Tuatha-Dé-Dananns, and they ruled Ireland until they were conquered by the Milesians. The Tuatha were skilled in all magic, and though the Milesians wanted to destroy them, they became fascinated by the Tuatha's powers—and especially the superior breed of horses they reared. The animals could not be surpassed. They were fast as the wind and had arched necks and broad chests. Some said the horses were made of fire and flame, not of dull, heavy earth.

"It's awful quiet over there." Joseph walked around the trailer, leading his saddled horse. He tied the gelding to another bridal hitch by the tailgate and turned to Shotgun, stroking her back.

"I remembered an old legend my Irish grandfather told me."

"Since your picture books are mainly about Irish folklore, I'm not surprised. So this legend was about horses?" He continued stroking the animal.

"Yes." Tara pictured the scene Grandfather had painted with words. "These horses were owned by Tuatha, cave fairies. Their hooves were shod with silver, and they had golden bridles. With star-shaped jewels on their foreheads, they were quite a sight."

"Sounds like it. Have you drawn them in a picture book?" He made his way around Shotgun, still petting the horse.

"Not yet. I can't help but wish I could cast a magic spell and become a Tuatha-Dé-Danann knight. They weren't afraid of anything, especially not their horses."

He stroked down Shotgun's neck. "Don't be afraid. Shotgun won't hurt you once you earn her trust. And to do that, she needs to know you like her."

She wondered if this simple concept applied to humans. Would he have to truly like her before he could trust her? Silly thought. Why did she think that? She rubbed her eyes and tried to remain focused on what the horse and Joseph were doing.

He opened a compartment near the front of the trailer and pulled out a reddish-brown leather saddle and a colorful Indian-rug-like saddle blanket. Leaning them against the fender, he reached back inside and drew out a squirt bottle. "First you need to spray her with this insect repellent. It will keep the ticks and deerflies away. Brushing it on the horse with your hands will show her you care." He handed Tara the bottle. "I wonder what those cave fairies did for pests."

"Used magic, I assume. Just squirt it on?" She looked at the horse's twitching muscles.

"Here, I'll show you how." Joseph sprayed the animal and rubbed repellent over its withers, belly, and legs, talking and cooing to the Appaloosa all the while. Tara rubbed repellent over the horse's neck and forehead.

He set the bottle on the trailer's fender and hefted the blanket and saddle onto the horse. Catching the stirrup on the saddle horn, he cinched the saddle and placed the stirrup back in position. "Whenever you're not riding a horse for a while but are leaving the saddle on, you should loosen the cinch. I'm going to leave the hackamore on her. She'll do what you want without a bit in her mouth. The important thing to remember is to relax."

The moment of truth had arrived.

"Wait a minute." Joseph held his hand up. "You need to be sprayed too. Don't want wood ticks on you."

Joseph sprayed her pants with the musty-smelling repellent, starting at her calves and spraying up her body. Taking a firmer hold on the bottle, he said, "Hold out your arms." He sprayed down each sleeve, then said, "Turn around and keep your arms out." He repeated the process on her back, except this time he worked from her top down. Once finished, he turned her around to face him. With repellent on the palm of his hand, he wiped her cheeks and across her forehead. He paused a moment, staring into her eyes. His gaze went to her lips and didn't waver.

Joseph drew closer, and Tara felt like he was going to take her in his arms and kiss her. But how could this be possible? Last night he said there was no affection between them. Yet every nerve in her came alive. She remembered the kiss they'd shared on the garden bench, the feel of his lips on hers, and how something had awakened inside. Whether he was acting or not, she couldn't let that happen again, especially since no one else was around. They had to remain friends. "Joseph?" Tara took the bottle from him. "Should I spray you too?"

She wanted to show him she wasn't upset and she could do this cowboy stuff without batting a citified eye. She didn't know what force was driving her. Was it the way he'd looked at her, or was it because she felt he needed her?

What an odd concept—his needing her.

He gave her the go-ahead nod.

Spraying his pant legs, she worked her way up the same way he had. He held out his long arms, allowing her to spray his front and back. Nearly finished, she squirted liquid onto her palm, ready to do his face, but she hesitated.

He stood still, gazing down on her, his face expressionless. Her hand trembled as she wiped over the scar on his right cheek. What had happened to him? Did he get the scar while working as a police officer or on the ranch?

He flinched.

"Does it hurt?"

"No." He took her hand in his and held it.

She should pull away, should step back. But she didn't want to. She felt like she belonged there.

Joseph pulled away, breaking the spell. He took the spray bottle from her, set it inside the compartment, grabbed his leather work gloves, and closed the hatch.

He untied Shotgun and handed her the reins. "She's all yours."

The feeling of belonging she'd had a second before vanished.

* * *

As Joseph tugged on his work gloves, he knew he had to take control of his emotions. When he looked at Tara, he no longer thought of Jenny.

No, instead he saw a beautiful, trusting woman, and he was becoming mesmerized. Her eyes were as green as polished malachite in the midday sun, and his arms yearned to hold her. The feelings he was experiencing for Tara were new, different, fresh, and alive. No, Tara wasn't Jenny, and he was glad.

Guilt roped him in. Though Jenny had been dead for five years, he felt he was betraying her. What was wrong with him? He was supposed to keep Tara safe, not . . .

"But . . ." Tara stared at the horse. "I've never . . . ? I mean . . . How do you . . . ?"

Against his better judgment but wanting to get on their way, he said, "I'll help you into the saddle."

He guided her hands to the saddle horn and cantle. She tried to step into the stirrup but couldn't quite reach. Threading his gloved fingers together, he stepped forward. "Put your foot here, and I'll give you an added push as you pull your other leg over the horse."

She stepped on his hands, and he boosted her up as she swung her leg over the horse's rump and landed squarely in the saddle.

Joseph got on his horse and tried to think beyond the new emotions churning in his gut. "First, you need to get used to the motion of the animal. This will help you relax. Sit deep."

"How can I sit deeper than I am?" She squirmed, trying to do what he said.

She wasn't doing it right, and he knew he'd have to ride closer to show her what he meant, like he had with Katelen. Without thinking, he leaned from his saddle, reached over, and placed his hand beneath her bottom, sliding her down a bit.

Her eyes widened, and he suddenly realized he shouldn't have done that. He pulled his hand away and tried to act cool and calm. "Try to sit on the back pockets of your jeans. That gives you balance for the quick, hard moves Shotgun might make." Wanting to draw her attention to something else, he said, "Those stirrups feel all right?" He studied her legs. They appeared slightly bent, which was how they were supposed to be.

"I guess." Tara looked at her knees.

"You're using one of my mother's saddles. I let the stirrups down a couple of notches before leaving the ranch." He reached over and took the reins from her. "I'm going to lead your horse for a while. I want you to close your eyes and concentrate on the motion of the animal. Try to relax. A horse can sense if you're afraid through the pressure from your legs and behind."

"The horse can feel fear through the saddle?" Tara didn't sound like she believed him.

"The horse can smell your fear." Joseph clicked his tongue and kneed his horse into a slow walk. "Horses are pretty smart. A sure-footed horse can generally find his way home by himself."

Tara held on to the saddle horn for the first few jarring steps. Gradually, she appeared to relax and feel the rhythm. "This reminds me of when I was a child. I would sit on Grandpa Kelly's lap and he'd rock me."

"Uh-huh." Joseph scanned the area, searching for the herd and anything out of the ordinary. His hand drifted to the rifle in its holder attached to his saddle just to assure himself the weapon was there. Even though he had work to do, he had to keep Tara safe.

But was *he* safe from becoming involved with her? That was the question, and he had no answer. Off in the distance were brown and white dots—his cattle. Scrap trotted nearby, watching Joseph for a command. The border collie's herding ability was a godsend. Joseph was grateful to have such a darn good dog.

Joseph reined back, stopping his horse. Tara's walked up alongside his. "Have a good feel for it now?"

"I guess."

"Good." He handed Tara the reins. "When you want the horse to turn right, pull the rein in your right hand and nudge with your left knee. When you want to turn left, pull the reins left and nudge with your right knee. When you want her to stop, say 'whoa' and pull back on the reins, and when you want her to go, click your tongue and nudge with both knees. Shotgun will follow Copper, so don't worry." He gave his horse a light tap with his heels, and they started down the trail.

The sun bore down on them, and heat waves rose from the desert floor. They rode for nearly an hour, drawing nearer to the herd. Joseph half expected to run into Wes and Digger—they were supposed to bring the bull, Beelzebub, out here—but Joseph could see no sign of them. He checked on Tara several times, and she dutifully followed.

Again, he surveyed the area. In the distance, he thought there was a reflection but decided it had to be the sun's rays bouncing off the windshield of his truck. They rode a while longer before he spotted the cow he wanted.

Joseph waited for Tara to ride near him. "Sometimes when we try to graft an orphaned calf to another cow, we have a hard time because the mama can be ornery. This one is different. Her calf died a couple of days ago, so I think she'll welcome Shamrock. All we have to do is load her in the trailer and take her back to the ranch. How are you doing?"

Tara seemed reluctant to answer. A rookie in the saddle, he knew her hindquarters and knees had to be smarting, but she answered, "I'm fine."

"I'll cut the mama cow from the herd, and we can head back to the truck. Do you think you can hang on a while longer?"

"Sure. Why not?"

"Take your feet out of the stirrups and let them dangle for a bit," he said, sympathizing. "That will help your knees." Joseph showed her how.

She copied his actions and sighed.

A loud bellow drew their attention.

"That's Beelzebub."

"With a name like that, he must be related to the Dark Druid. What's the matter with him?" Tara put her feet back in the stirrups.

"He's searching for a lady friend." Joseph had already put his feet back in the stirrups and was untying his lariat from the saddle.

The large, muscular bull trudged over a lava rim and headed straight for them. His enormous clawlike horns curled around his face.

"I'm going to herd him toward the rest of the cattle. Sit tight. I'll be right back." He galloped ahead, circling behind the cantankerous bull. "Head up there," Joseph yelled at the bull, slapping the lariat against his leg.

Beelzebub whipped around, flipping clumps of sand and weeds high in the air and making a swirling dust cloud. Snorting, the animal burrowed his forehead in the dirt, raised his head, shook, and zeroed in on Joseph. With one powerful burst of energy, the bull charged.

Joseph's horse danced around the frustrated bull, and Joseph yelled to Tara, "Ride over to that bluff." He pointed in the direction he wanted her to go. "He's mad. I don't want you in his way."

Tara kneed Shotgun. "Come on, girl."

Again, the bull bellowed, snorted, and flipped dirt in the air. Joseph rode ahead of him, teasing the ornery animal in the direction he needed him to go.

All at once, a sharp startling sound of rifle fire echoed through the air. A bullet hit the ground, and Joseph scanned the area to see where it had come from. All he could see was sagebrush.

"Get down!" he yelled.

Tara turned and looked puzzled. He didn't have time to explain. Joseph kicked Copper to a run, leaving the bull to fend for himself. Drawing up to Tara, he lunged from his horse, tackling her. They tumbled to the desert floor, and she gasped for air. He didn't have time to calm her. Joseph pointed to a small protective crevice of lava rocks and shielded Tara as he got her to cover. Though the rocks made them safer, Joseph had her lie facedown. Was the shot meant for him or her or the bull?

Another bullet ricocheted off the rocks. This time the horses took off at a dead run.

Tara's entire body trembled. She turned sideways and glanced at Joseph. Wild fear clouded her eyes. He couldn't risk her getting hit, so he bear-hugged her from behind, forcing her to stay down.

If only he hadn't left his cell phone in the glove box of the truck. The only help he could count on was from above. *Please, God, help me know what to do.*

CHAPTER TEN
Too Much Information

THE ECHO OF RIFLE FIRE threw Tara's mind into another time, another place where all was dark. She turned on her side. Next to her lay a body.

Rosalie.

Blood smeared her aunt's face. Her eyes were frozen in fear.

Wanting to comfort her, Tara tried to reach out but couldn't. She held something in her hand. Something heavy. When she looked down, she was holding a gun—Rosalie's gun.

The image melted away, and Tara was in bright sunshine, lying on sandy ground, the scent of sagebrush in the air. Something heavy lay on top of her.

No, not something . . . someone.

A person.

The killer?

Panic flew through Tara. Rosalie was dead, and Tara was next. She reared back as hard as she could, and her head collided with her attacker. He rolled off, recoiling in pain and giving her a chance to escape. Tara scrambled to her feet and ran.

* * *

Stunned, Joseph fell backward, pain numbing his nose and mouth. The coppery taste of blood assaulted his tongue, and he rubbed the back of his hand over his smarting upper lip as he watched Tara frantically race through sagebrush. Scrap was trying to herd her back to Joseph, but she didn't seem to recognize the dog as she stumbled on rocks and tripped over ruts. If she didn't get down, she'd get shot. Joseph leaped to his feet.

A bullet zinged overhead and hit the dirt just as he tackled Tara. He lay on top of her again, shielding her the best he could.

She twisted and squirmed until she turned onto her back, coming face to face with him. No recognition flickered in her eyes. She thrashed about, and Joseph cupped his hands to her face, making her look at him. "Knock it off. It's me, Joseph. You're going to get us both killed."

Tara stared at him. Her breath came in short, desperate bursts.

Her fight stopped. Her arms slowly wrapped around him. "Joseph." She whispered his name, hiding her face in his neck. He knew he had to be crushing her. He eased to one side while still covering her. She didn't let go. She was so small, so fragile. He wanted to kick himself for bringing her out here, but he truly thought whoever was shooting was after him, not her. And he had to believe the shooter meant no real harm but was delivering a message. He just couldn't figure out what the message was.

The lack of gunfire was almost deafening. What was going on? Still lying on the ground, Joseph stole a quick glance around. Scrap was by his side, and he could see little else lying down. Rising up on his elbow, he saw no sign of their horses or the cattle. It was just desert with the mountains in the distance. Whoever had been shooting had to have been far away. Maybe that windshield shining in the distance hadn't been his truck. Could it have been the shooter? They were well within shooting range on the valley floor. The bullets had come from that direction. As hard as he tried, he couldn't see a visible threat. He needed to stand up.

Joseph carefully eased completely off of Tara. "Stay down, okay?"

"Don't leave me."

Joseph'd seen fear like this before, many times as a cop. He leaned close. "I won't. I'm just going to take a look." He started to rise, but Tara pulled him down.

"Please!" Worry pinched her forehead.

She was trying hard to be brave, but he could see the war going on inside her. Joseph pulled her into his arms, holding her tight. "It's all right. I really think the shooter is gone now."

"But you're not sure." She spoke into his chest.

No, he wasn't sure of anything.

The sound of galloping horses made him look up. "Someone's coming."

"The killer?" Tara shuddered.

Joseph had nothing to defend them with. His gun was on his horse, and his horse was long gone. He had to put himself between the shooter and Tara.

"I've got to stand up. Stay behind me." He peered deep into her eyes. Something new threaded through them: gratitude, amazement, and . . . He wasn't sure what else, but she released him. The urge to pull her to him and never let go swelled inside his chest. Fighting his emotions, Joseph rose to his feet.

Digger rode up with Joseph's and Tara's mounts, and relief flooded Joseph.

"Hey, Chief. Wes and I heard gunshots. He's scouting the area, but I wanted to make sure you're all right. Found your horses."

Joseph surveyed their surroundings, looking for anything out of the ordinary—the shine of a windshield, the movement of bushes, even dust from the road. Nothing stood out.

He gave Tara a hand up. Her face had paled, and she avoided eye contact as she brushed sand and dried weeds off her knees and backside.

"Was he shootin' at you and the little lassie?" Digger's whiskery face twitched with concern beneath the tattered baseball cap resting backwards on his head.

"Think so." Joseph brushed dirt and twigs off his own pants.

A timid Tara handed him his hat. He hadn't noticed while trying to save their lives that it had fallen off his head. Tara's eyes rested on the Stetson. Wanting to ease her mind, he put it on his head, gave her a thank-you nod, and winked. A slight smile tugged at the corners of her mouth, though her smile quickly faded.

Wes rode up on his lathered and tired horse.

"Did you see anyone?" Joseph asked.

"Just dust flyin' up from the dirt road over the hill. That no-good son-of-a-poacher is turnin' tail and runnin'." Wes squinted as he scanned the hillside.

Joseph noticed Digger studying Tara. The old man wouldn't miss her pale complexion or her trembling.

"We'll never catch him now." Joseph rubbed his throbbing nose. He'd forgotten momentarily about Tara knocking him good with the back of her head and how she'd appeared confused. She'd been fine up until the bullets had started flying and he'd tackled her off the horse. Many times when he'd worked on the force, he'd find victims dealing with PTSD. When Tara heard the gunfire, it must have stirred up memories of her aunt's murder.

He wanted to ask Tara but couldn't in front of Digger and Wes. Trying to act normal in a situation that was anything but, he said, "I was trying to herd Beelzebub over the rise." Joseph pointed to the lava ridge where the cantankerous bull had come down. Something huge was lying on the ground.

No, it can't be.

Joseph's heart raced, and his skin prickled. He rushed across the distance, each hurried step filling with dread until he stopped in front of the bull's body. A bullet had hit the animal in the head. Here, lying at Joseph's feet, was his prized breeding bull. Dead. Another financial blow. Anger churned Joseph's gut and pulsed in his veins.

Wes and Digger had climbed down from their horses and now stood shoulder to shoulder staring at the animal. They knew the financial strain this would put on Joseph. Tara took Joseph's hand, her touch gentle, soothing. He realized this could have been Tara lying here dead. Immense gratitude filled him. His insisting she learn to ride nearly got her killed. When would he ever learn not to be so muleheaded? He thought a ride would be good for her. And he had to collect the cow. The cow . . .

What had happened to the mother cow?

He scanned the landscape for the Hereford. Through the brush, he caught sight of her. She'd wandered at least three quarters of a mile away.

"Thank goodness, she's all right. We can't afford to lose more cattle." Joseph looked at Wes and Digger. "That shooter was on a mission. We need to act, and fast. I know it's early, but we have to move the herd up to summer grazing in the next couple of days. We can't wait until June. Someone's picking off my cattle in the valley. The mountains will give them safety. Could you two spread the word to the part-timers that we're starting roundup in the morning? It may take us a couple of days, but we can put cattle in the north pasture and leave some hands camped on guard duty twenty-four-seven."

Wes's Adam's apple dropped to the base of his throat as he gulped, but Joseph knew his men would move a good chunk of heaven and a large parcel of earth if he asked. He also knew if given the chance, these two would chase down the shooter and show him how real cowboys delivered justice.

Joseph knew the time had come to call Sheriff Conrad and Mac. The sheriff needed to be aware of the trouble, and Mac needed to know the danger Tara was in.

"You got it, Chief." Digger mounted his horse, and so did Wes. Without further questions, they left.

Joseph turned his full attention to Tara. "Are you all right?"

She smoothed a strand of fine hair away from her eyes. "I think so. I'm sorry I ran and put us both in danger. Sounds crazy, but for a moment, I saw Rosalie dead on the floor." She stared at him like she desperately needed him to say something encouraging.

He put his arm around her shoulders, hugging her briefly. He had to let her know he understood. "You've been under tremendous pressure. You witnessed a murder less than two days ago that you can't remember, and now today you've been shot at. I think you're allowed a moment of confusion." Her bandage had fresh blood. "Your cut is bleeding again."

Tara stared at the bandage as if remembering something else. Dreadful memories were eating her alive. He wanted her to talk about them, but first she needed to get out of the sun and relax a little. "We'll take care of it as soon as we get home. Why don't we get the mama cow into the trailer and head back to the ranch."

Tara heaved a sigh of relief and nodded.

Once they loaded the cow and were on their way back to the ranch, Joseph reassured her that the shooter couldn't have been Garrett, hoping to lay the groundwork for her to tell him more about what she remembered. But she hardly said a word, so he talked to her about her picture books and art. She only answered with yes, no, and maybe, and every time he tried to get close to the subject of her aunt, Tara clammed up and merely shrugged. He'd have to wait until later.

Later, she would have time to relax and begin to deal with her loss.

Later, Joseph could reassess the new feelings he was having for this woman.

Yes, later would be much better for both of them.

* * *

Tara closed her eyes and let the warm shower caress her. She wished she could have told Joseph more on the way home, but her emotions were too fresh to put into words. Her head throbbed, and she could still hear the sounds of gunshots, feel the flush of fear ripple over her skin. What troubled her even more was how she'd mentally checked out and thought she was at Rosalie's and that it was the night Garrett had Rosalie on the floor, beating her.

And the gun!

Tara had held a gun in her hand. Where had that memory come from? Joseph insisted the trauma of being shot at had thrown her into the delusion, but Tara didn't believe him. He didn't know her history. He didn't know she'd had a breakdown before.

On the ride home, Joseph had tried to persuade her that whoever had shot at them wasn't Garrett, that someone was trying to scare Joseph and ruin him financially, and for a while, she'd tried to believe him. But as he'd talked, her thoughts had drifted back to the night Rosalie died and the taunting memory of holding a weapon in her hand.

Joseph had said that when something horrible happened to a person, their mind sometimes played tricks on them. Maybe he was right. Garrett had been the one with the gun. He'd killed Rosalie and was now after Tara. Deep down, the fear that Garrett could have somehow tracked her here remained alive. After all, he was an Internet expert. His main responsibility on the force was using the web to find people. Ripples of water slid over her skin, and she wished with all her heart that her doubts would flow down the drain with the water.

Her upper arm was still sore where Irene had given her the tetanus shot, and she carefully peeled off the dressing over the barbed-wire cut. Her pink, raw skin had torn a little, but the bleeding had stopped.

Trying to forget her aches and pains, she lathered apple-scented shampoo into her hair. Her mind drifted back to Joseph and how he'd looked concerned about her arm. She also thought about how he'd tried to protect her, putting himself in the line of fire when the bullets were flying. His courage was amazing.

Courage had once again eluded her. What she'd give to be able to act with valor and face fear head-on. Maybe if she stayed here long enough, she would learn to be brave from Joseph. He didn't seem rattled by the event in the least.

After they'd arrived home, he'd told her to get some rest, but he'd remained outside, caring for the animals. She remembered before leaving him to go into the house how he'd looked at her with deep concern. His worries would grow exponentially if he knew about her past.

Rinsing the suds from her hair, she turned off the brass faucets and put her hair in a towel turban; then she wrapped another towel around her body.

She softly stroked the pink, sensitive skin around her wound, remembering what Irene had said about a trail of red being a sign of infection. No trail of red. Tara moved her jaw. No soreness, so no lockjaw. She was worrying needlessly. Of course, that was what she did best: worry.

A knock came at the bedroom door. She'd only brought her underwear into the bathroom with her, leaving her jeans and shirt on the bed, but maybe she could quickly towel off and slip on her clothes before answering. She caught a glimpse of herself in the mirror. No makeup! She hated anyone to see her without it. Makeup was her shield, something to hide behind, something to make her feel normal.

Another knock sounded, this time louder.

She had to answer. She hurried to the door. "Joseph, is that you?"

"Yes."

The door began to open, but Tara stopped him from coming in. "I'm dressing."

"I'll wait. I want to make sure you take care of that cut on your arm."

"Let me slip into some clothes." She closed the door, scooped up the clean jeans and shirt she'd laid out, and hurried to the bathroom. Her fingers fumbled over everything—the zipper in her pants, the buttons on her shirt, and even the socks she tugged onto her bare feet. Pulling the towel from her hair, she grabbed the pick off the counter and drove it through her long wet strands. Gazing in the mirror, she looked like a lost waif. She was tempted to put on eyeliner but thought better of it. In her state of mind, she'd probably poke out her eye. Still, she hated him to see her like this, but she had little choice.

As she opened the door, Joseph stood in the doorway. Desert dust covered his clothes and boots and even his black Stetson. She remembered handing the hat to him once the danger was over and how he'd chuckled. She couldn't be sure, but she thought he had added dodging bullets to his list of times he took off his hat. She could plainly see his nose and upper lip were a little swollen. He must have been hurt in the commotion.

His lips curved into a lopsided smile. "Sorry to bother you." In one hand, he held the handle of a large white box with a red cross on the lid.

"I'm fine, really. If you could leave a bandage, I'll take care of my cut."

"I want to take a look at it."

How could she say no to the man who had saved her life? And she couldn't very well ask him to wait while she put on her makeup and did her hair. Whether she liked it or not, she had to talk with him barefaced and wet-haired. Tara moved aside, letting him in.

Joseph set the medicine chest on the bed and looked around the room as if he noticed she'd cleaned it. His gaze stopped on the dresser top, where the picture of his late wife had been.

Worried he might be upset, she said, "I hope you don't mind, but I put the picture in the drawer."

Hurt flickered in his gaze for a second. "Let's see that arm."

She pushed her sleeve up. "Really, I can take care of it." She was uncomfortable having him in here alone with her. Even though they were supposed to be engaged and others probably thought nothing of it, Tara knew differently. There were no feelings between Joseph White Eagle and her. No feelings whatsoever. But having the man in her bedroom bothered her.

Silly. This is Joseph's house, his bedroom. He has every right to be in here. But uneasiness settled over her. Was it because the more time she spent with Joseph, the more she found herself attracted to him?

No.

Was it because she hadn't been completely truthful with him?

Partly, but still no.

The real reason for this uneasiness was she was relying on him to keep her safe when she needed to be strong and stand on her own. Yet with Joseph by her side, she felt complete.

Complete? The thought rattled her to her toes. This man was temporarily helping her. That was all. She could not rely on him to always be there for her.

But what if he was? Tara couldn't allow herself to entertain such thoughts. Besides, she could never feel complete while she was withholding the truth from him.

But what if she told him everything? Was there a possibility she could feel totally and blissfully whole in a real relationship with Joseph? She became aware of him watching her, waiting for her. She should tell him everything now. They were alone. And once she did, she'd be rid of the guilt. She could do it. Just tell him. Tara cleared her throat. "Joseph?"

"Yes?" His brows slanted with empathy, his dark eyes full of concern.

Once she told him, he'd never look at her the same. He'd see a crazy person, not her. She couldn't risk it, not yet. So instead of telling him what she knew she should, she dutifully held out her arm.

He guided her near the bed, where a lamp sat on the nightstand. Even though daylight lit the room, he turned on the lamp and took hold of her arm. She watched his large cowboy hands tenderly touch her skin as he studied her cut. His soft strokes were nearly hypnotic, magical.

Joseph opened the first-aid box and searched through the contents. Small brown bottles labeled Hoarhound, Nettles, St. John's Wort, and Wood Sorrel filled the white box.

"What kind of first-aid kit is that?" It looked like Grandpa Kelly's medicine chest, except he filled his with green and black stones, bird feathers, and tree roots, almost anything that would help him with his charms and ancient cures.

"I brought Digger's kit this time. He has all sorts of Indian medicine. There's also some white man's potions in here." He pulled out a small bottle labeled iodine.

"Wait a minute." She stepped away from him. "You told me iodine stings. The cut isn't that bad."

"I'll be gentle." He chuckled and peered once again into the box. Watching his seriousness as he searched through the trays, she knew this man had depth. He was a father, a son, and a widower. He was also a cattleman, an ex-cop, a protector, and even a stand-in doctor. She wondered what it would have been like to have been married to him. He had been deeply in love with his late wife; that was evident because he'd shut this room off in her memory and still looked for her picture when he entered the room.

Once again, he took her arm. "I just want your wound to be well on its way to healing before we leave for the drive. That is if Mac doesn't have me send you home after I tell him what's been going on."

A new fear welled up within her. What if Mac told Joseph about her breakdown?

"This will help speed the healing along." He poured a little iodine on a cotton swab he'd found and gently pressed it on her cut.

To her surprise, it didn't sting as badly as she'd expected. Maybe the soap in the shower had done most of the work. She relaxed and let him finish by putting clean gauze over the site and taping it in place. His magical fingers lingered on her arm. "There now. You're good as new."

She only wished that were true. "How's the mama cow?" She pulled down her sleeve, careful of the bandage.

"I put her in the pen next to Shamrock to let them get used to each other." He closed the medicine box and picked it up. Opening the door, he paused and turned back to her. "I'm going to try to put them together after supper. You can help if you want."

"Yes, of course. Anything." Her eyes went once again to his hat. He noticed, and a smile teased his lips before he closed the door.

She couldn't help but wonder if staying close to Joseph was helping him become more used to her, like the mama cow and the calf. And when he was used to her, she'd inform him about her breakdown and her crazy memory of the night Rosalie died.

Wait a minute. What am I thinking? No amount of getting used to a person could prepare him to learn about her past, nor her dysfunctional memory. She dismissed the idea of telling him anything more. That would be too much information.

CHAPTER ELEVEN
GETTING PAST IT

"Ms. Smith, you didn't see the shooter?" Sheriff Conrad's droopy bloodhound eyes studied Tara as he stood with her beside his patrol car parked in the barnyard. Joseph watched her bite her bottom lip. She looked up at him in a plea for help.

"She saw what I saw, which wasn't much." Joseph had not shared with the sheriff Tara's true identity. Since Tara wasn't a criminal, like many of the people in the federal protection program, there was no reason for the sheriff to know. And since Mac and Joseph weren't using the program but were protecting her on their own, telling the sheriff who Tara was would only increase the risk that Garrett might find her. So Joseph had stuck with the engagement story. Of course, Sheriff Conrad had been as surprised as everyone else by the news.

"If you don't need me any longer, I'd best help Digger with the supper dishes." Tara waited for the sheriff to dismiss her.

"Go ahead. And once again, congratulations on your engagement."

Tara made her way to the back door and disappeared inside the house. Conrad stared after her, deep in thought.

Wanting to take the sheriff's mind off of her, Joseph said, "Are you going to talk with Lester Fimble and Denver Harris?" Joseph had already explained his early-morning encounter with Lester, which surprised the sheriff, and he knew about the bad blood between Harris and most of the ranchers.

"Looks like I'd better."

Joseph handed Conrad the cartridges he and Bear had collected. "You might want to take a look at these too."

"Handling them like you have, you've probably destroyed any evidence." Conrad looked them over. "However, each gun shoots differently. I'll have them examined by an expert." He pocketed the shells and walked to his patrol car.

Joseph followed. "I sent Allen up to the summer grazing land to check on the fencing by the creek. What Harris doesn't understand is moose are the culprits knocking down those enclosures. Cows do too, but not like moose."

"We all know Harris's main objective is to keep cattle out of the high country no matter what. He needs to realize there's plenty of land for everyone. I just have a hard time believing he would kill cattle and shoot at people over it. But again, if this job has taught me nothing else, it's that people are unpredictable." Conrad opened the door and got in, then rolled down his window. "Take care, and let me know if anything else out of the ordinary happens." He started his car and drove off.

With the sheriff gone, Joseph breathed a sigh of relief. He'd done everything he needed to. He'd even tried to call Mac to let him know what was going on but didn't get an answer. He'd have left a message, but what he had to say should not be left in a voice mail. He needed to explain things. He could send an e-mail, but Mac didn't want him using the Internet in case Garrett hacked him.

Joseph's Appaloosa stallion, Wallowa, pranced up to the fence. The animal stretched his head and neck over the top rail and sniffed.

"Well, old boy. What do you think of the filly?" Joseph pointed to Odell's mare in the adjacent pasture. Joseph would put her in with Wallowa in a day or so.

The stallion lipped Joseph's hand. He didn't have the usual apple treat the horse was looking for, so he rubbed between the animal's ears and patted his neck. "I'll get you something. I know you're pretending you're not interested in the filly, but you are. You're such an actor."

"The same could be said about you." Bear walked up behind Joseph. The customary cigarette hung from her mouth. Smoke hovered over her like a cloud.

"What do you mean by that?" He knew he was in for a grilling about the shooting, the rush of the cattle drive, and Tara.

Wallowa walked to the other side of the corral as if he knew what was about to be said and wanted to be a safe distance away.

Bear took the cigarette from her mouth. "While you and Sarah were out here and while Katelen was involved with a video game, Digger told me what happened this afternoon. We have enough on our plate without dodging bullets." She paused a moment, staring at him. "Did you tell the sheriff you're trying to keep Sarah safe from a murderer?"

"No."

"And why not?"

"Because if I had, he wouldn't look into other possibilities." Joseph stared at his mother, hoping she knew what he meant.

"Harris?"

His mother was a smart woman. "And maybe Lester Fimble."

Bear shrugged but didn't look too surprised. "While we were checking the horses, Irene mentioned her father was upset that you're engaged to someone else."

"In front of my daughter?" Joseph didn't want Irene talking about such things where Katelen could hear.

"No. Katelen had ridden ahead of us. You know, son, that Lester hoped if you and Irene married, we would merge the White Eagle Appaloosa with his ranch, don't you?"

This was news to him. "No, but I should have realized money was the real reason he was all fired up this morning."

Keeping her eyes on him, Bear took a puff of her cigarette and blew it out the side of her mouth. "What if whoever shot at you two really was this Garrett person who could have followed Sarah from California? The sheriff's going to be more than a little ticked you didn't tell him. Plus, you're putting your family at risk. I'm not worried about me, but Katelen is a different story."

His mother hit bone with her comment, which was what she'd meant to do. Joseph glanced down at the ground. "It can't possibly be him. He'd have to have known Sarah was coming here, and there's no way he could have known that." Yet, Joseph's mind reeled with worry that he could be wrong. Panic couldn't rule his thoughts. He had to be logical. "No, this is local. And I'd send Katelen away until things settled down if I could, but where?"

"Digger and I could take her on a trip through Yellowstone." Bear stared at him.

He shrugged. "You may have to. I'd never do anything to hurt my daughter, my family, or the people who work for me. They're all in danger until we find out who is behind this. But I can't fight what I can't see. I can't very well shut down the ranch so no one will get hurt. Cattle need to be fed. A ranch goes on. The best thing I can think to do is get the cattle to higher ground."

"I only brought it up because you have a tendency to be stubborn and want to right the wrongs of this world, and when it backfires, you blame yourself." She grew quiet, staring at the lake beyond the corral.

Joseph knew she was thinking about Jenny and how she'd died while Joseph was trying to right the wrongs five years ago. "Ma . . . I'm just trying to do what I think the Lord wants me to."

She rolled her wrinkly lidded eyes heavenward.

He'd tried several times to explain his belief in God but had gotten nowhere. He had to make his case more personal for her. "If Mac had called you two nights ago and asked you to take Sarah in, what would you have done?"

She took another drag on her cigarette and blew it out. "Probably the same blasted thing you did. See, we're cut from the same cloth, you and me. Suckers to defend those who can't defend themselves, no matter who it hurts." His mother brushed her knobby knuckle beneath her chin. "We need to work together on this one to protect our loved ones and our livelihood." Deep worry lines creased her forehead. "It's good we're moving the cattle early. If the shooter's the same person who is after Sarah, he won't look for her in the mountains. And if it's someone else, it's better so the cattle won't be easy prey. Our problem is breeding the mare and grafting that calf to another mother cow." Bear rubbed grit from the corner of her eye. "I had hoped to get those tasks done before we left on the drive."

"Wes can stay behind and watch the horses. I'm going to try to take care of the calf tonight. Sarah's going to help." Joseph added the last sentence so his mother would know Tara was trying to fit in the best she could.

"Really? She's going to help?" Unbelief and doubt showed in his mother's tired eyes. "That's not going to set well with Katelen. She's your helper." She flipped ash from her cigarette.

"Would you mind running interference and keeping Katelen busy? She's helped graft calves dozens of times, and it seems important to Tara— *Sarah*—to do this." Joseph hoped his mother would let his slip of the tongue go.

She stared at him. He stared back.

His mother knew enough about police work to know not to press him to confirm Tara's real name. At least he hoped so.

She cleared her throat. "Digger needs to stock the camp trailer. I can keep Katelen with us while we figure out what we need to pack. By the way, when you were in town yesterday, did you buy the salt licks? We can't leave those cattle on the open range without them."

Grateful that before meeting Tara at the airport he'd stopped by the Mercantile and picked up salt blocks, he nodded.

His mother squinted at the setting sun. Her mood mellowed. "We'll make it." She patted Joseph's scarred cheek. He wondered if she'd said those words to convince him or herself. His mother had a gold-mine heart. She backed his decision, but he needed more than his mother's reassurance that moving the cattle would keep everyone safe. He needed guidance from above. Tonight after everyone was asleep, he would go to his spot on the lake, where he felt close to the Lord, and seek His help.

* * *

Tara was just finishing putting the pots and pans away when Joseph entered the kitchen. In his hand was a bottle of Vicks Vaporub, which seemed peculiar, but she was more interested in what had happened after she had left Joseph with the sheriff. "Did Sheriff Conrad leave?"

"Yeah." He opened a cupboard and pulled out a bottle of molasses. "He really didn't say much else after you went inside." He paused a moment. "I tried to call Mac a minute ago while I was in the den, but he didn't answer. He must be neck deep in the investigation. He should know what's going on here." Joseph's dark eyes turned kind and caring.

Tara knew he was right. Wanting to talk about something else, she asked, "When are you going to try to get the mother cow to nurse Shamrock?"

"Right now. That's why I need these." He held the bottles up.

"Vicks and molasses? This is going to be interesting." She chuckled.

"Yeah . . . well, if we're lucky, what I have in mind will work." He opened the back door for her and followed her out. Scrap joined them.

Once they were in the barn, Joseph handed Tara the Vicks and entered the calf's stall. He proceeded to put molasses on Shamrock's rear end and down the animal's upper hind legs.

"This is the weirdest thing I've ever seen," Tara said.

Joseph winked at her. "I put molasses on the calf so the mama cow will lick his bottom. Taste is what will bond her to him." He carefully screwed the lid back on without getting the sticky substance on it and made his way out of the stall while tugging a bandana handkerchief out of his hip pocket. He handed the molasses bottle to Tara and wiped goo off his hand.

"What's with the Vicks?" Tara held the bottle up.

"That's for the mama cow." He took the Vicks, and he and Scrap went into the stall where the cow stood munching on hay, totally content. Joseph stroked the cow's neck and backside. Standing close to her, he unscrewed the Vicks and dug out a glob of ointment. He reached in front of the cow and rubbed Vicks on her nose.

The animal shook her head and backed up.

"It's all right. There's a little one here that's hungry." He screwed the lid on the Vicks and motioned for Scrap to do his work. The dog went behind the cow as the animal followed Joseph from her stall to Shamrock's. Scrap herded her over to the calf, and Tara was amazed at how well Joseph and his dog worked together.

Joseph came to stand near Tara, though the stall fence separated them. "Come on; give him a chance," he coaxed the cow.

The mama licked the hind quarters of the calf. Shamrock liked the attention and made his way to try to nurse. The mother cow stood there and let him.

"And the Vicks on the cow's nose does what?" Tara was curious.

"Makes it so she can't smell the calf. And if she can't smell him, she's more willing to lick and accept him as her own."

"If all of life were only that simple," she said without thinking.

A smile gentled Joseph's face. The scar on his cheek faded away. "Life has been pretty bumpy lately, hasn't it?"

She gave a slight nod. He didn't know the half of it. Joseph tilted his head to the side, his dark eyes filled with empathy. Maybe it was because of the turbulent day they'd been through or the way his cowboy hat sat on his head or even the tiny fracture lines at the side of his eyes, but the old country song of heroes being cowboys came to Tara's mind. And in that moment, she knew she wanted him to kiss her because he wanted to, not because he was forced to convince other people they were in love.

She realized she needed him to kiss her before she confided in him her dark secrets.

Joseph must have sensed what she yearned for. He leaned toward her. At any moment, their lips would touch; at any moment, her deep-seated wish she'd fought and tried to ignore would be granted. His breath caressed her cheeks. A shiver raced over her skin. She tightened her hold on the bottle of molasses, afraid if she let go her arms would wrap around him. She dared not breathe, transfixed in his stare—his heated, intoxicating stare.

Joseph's lips met hers softly, gently. An electric feeling swirled in her chest, skittered to her limbs, and raced over her skin. The kiss deepened as he tried to pull her close, but the fencing stood between them. One of his hands slid to her face, lightly holding her cheek.

"Daddy?" Katelen's voice startled them as if a bucket of spiders had been set loose at their feet.

Joseph and Tara jumped apart. Tara nervously rubbed her brow, avoiding Katelen's condemning glare.

"Katelen, what do you need, sweetie?" Joseph acted as though nothing was wrong.

The seven-year-old's anger fixed on Tara. "Daddy, how could you kiss *her*?"

Joseph opened the gate and came out. Scrap followed him. Stroking the top of his daughter's head, he said, "Tara and I are engaged. Of course we kiss."

Had he kissed her because he had seen his daughter coming? Had it all been a show?

Katelen whirled away from him, tears brimming in her eyes. "Irene's supposed to be my mother, not her!" The child kicked dirt onto Tara's boots and took off for the house.

"Katelen!" Joseph shouted. "Come back here, young lady."

His daughter's answer was the banging of the screen door as she went inside the house. He breathed a heavy sigh. "I apologize for my daughter's temper tantrum." He looked directly at Tara. "And I should apologize for kissing you, but I won't. Truth be told, I wanted to kiss you."

Tara was glad he felt the same way she did.

He glanced down. "I didn't know Katelen was watching us, but in a roundabout way, Katelen's anger over us kissing strengthens our engagement story. See, she thinks we're really a couple, though I hate deceiving her."

Tara didn't like deceiving people either, and she hated that she and Joseph had to pretend to be engaged, but he had been the one who put them in this situation. Her hand tightened around the molasses bottle. She wondered if he had enjoyed the kiss until Katelen had made her presence known. Was she selfish for hoping he had?

More guilt piled onto Tara. Maybe he'd decided he wasn't attracted to her. And maybe now they could be friends. She shouldn't let one little spontaneous kiss make her think differently. "I'm sorry you have to deceive your daughter to protect me."

He shook his head. "Don't worry. It will iron out in the end."

Tara didn't know what else she could say or do. "I'd better call it a day. Sounds like tomorrow is going to be very interesting."

She walked away, feeling Joseph's gaze on her back. She was tempted to turn around, but she willed herself not to. She had to be strong, had to resist temptation, and had to figure out what she should do about the mess she was making of Joseph's life. She just didn't know if she could do it on her own.

CHAPTER TWELVE

A Newfound Truth

WHEN THE HOUSE WAS FINALLY quiet, Tara tiptoed down the hallway to Joseph's den. He'd told her he'd tried to call Mac while in here, so there had to be a landline available. After everything that had gone on today—the shooting and the kiss—she thought it would be best if she called Mac and asked him if she could go home. She still felt strongly that she didn't want to put Joseph's family in any more danger, plus she couldn't shake the guilt she felt over Joseph's deceiving his daughter and his friends by protecting her. Pressing her ear to the wooden door, she listened for any noises from within.

Nothing.

She slipped inside and flipped on the light. Glancing around the room, she noticed the wall where a floor-to-ceiling shelving unit held leather-bound books. Another wall had a sprawl of sheepskin chaps and old, fancy riding gloves with beaded cuffs and leather fringe in large shadow boxes. Next to those were sepia pictures of Indians in front of tepees. They must have been Joseph's ancestors.

A sound in the hallway made her pause. She listened, careful not to move. Footfalls passed the door. Relieved, she set about doing what she'd come in here to do. She spied the phone on the desk and quickly made her way to it.

She dialed Mac's number. As it rang, Tara looked over the desk. Pens and pencils were crammed into an old coffee mug. A stack of copy paper rested near a printer. The desk was neat and orderly, too orderly compared to the rest of the house. On a corner stood a small wooden statue of a bear rearing up on its hind legs with a savage snarl on its face. An odd memento.

She waited for Mac to pick up. Finally, she heard a "Hello."

"Mac, this is Tara."

"I'm unable to come to the phone right now. Please leave a short message after the beep, and I'll get back to you as soon as possible."

Tara took a deep breath. She hated to leave a message, but she wanted Mac to know she had called. "This is Tara. Sorry to call again. I hope you're all right. Do you know where Garrett could be?" Feeling she shouldn't stay on the line, she said, "Stay safe, and I hope to hear from you soon." She hung up. Why did she ask about Garrett? Mac had enough pressure on him without Tara adding to it. Had she done more damage than good? She decided to hurry back to her room before someone discovered her.

She passed a door cracked open to another room, and Tara recognized Joseph's deep voice. She peeked through the slit. He sat beside Katelen on her small twin bed and had his back to the door. His daughter was snuggled down with a teddy bear that strongly resembled her grandmother under one arm. She smiled up at her father with deep love in her eyes. He must have made amends with Katelen over her catching them kissing. On the nightstand rested one of Tara's picture books. It warmed her heart to know one of her books held a special place on Katelen's nightstand. At least Katelen liked her stories.

By the way Joseph's shoulders were slumped, Tara could tell the tired cowboy was ready to call it a night. His hat sat on his lap. So this was another time he took it off. It seemed fitting to remove his hat for his daughter, someone he loved and cherished.

"Promise you'll go right to sleep?" He waited until Katelen reluctantly bobbed her head. Clearing his throat, he began, "There once was an old man and his daughter, who were all alone in the world. The daughter was filled with anger because her mother had died. Sometimes the old man would be so lonely that when his daughter slept, he would go to the mountain peaks and sing to Father Sky. 'Ha-no ha-no hi-hi-ye-ee.' Over and over he sang of his grief.

"From afar, his sad and lonely words were heard by a great bald eagle. The eagle swooped down from Father Sky and asked him, 'Why do you sing of grief?' The old man replied, 'Because my daughter and I are alone in the world and I miss my wife, her mother.'

"The eagle told him, 'Take hold of my wings.' And when he did, the bird flew up into the heavens, taking him so far into the sky that they reached the home of the celestial dwellers.

"Among the dwellers, the old man saw his spirit wife. She was happy that her husband had arrived. She asked, 'Does our daughter know I watch over her night and day?'

"The old man said, 'No. There is no sign to show her.'

"The spirit mother scooped many bright, shiny stars into her arms and formed them into a glowing ball of star beams, then tossed it to the eagle. The glowing beams rained over the bird until all of his feathers turned white. Spirit Mother said, 'Tell our daughter this eagle is her sign that she is being watched over by someone who loves her very much.'

"The old man was so happy. He could hardly wait for the eagle to take him home so he could tell the daughter that when she saw a white eagle, she'd know her mother was watching over her, always and ever more."

Tears pooled in Tara's eyes.

Joseph pulled the covers up to his little girl's chin and kissed her on the forehead. Katelen said, "Why can't *I* see a white eagle?"

Joseph settled on the side of the bed. "We've discussed this before. Real white eagles are ill, so it's a good thing not to see them. I only tell you the story of the white eagle because White Eagle is our family name. And besides, you know Heavenly Father watches over you, and the only signs He gives us are . . ."

"Sunsets, rainbows, and the beauty of the world," Katelen said, her voice monotone.

Joseph placed his palm against her cheek. "Someday you'll understand God loves you more than even I do." He tweaked her nose. "My love for you fills the oceans."

"My love fills the sky," Katelen replied.

"My love fills the universe." Joseph rose from her bed and turned out the lamp on the nightstand.

Tara dashed down the hall. A second before she closed her door, Katelen's open. That was close. Too close. She had narrowly escaped Joseph's catching her eavesdropping. Thinking over what she'd heard, an idea came to her for a picture book, a different kind of picture book than she'd ever drawn.

She yearned for a pencil and paper so she could sketch the scenes coming to her: a white eagle and an angel mother. Remembering she'd seen paper and pencils in the den, she realized she could draw a little book about the white eagle story and give it to Katelen. Pleased with the idea, Tara hoped her effort would go a long way toward making the child think better of her.

* * *

Joseph headed for the kitchen. Digger was there peering into the cupboard, then scribbling on a notepad as he finished the grocery list for the drive. Joseph knew Digger had included ingredients for snakebite kidney bean stew.

Digger glanced at Joseph. "That skinny little woman of yours didn't eat much supper. Course, it's not every day a person gets shot at."

The man was poking around, wanting to know more about Tara and what had happened before he and Wes arrived. "She'll be all right. Just needs some rest." Joseph glanced at the list and noticed ten cans of kidney beans written on there, confirming his assumption. "Did Bear talk to you about the cattle drive menu?"

Digger flipped his hat around to set it properly on his head. "Don't worry. I promised your mom I'd only serve my stew one night. Irene and Katelen were with her, so I didn't argue. Before Irene left, your mom asked her to pick up the cattle vaccines. You know, Chief, Irene is still a part of this ranch even though you went and found yourself another filly."

"Irene is always welcomed here. And I appreciate that you're making Sarah feel welcomed too." Joseph didn't want to discuss his personal life with Digger. "So Irene said she'd get the vaccines?" Joseph was pushing the cattle, and they could lose a few calves taking them to the high country this early. But better to lose a few on the drive than have someone shoot them one by one here in the valley.

Digger closed his notepad and started for the door. "Said she'd bring the vaccines by in the morning. I'm so tired my eyelids feel like they're work-worn horseshoes. See you in the morning, Chief." The old man shut the door behind him, heading for the bunkhouse.

Joseph enjoyed Digger's company but was grateful he'd left. He grabbed the kitchen phone and dialed Mac's cell.

"Hey, what's up?" Mac sounded like he was in a hurry.

"Had an incident at the ranch."

"What happened?"

Joseph proceeded to tell him about the day and added. "I wanted you to know."

"Well, I was about to return Tara's call, but I'd rather give you the bad news."

Joseph wondered when she'd called him, but Mac's tone was grave and stopped him from asking.

"We had a lead that Garrett was staying in a motel in Whittier. I'm leaving it now. Needless to say, he wasn't in his room. Clerk said she hadn't seen him since late last night."

"Do you think he could have been the one shooting at us?" Joseph had a hard time thinking it possible.

"Doubt it. If it was him, he would have had to book a direct flight and drive like mad to get to the ranch in time to shoot at you. Not saying it's impossible but very unlikely, though I'm worried he's heading your way. Tara's called me twice today. First one was early this morning. He may have had a trace on my cell. I'll get a new one as soon as possible."

"I thought your cell was untraceable." Joseph leaned against the wall.

"He's the cop who wrote the manual on tracing calls, remember?"

"Should I send Tara home?"

"Not yet. I have one of my guys looking into Garrett's parents. They live in Seattle. Could be he's heading there. Don't worry Tara about this. It will only cause her more stress."

"So how are you doing?"

Mac didn't answer. He was probably working around the clock trying to gather evidence against Garrett. Joseph remembered working a hard case twenty-four-seven. He also remembered how it felt to have someone he loved murdered.

The first few days after Jenny's death, Joseph spent every waking hour trying to figure out who the bad cop was. For a moment, Joseph was back at the police station—Jenny's blood on his clothes—holding a crying and scared two-year-old Katelen. Jenny's death was his fault. If he'd turned left instead of right, the bullet would have hit him instead of her. If he'd just followed Jenny's intuition, she would still be alive. If only he hadn't been stubborn but had listened to Mac, who'd asked him to steer clear of investigating the bad cop feeding information to the Martinez gang, maybe the killer wouldn't have come after Joseph.

In the end, Mac had been the only person who had understood the guilt and pain Joseph had carried. After Joseph had worked the case day and night for months, Mac had helped him understand the need to let it go. Other cops who weren't personally involved would do a better job. Joseph's daughter needed him. He encouraged Joseph to raise Katelen somewhere else, that moving to Idaho was the best decision Joseph could make. Joseph owed Mac.

Mac cleared his throat. "I now understand how you felt when Jenny died. Feels like someone gutted me."

Joseph rested his head against the wall. Yes, he knew exactly what Mac was going through. "Just remember we're keeping you in our prayers. You have good men working for you. Rely on them."

"Thanks." Mac ended the call.

Joseph placed the phone in the cradle and rubbed the back of his neck. This had been one long, hard day. Still, he wanted to go where he could find the peace he needed to get through whatever was coming. But he'd wait a couple of hours to make sure everyone was asleep.

* * *

Tara sneaked back to the den, grabbed some paper and pencils, and rushed to her room. Settling on the bed, she immersed herself in her art. A couple of hours ticked by, and when she finally laid her pencil down, she appraised her work. She'd sketched several good roughs and a few extremes of an old Indian man with a likeness of Joseph, as well as his daughter with a likeness of Katelen and a white eagle. Staring at the images, she believed this could be her best work to date.

Stretching, she stood and went to the bathroom to look in the mirror. Dark, ugly circles framed her eyes. After a day like today, she knew she wouldn't fall asleep without taking a pill.

She worked hard to put distance between herself and the scenes of the day: riding a horse, being shot at, and Joseph's kiss. Of course, being shot at had scared her plenty, but the kiss—that was fear on another level.

Sheesh, who knew so much could happen in only seventy-two hours? Tara thought of Rosalie. Her aunt was dead—had died right in front of her— and she couldn't remember anything after that except darkness, voices, fear, and the deafening sound of a gunshot. But she did have that weird memory of holding a gun.

What if she had held it? If so, had she fired the weapon?

Had she killed her own aunt?

If she had, she'd remember, wouldn't she? Joseph had told her trauma could make a person forget, and he could be right.

It troubled Tara greatly that Mac had found her outside in the flower garden when he'd arrived home. *So strange. If Garrett came to kill me, what made him run off after he killed Rosalie? Why didn't he kill me too? It doesn't make sense.*

Unless he saw me shoot Rosalie and feared for his own life.

She grabbed hold of the vanity and stared in the mirror. *Am I a killer?*

A surge of heart-stopping anxiety washed over her. Nausea pressed at her throat, and perspiration beaded on her brow. *No! I know I didn't do it.*

I am not a killer!

I am a good person.

Tara picked up her brush and began her nightly ritual of brushing her hair from the roots to the ends to calm her nerves.

She got ready for bed, then pushed the window open a crack, letting the cool country air laced with the scents of grass and pines, with a hint of lilacs, float in and fill the room. She filled a glass with water. Grabbing her bottle of sleeping pills, she twisted off the cap and let one pill drop from the bottle onto the palm of her hand. She was ready to wash the pill down with the water when, out of the corner of her eye, she saw a shadow pass by the window.

Immediately, she jumped and dropped the glass she'd had in her hand, shattering it on the tile floor. Her heart pounded against her ribs and thundered in her ears. Was Garrett out there? Had he been watching her through the window?

No! He doesn't know where I am. The chances of whoever was out there being Garrett were miniscule.

Pushing the lace curtain aside, she peered into the darkness lit only by the barnyard light and saw Joseph walking toward the lake with a large bundle under his arms.

Relieved and perplexed at the same time, she set the pill on the counter and carefully picked up the large pieces of broken glass, putting them in the wastebasket under the sink. She didn't want to risk waking anyone by vacuuming the small bits, so she wiped them up with a wash rag the best she could. She'd vacuum in the morning.

Her mind returned to Joseph. Why was he going to the lake this time of night? She knew he was tired. *Strange.* She really didn't know anything about ranch life and the people here.

And yet she did.

After all that had happened today, she knew Joseph was a kind and giving person, a loving father, and a devoted son. For a moment, she felt the warmth of his lips on hers and touched her mouth as if to bring the moment to life; then she realized what she was doing and dropped her hand.

What was wrong with her—constantly thinking about the kiss, about him?

Sheesh! Only moments ago, the unthinkable had crossed her mind: that she could have killed her aunt. Rubbing her forehead, she knew what she had to do. First thing in the morning, she would tell Joseph what might have happened. It was the only honorable thing to do. Then she would ask him to take her to the airport. No matter what Mac thought, she needed to go home.

Tara crawled into bed, fluffed her pillow, and positioned the blankets so the sheet overlapped. Then she lay back and closed her eyes.

Maybe she should tell Joseph now what she planned to do in the morning. He was down at the lake by himself. It would be the perfect time because no one would interrupt them. No one would overhear. But could she go near the lake without remembering how she'd found her grandfather dead in the water? That was a different lake, a different time. And besides, Joseph would be there. Before she could talk herself out of it, she leaped out of bed and got dressed. She had to see this through while her courage lasted.

* * *

When Joseph was a boy, his father built a sweat lodge to pray in. His father's belief in God was based on teachings of a Great Spirit that had been passed down for generations. His father had used the sweat lodge to feel close to the Great Spirit, but years ago, the lodge was destroyed by a bad winter storm. Because Joseph had converted to the LDS faith, he didn't rebuild it, but in a way, he wished he had so he could have kept something that meant so much to his father.

Joseph didn't need a sweat lodge to feel close to God, but in the tradition of his father, he built a small fire of pine and aspen wood. Once the flames were strong, he gazed out at the lake and thought of his heritage, as well as being here beside the water—where he and his father had spent so much time—which turned his thoughts to the story of Wallowa Lake in Oregon, the lake his black Appaloosa stallion was named after.

Legend said the hand of the Almighty had lifted hills near the lake so high that glaciers with eternal snow still remained. The deepest gash on the surface of the earth was to the east, where the Snake River flowed. There the Nez Perce hunted deer drawn to the lake and river. He remembered his father telling him he was named after Chief Joseph, whose Indian name was Thunder Rolling in the Mountains. Joseph was a mighty chief, who, when pushed by the white man, rose up to defend his people, but his people lost the battle, and the government allowed only a few to return to their homeland at Wallowa Lake, where their teepees once crowded the shores. Joseph's father left the area when he married Bear, and they settled here. This small lake must have reminded his dad of Wallowa. Joseph wondered if he should put up an old-fashioned teepee. Katelen would love to play in it, and it would serve as a reminder of her heritage.

The moon glittered off the shimmery water like fireflies dancing on ice, and he looked up to embrace the majesty of the sky. Sparks popped from the flickering fire, rising high on wafting air currents and then disappearing into the thick, black night. The scent of campfire smoke made him realize how much he missed coming here.

He placed the revered buffalo robe bundle on the long grass and unrolled it. On the smooth leather inside were drawings symbolizing four life circles. Two bags lay before him: one large, one small. He opened the large doeskin bag. Inside was the ceremonial double-tailed golden eagle feather headdress his great, great-grandfather Totoken wore. Carefully, he lifted it and ran his hand over the soft downy feathers, thinking of his father and how important ceremonies had been to him.

One important ceremony happened after a kid at school fought with Joseph. Joseph had received a severe cut on his right cheek, and his father had taken him down to the lake, where he'd made a fire like the one burning now. Joseph remembered the reverence in his father's eyes as he spoke to the spirits in their native tongue. Afterward, he told Joseph the wound would make a scar that would become a badge of honor and give him power throughout his life.

His father had stood, lifting his pipe to the moon. He'd seemed as tall as a teepee. Dressed in his white ceremonial robes and the golden eagle headdress, he'd looked like the mighty warrior he was meant to be—strong as a mountain lion and noble as an eagle.

That night his father had passed the headdress on to Joseph, telling him Totoken had worn it in the mighty counsel of the Nez Perce chiefs over a hundred years ago.

Now, Joseph felt humbled as he gazed upon the eagle feathers. Totoken had earned every feather by his acts of bravery. This very headdress had been carried over the Lolo Trail and even into Canada, where some of the Nez Perce had fled.

Joseph's index finger trailed over each feather. He thought of the eagle, how his people considered it to be a sunbird and a messenger for the Great Spirit. Out of reverence for his father's old belief, Joseph put on the headdress and then glanced at the small mink bag that held the sacred pipe. Joseph pulled the pipe from the sheath. Beaver hide wrapped the center of the thirty-inch shaft, and a double row of translucent beads ran along the sides. His ancestors believed the calumet possessed the power to call upon the spirit for blessings. A small deerskin pouch of Indian tobacco lay next to it, and he drew the pouch to his nose, smelling the scent of dogwood bark and sumac leaves, a mixture his father had made. Another pouch held a fragrant herb that tempered the bitterness and was to be added during ritual.

Joseph set the pouch down and reverently took off the headdress and laid it on the buffalo robe. He longed for his father's guidance. However, since converting to the Church, Joseph had learned to lean on a higher power. He'd pray to his Father in Heaven for help.

By the flickering firelight, he knelt down, folded his arms, and silently poured out his heart to God. Prayer calmed him as though Heavenly Father's warm embrace of love and understanding held him. As he concluded his prayer, a twig snapped from behind, and he whirled around.

There stood Tara.

For a brief moment, he thought he saw white eagle wings fluttering protectively above her. The image settled into the incandescent glow of firelight, and her big, bright, malachite eyes peered inquisitively at him, full of wonder and awe but also underscored by wariness and grief.

Mac had said Tara had no family now. She was alone, with no one to watch over her. No one to turn to. Grief her only companion.

Joseph understood her grief and shared it with her. But they also shared something else: growing feelings for each other. He had pretended his advances were merely for show . . . and they were at first. But tonight in the barn was not.

He knew it then, and he knew it now. This woman had come into his life for a reason.

A burning ignited in Joseph's gut, and in that moment, he knew he was meant to help her. She was *meant* to be in his life. The strong knowledge nearly stole his breath. He didn't understand this feeling, but he couldn't deny it either. Maybe those white wings he'd seen for a second had been a combination of moonlight and firelight, but whatever they were, they were a sign.

He stretched his arms out, beckoning her. A magnetic force more powerful than mere words pulled her to him, and she stepped around the fire and into his embrace, melting against him. Her awestruck eyes looked up. She was suddenly as much a part of him as his own heart. He'd destroy whoever dared threaten her.

But she was keeping something from him. Fear was eating her up, and she didn't dare face it alone. He pressed his lips gently on her forehead and cradled her face in his hands. "Tell me what your heart fears."

Her brows pinched together, and her bottom lip trembled. Tears puddled in her eyes.

Leaning close to her ear, he softly said, "Trust me."

She opened her mouth as if to speak, but before she could utter a sound, torture claimed her face, and she turned away from him. "I can't," she choked. "I'm so sorry, Joseph." She fled from his arms and ran toward the house.

He wanted to chase after her and make her tell him what was wrong, but a strong premonition kept him there. He had no idea why he was being held back except that she needed to come to terms on her own with whatever was tormenting her. Only then would she be ready to face the truth she was hiding from. And when she faced that truth, Joseph would be there for her.

With sudden clarity, he knew it had also been a sign when he'd first laid eyes on Tara Kelly and thought she looked like his wife.

She was here not only to keep safe but to become part of Joseph's life—and to become his wife.

CHAPTER THIRTEEN
THE SOUL OF A CHARACTER

TARA LEANED AGAINST HER BEDROOM door and took a deep breath. *Joseph knows I'm hiding something from him.* She should have told him about her breakdown and that she thought she might have been holding a gun. That was why she had followed him out there. Once again, courage had failed her.

Failed her big time.

But she'd expected to find him merely sitting on the dock, not kneeling in what looked to be prayer.

In prayer? Who does that anymore?

Her grandfather had prayed a lot but in short prayers, and they were more like sayings, not getting-down-on-bended-knees-and-folding-his-arms kind of prayers. Finding Joseph the way she had had brought her up short. She didn't know what to think except that the image of him praying would be forever burned in her memory.

Religion had never played a role in her life, especially after her breakdown when her grandfather had died. For years, Tara had felt that if there was a God, He was mean and selfish for taking Grandfather from her. And not only him but her parents as well.

Sure, her picture books were full of magical Irish tales with religion in them, but she didn't believe any of it. She'd drawn them as a tribute to her grandfather. And she may have said that Irish blessing over the calf when she'd thought it was dying, but that was different. For a person to go out in the middle of the night, build a fire, and say a prayer, that was serious belief. It made her wonder about herself.

Just what did she believe?

And why did she believe it?

Somewhere from inside the house, the deep bong of a clock rang twelve times. Midnight. At least this harried day was finally over. For a moment, she thought of the pill she'd been about to take before she went to the lake. She didn't need it now. She was tired enough. And too tired to find answers for deep questions, so she tugged off her boots and clothes and crawled into bed wearing only her underwear, not wanting to put on Jenny's nightgown. She needed to feel like herself and to rest her mind, body, and soul. Maybe tomorrow things would fall into place.

As she drifted to sleep, she remembered the feel of Joseph's arms around her like he'd known her forever, like he'd always been there waiting for her.

And for the first time in a long, long time, she was comforted.

* * *

Joseph got up at five o'clock before everyone else to prepare for the day. He was heading out to the barn when the phone rang in the kitchen.

"Joseph, this is Mac."

"I'm surprised you'd risk calling. If Garrett tapped your phone—"

"Got a new one. Supposed to be untraceable." He rattled off the new number.

Joseph jotted it down without responding, even though he wanted to remind him the last one was supposed to be untraceable too, but why state the obvious. "You're up early. Get any rest last night?"

"Not much."

Joseph could relate.

"My conscience has been bothering me. I should have told you something about Tara before I sent her to you." Mac cleared his throat. "Rosalie told me when Tara was in her teens, after her grandfather died, she had a nervous breakdown. She was the one who found him in the lake."

Joseph didn't know what to say. He knew she'd been the one to find her dead grandfather, but he'd had no idea she'd had a breakdown.

"Her problem was acute depression. She didn't hear voices or anything, and Rosalie swore me to secrecy, but your call last night got me thinking I've been wrong." Mac sighed. "With what's going on at the ranch, you don't need the worry of taking care of a woman who may or may not have another breakdown. I'll see if I can find another place for her. I was just hopeful to keep Tara close to some type of family even if it was mine. Since I never married Rosalie, I'm not really related to Tara, but I'm the only family she has."

Joseph knew many people who suffered from depression after a loved one passed away, himself included. "If anyone can help her get over her aunt's death, I think I can. And I only told you about the shootings because it's something you need to know, but I'm more than willing to keep her here as long as you need me to. Like I said, I'm moving the herd to a safer place. I'll keep Tara with me." Even as the words left his mouth, he realized how hollow they really were. Jenny had been with him when she'd been shot, and he had been helpless to save her. What made him think he could keep Tara safe? But his prayer last night and the feelings he'd had made him believe he could.

"If you can hang on for a week or so . . ."

"Longer if you need," Joseph added. Remembering Tara's concern over her aunt's funeral, Joseph asked, "What have you heard from the coroner?"

"They've gathered all the evidence they think they need and will release a preliminary report anytime now, but the final word will take a while longer. We're trying to hurry them along because Rosalie was a cop, but some tests take longer than forty-eight hours. They won't release the body for another week. Rosalie once told me if something should happen to her, she wanted to be cremated." His voice cracked. "I'll wait and talk it over with Tara."

"Do you want to talk with her now? I can wake her up."

"Ah . . ." Mac seemed to be having a hard time talking.

"Don't worry. It can wait. Let me know if I can do anything else."

"You're helping a lot by keeping Tara with you." Mac sounded more like himself. "I'll keep you posted. Take care."

"You too." Joseph hung up.

Leaving the house and heading toward the barn, he looked toward the lake. He remembered the surprised expression on Tara's face when she saw him last night. He was sure many questions had swirled around that pretty head of hers. And the way she'd left when he'd tried to talk with her; she'd been troubled about something.

As soon as he could, he'd take her aside to tell her about Mac's call and let her know he knew about her past and it didn't matter to him. But how was he going to say it? Broaching the subject of depression could be tricky.

The sound of vehicles pulling into the barnyard drew him away from his thoughts. Some of the crew had arrived to help with roundup, and a few others were due later in the day. Part-time help came when they could, which was all right. Everyone would be here by tonight for the annual night-before-the-drive dinner at Qualey's Café.

A night away from the ranch might be what they all needed, even Tara.

* * *

Tara heard a number of trucks pull into the barnyard. Today would be a busy day, and Joseph wouldn't have time to spare to take her to Idaho Falls so she could catch a plane. Still, she was determined. She had to go home to tell Mac she could have been holding a gun and that she might be the reason Rosalie was dead. If Irene showed up, she'd be more than happy to give Tara a lift to town to get rid of her.

Tara showered and put on Rosalie's suit. She couldn't very well leave wearing Joseph's late wife's clothes. She applied her makeup and, with firm determination, left her room.

Digger was in the kitchen taking pots and pans out, preparing to make breakfast. "We're going to have quite a crew to cook for . . ." His voice faded as he noticed what she was wearing. "You all right, little lassie?"

"I need to speak with Joseph. Have you seen him?" She had no intention of telling Digger what she planned to do. She'd leave the explaining to Joseph.

"Suspect he's out with the newly arrived men, givin' them the skinny on what's been goin' on and what we need to do today."

She didn't wait to hear more. Trucks and horse trailers littered the drive. Men were unloading horses and saddling them up. Many gave her sideways looks, but she kept walking. She finally found Joseph alone in the barn checking on Shamrock and the mother cow. His back was to her as she walked up beside him.

"Joseph?"

He turned, and when he saw what she was wearing, he frowned. "What's going on?"

"I have to go back. I haven't been truthful with you." She didn't want to tell him about the gun—she couldn't tell him. She'd need all the courage she could muster to tell Mac, let alone Joseph. No, she'd tell him about her breakdown. That alone should make him want to send her home.

"By the way, I've spoken with Mac." Joseph rubbed his chin.

"You have?"

"Yeah. He told me when you were a teenager you had a breakdown. That's what you tried to tell me down by the lake, isn't it?" He smoothed her bangs away from her eyes.

"Well . . ."

"Don't worry. I understand perfectly. I darn near had one myself after my wife died, but I had my daughter and mother to turn to. After your grandfather passed away, you only had your aunt. And I bet the two of you weren't close, were you?"

"She took care of me after Grandpa died, but, no, we were never really close. Joseph, there's more you don't know." Tara didn't know exactly how to tell him.

Joseph must have sensed her trepidation. "Look." He placed his hands on her shoulders. "I know plenty."

She shook her head.

"You're scared and alone. But you have me. I understand if you want to bolt because of the shooting yesterday, but I promise you I'll do everything I can to keep you safe. Mac said they think Garrett left yesterday and could be heading to his parents' in Seattle, but there's a chance he could be coming here."

She hugged her arms to her body.

"Odds are he's going to his parents'. They aren't far from the Canadian border. If he can cross over, he'll be safe for a while." Joseph seemed confident that was the case.

Why would Garrett run unless he was guilty of killing Rosalie? Maybe Tara's worry that she'd been the one who had killed her aunt was way off base. After all, the only thing Tara remembered was that she might have been holding a gun. And that memory was shaky at best.

"I doubt that whoever was shooting at us yesterday was Garrett." Joseph folded his arms. "He wouldn't have had time to fly from California and drive out here. The shooter was more likely someone trying to ruin me financially, and I must say they're doing a good job."

Even though Joseph didn't seem bothered that she'd had a nervous breakdown and even though she'd reasoned that Garrett was only on the run because he was guilty, she still felt she needed to leave. "But I need to take care of my aunt's remains."

"You don't need to worry about that."

"Why?"

"Mac said they weren't releasing her body until they were finished with tests. Guess she told Mac if something should happen to her, she wanted to be cremated, so there won't be a lot to do." Joseph took her hand. "When you go back, you can spread her ashes on her favorite beach."

Unable to look directly at him because tears clouded her vision, she said, "She'd like that."

"So you'll stay?" Joseph sounded hopeful.

Before she could answer, Wes came in. "Chief, some of the guys are waitin' for you to explain how you want to handle the workload today." He noticed what Tara was wearing and seemed to realize he'd interrupted something important.

Joseph didn't turn away from her. "Tell them I'll be right out."

Wes left as quickly as he'd arrived.

Joseph leaned near her. "Soooo, you'll stay?"

Her resolve to return to LA dissolved. Maybe she should discuss her odd memory of holding a gun with Joseph. After all, he was the one who had told her that grief could blend reality with nightmares and create false memories. If she told him, he'd know whether she should report this or not. Yet the words choked in her throat. She couldn't tell him right now with the cattle drive pressing on him, so she reluctantly nodded.

He winked. "Good. I want to talk to you about last night and explain a few things, but the men are waiting."

"Why don't we talk tonight? There are things I need to discuss with you too."

"Tonight will work. The night before a cattle drive, Ma and I take the entire crew out to eat at Qualey's. We can talk after."

She gave a slight nod.

"All right, then." He gave her a quick peck on the cheek like they truly were engaged and left to take care of his crew.

As she watched him, she marveled at how fast things had turned around. When she'd gotten up, she'd thought she'd be heading to LA, but now she was going back inside to change her clothes so she could help Digger fix breakfast. She'd worry about how she would tell Joseph about the gun memory after breakfast was cleaned up.

* * *

Not only were they feeding the family, but they were also feeding a crew of twenty more hands. Digger and Tara worked hard making cowboy hash, biscuits and gravy, and griddle cakes. As soon as breakfast was over, Joseph disappeared outside with the others. As soon as the dishes were washed and put away, Tara helped assemble sack lunches for the crew.

Digger and Tara were on their way back to the ranch after delivering the food when he asked her if she'd like to go to Idaho Falls with him to do the grocery shopping for the cattle drive. Wanting to work on her drawings for Katelen, she begged off, and Digger didn't seem to mind, saying he usually went by himself anyway.

For the rest of the day, Tara stayed in her room working on the picture book. When she finished all the sketches, she leaned back against the headboard and studied her work. She was darn proud of what she'd accomplished in so little time. And if she had her paints and canvas, she would start on the actual proofs, adding color to the scenes.

As she tucked a pillow beneath her head, she thought of the few times she'd seen Joseph today. He was always helping someone, too busy to speak with her, but his smile was enough to make her feel as if she belonged. She was looking forward to having that talk with him. And yet she wasn't. Her emotions were all over the place when it came to Joseph White Eagle.

She pictured him beside the lake. When he'd discovered she was there, he'd risen from his prayer and beckoned her to come to him. The comfort and peace she had felt as he'd folded her in an embrace had been phenomenal. She had felt whole. She had felt loved. And she had felt valued. The warmth of the memory lulled her to sleep.

A knock at her door awoke her, and Tara swiped her palm across her face and glanced at the clock on the nightstand—six o'clock.

Six! Good grief! She'd never taken such a long nap, but she'd never been through the stress and strain she had the last few days either. It had finally caught up with her.

Finger-combing her hair away from her cheeks, she rose and opened the door. Her heart leaped at the sight of Joseph. He was clean shaven and wore a fancy Stetson; a crisp, white, long-sleeved, Western shirt with pearl snaps; black jeans; and fancy cowboy boots. A smile claimed his face. "Are you ready to go?"

"Go?" Tara had no idea what he was talking about. Then she remembered Qualey's for supper. "Oh, Joseph, I fell asleep." She stepped away from the door, allowing him to enter.

His dark brows crowded together as his eyes went from one sketch to another. A smile gradually came to his lips. "This is the White Eagle story I always tell Katelen."

"I overheard you last night before you went to the lake and—"

"Listening at keyholes, are you?" He smiled, so he wasn't upset. In fact, he looked genuinely impressed. "These drawings are better than anything I could have imaged. When this is over, you have to tell Katelen who you are. She loves your books. I'm sure she'll be impressed."

"I want her to like me. Right now, I'm the *other* woman who has intruded her life. After I leave, everything can return to normal, but until then—" She brushed a possessive hand over the sketches, rubbing the papers here and there where undesirable smudges had appeared. Joseph was deep in thought. Was it about her leaving or something else? Maybe he was upset because she'd taken supplies without asking. "I hope you don't mind that I borrowed the paper and pencils from your den."

"Of course not." He stared at the sketch of the old man. "He looks very familiar."

Tara chuckled. "He should. I used you as my inspiration."

He did a double take, and slowly, recognition lit his eyes. Staring at the young girl in the picture, he said, "And Katelen too, I see."

She cautiously nodded.

He flipped through the papers, coming to the picture of the angel mother. Tara had decided to make her likeness Jenny. It seemed fitting. But now, as she watched Joseph's reaction, she worried. Maybe he thought using his late wife's likeness was going a step too far.

When he glanced up, his eyes had softened with gratitude. "Thank you. This means a lot to me and will to Katelen too when she sees it."

"I'm relieved. I tried to catch Jenny's likeness from that picture you have of her. The soul of a character is reflected in the eyes, don't you think?"

He stared at her. "Oh, I heartily agree. The eyes mirror the intent of a person's heart."

The way he gazed at her, she felt awkward and didn't know what to do, where to look, what to say.

He reached out and took her hand. "Don't you wonder why we've been drawn to each other? Or why last night you went to the lake when you could have been safely in bed?" His brows slanted, his demeanor sincere.

She had no idea why the events had unfolded the way they had or why she was in Idaho grieving her aunt and becoming indebted to this rancher. Sure, Mac had sent her, but he could have sent her anywhere. And on top of that, she was trying to come to grips with her feelings for Joseph, feelings that should have taken time to develop but had instead instantly ignited. She didn't want to put a name to those emotions. She was afraid to. But here she was anyway, standing before him, and words failed her. Finally, she gave a lame reply. "I don't know."

"Think it over, and then we'll talk." He set the sketches back on the bed and went to the closet and pulled down a hatbox. Opening it, he drew out a woman's Stetson. "Here." He handed it to her. "After your drawing Jenny's likeness to the angel in your story, I'm sure she'd want you to wear her hat tonight. See if it fits."

The hat was the usual straw Stetson, but the hatband was made of bone and turquoise. Hesitantly, Tara took it from him. She already felt uncomfortable wearing the dead woman's clothes. No one seemed to notice, probably because they hadn't seen them for so many years, but they would definitely remember the hatband and realize she was wearing Jenny's hat. When she placed it on her head, it was a little tight.

"Let me see." He took the Stetson from her and turned it over, then unfolded the inner band and pulled out a paper that had been placed inside.

"Try now." He handed it back. As she took the hat, he glanced at the folded paper in his hand like he recognized what it was, yet he didn't open it.

Tara once again placed the hat on her head. Perfect fit. "Still, I don't want to wear it. I feel odd wearing her clothes as it is." She took off the hat.

Joseph tucked the paper he held in his jeans pocket. "You don't need to wear it tonight if it makes you uncomfortable, but you'll need it tomorrow during the cattle drive. You'll be in the saddle for hours on end, and you'll be grateful for the small bit of shade on your face. Besides, it looks nice on you." He kept his eyes on her. Hope that she would accept the hat and not make a big deal of it filled his gaze.

She set it on the bed. Her eyes drifted to the sketches and the angel mother. "Don't you think Katelen will notice I'm wearing her mother's hat?"

"She's only really seen it in the hatbox."

"But I don't want her to think I'm trying to replace her mother or be her mother." Tara hadn't entertained the idea of being a stepmother to the little girl. With the engagement only a fabrication to keep her identity hidden, it had never been a possibility. But now she suddenly wondered.

"If it will make you more comfortable to wear one of my mother's hats, I'll ask her to rustle one up for you. Now hurry up, and get ready to go. People are leaving already." He tipped his Stetson to her and left.

Tara stood for a moment staring at the closed door, and for the first time, she allowed herself to wonder what really being part of Joseph's life would be like.

CHAPTER FOURTEEN
JUMPING TO CONCLUSIONS

QUALEY'S CAFÉ WAS A SMALL, family-type restaurant with a dance floor and space for a band. By all rights, it could have been a tavern, but the Qualeys valued families and wanted everyone to feel welcome. The twang of country music sounded in the background, and the tables were filled with ranch hands eating dinner while others who were finished danced across the hardwood floor.

Joseph, Tara, Bear, Katelen, and Wes sat at a table, each busy eating their different orders of porterhouse steak, fried chicken, and pork tenderloin. Joseph kept a watchful eye on the door in case a stranger came in or Lester or Harris turned up to cause trouble. Tara had been quiet most of the evening, which gave Joseph time to mull over what she had told him—that she didn't want Katelen to think she was trying to replace her mother.

When he'd first blurted out he was engaged, he hadn't taken his daughter into account. But to be fair, at the time, he'd been desperate to explain why Tara was there, and he hadn't had enough time to think up something else. Besides, in her nightly prayers, Katelen had always asked for a new mother. Joseph hadn't known her heart was set on Irene until she'd blown up when he'd introduced Tara.

Now, with the possibility that Tara could be going home soon, he felt a sense of loss. He'd been certain last night she was meant to be here, meant to be part of his life.

But what about Katelen? Such a strong premonition would mean the best for his daughter as well, right? He didn't know. He needed to sort out his feelings, needed to understand what he was supposed to do.

He was *supposed* to talk with Tara tonight sometime. He didn't have a clue what he was going to say or how to even bring up the subject, but he was hopeful together they might find some answers.

He thought of the folded paper in his pocket, the one he'd taken out of Jenny's hat. He'd put the paper in the lining so the hat would fit her better. She'd worn the Stetson only once and had told him it made her feel ridiculous. The hat had fit Tara perfectly, and though she didn't wear it tonight, Joseph was hopeful she would use it.

Most everyone at their table had finished eating. Katelen sat on one side of him, Tara on the other. Katelen grabbed her father's hand. "Daddy, dance with me." She gave him a cute please-Daddy smile, and he couldn't resist his little girl's charm.

The Wylon Wagner Band was playing a lively song. They were a colorful crew with beards, handlebar mustaches, and odd-looking hats with feathers. The only woman, a Reba McEntire look-alike, was their main singer, and she was dressed in normal western clothing. Katelen laughed and giggled as she and Joseph danced to the beat. Joseph loved to see his daughter smile and hoped she could forget her father was going to marry someone she didn't know or like. If only he could tell her what was going on. Even though she was only seven, if she knew, Katelen wouldn't be so brusque with Tara and perhaps might even like her.

If only . . .

He thought of the picture book Tara was making. She was very talented. Once Katelen saw her work and that Tara had made it for her, Katelen would let down her guard.

After the song finished, the lone woman of the band started singing a slow song. Katelen led him back to their group, and Joseph noticed Wes was gone. He'd probably headed back to the ranch to help Digger. Bear and Tara remained at the table. Wanting some time with Tara, Joseph leaned over and said, "You want to dance? I figure if we stick it out for three or four songs, we can go home without offending anyone."

Joseph glanced at Bear, hoping she wouldn't mind watching Katelen. His mother motioned for him to go ahead. "Katelen and I will be fine here. I'll order her a banana split."

Katelen clapped at the suggestion of ice cream and ignored her father completely.

Joseph guided Tara to the dance floor. His hand slid over her back, pressing her closer to him. She resisted for a moment, as if she didn't want others to know they were beginning to have true feelings for each other.

"We're supposed to be engaged, remember? We need to act the part," Joseph whispered to her.

Hesitantly, she leaned her head on his shoulder. It was all pretense on Tara's part, but still, it felt good to have a woman he cared for in his arms.

The rhythm of the song glided to a slow one-two beat. Joseph breathed in Tara's jasmine scent and closed his eyes, glad for this excuse to hold her close. For a few minutes, he could pretend she was his fiancée. He felt her hair play along his chin as she laid her head on his shoulder. The words of the song broke through his consciousness. "When love comes again . . . "

He couldn't help but wonder what she was thinking. Did she feel anything for him? He wished the song would never end, that his feelings for this woman could actually flourish into something more than he'd had even with Jenny.

The song ended, but Joseph still held her. Another slow song started, something about wild horses. He glanced over at Bear and Katelen. His daughter was enjoying the ice cream, and his mother seemed content to sit and watch Joseph and Tara.

Bear was a wise woman. She probably knew Joseph felt more than just obligation to protect Tara. As long as they didn't talk about it, he could keep his mother away from delving into his feelings. But he knew sooner rather than later, she would bring up the subject.

And *sooner rather than later* he would have to make Tara tell him what had scared her away from him last night. Was it only because of her breakdown, or was there more? He would reassure her that her breakdown didn't matter to him. He thought of what she'd told him about believing those closest to her died. He would have to help her realize how illogical that thinking was.

The song ended, and the lead singer spoke into the mic. "Let's do the cowboy boogie!"

The crowd seemed to buzz with excitement as they formed a line.

Tara nervously stood close to Joseph. "I didn't think real cowboys actually line danced. I thought that was only in the movies or on TV."

He winked at her. "Just follow what everyone else is doing."

While they danced, Joseph watched Tara try to keep up and mimic others, but she struggled.

"Hey, Joseph." Norman Beasley, one of his more friendly ranching neighbors, had made his way through the dancers to him.

Joseph followed the man over to the sidelines.

"I was driving by and noticed your truck parked out front. What's this I hear about you and your fiancée getting shot at and some of your cattle killed?" Joseph didn't want his time with Tara interrupted, but he had to warn Beasley about possible trouble. He wouldn't point fingers at anyone, but he could generalize and tell him to keep a close eye on his stock.

As Joseph explained what had happened, others quit dancing to listen. Joseph noticed Tara slip away. There'd be another time they could be together. He needed to be patient.

* * *

Making her way to the table, Tara sat next to Bear, giving Katelen space on the other side of her grandmother.

"I was wondering how long it would take for other ranchers to hear what's been going on and want to talk with Joseph. Word travels fast in the country." Bear held a lighter in her hand but no cigarette. Tara had noticed a "no smoking" sign as they'd entered the café. The woman's knobby-knuckled fingers flipped the lighter over and over.

"He asked Joseph about the shooting." Tara wanted to alleviate the woman's anxiety.

Bear leaned an arm against the table.

"Irene!" Katelen exclaimed, drawing Tara's and Bear's attention.

Irene wore a gold vest and no shirt. Her too-tight jeans emphasized her slim hips, and a fancy hat with a spray of pheasant feathers as the band sat on her cloud of long, fluffy, auburn hair. Tara had never seen her without chaps until now. Irene was a knockout, but her expression was filled with worry. "Where's Joseph?"

Tara pointed to the group of men around him near the dance floor.

Irene sat next to her and reached for a handful of mini pretzels in the center of the table. "I need to talk with him. I couldn't get the vaccines he needed." She looked at Bear as if to make sure she had heard.

Bear gave her an it-figures sigh.

"Allen is parking the truck. Just point him in my direction when he comes in." Irene took off, plowing her way through the dancing figures to Joseph.

"I was wondering if Allen'd make it off the mountain in time to help us. He's been checking the line shacks," Bear informed Tara.

"Grandma, you promised we could dance." Katelen had ice cream and chocolate all over her face.

"Not until you're cleaned up, we're not. Come with me, young lady." Bear pocketed her lighter and led Katelen to the restroom.

A foreboding feeling of being watched overcame Tara, and she turned around. In the open doorway stood a man silhouetted in the silver light sheen of the moon. His eyes were in the shadows of his hat. Was he staring at her?

He stepped farther into the room, and light hit his tanned and craggy face. He grinned at Tara and tilted his hat to her. He was a stranger and seemed nice enough, yet there was something not quite right. What was wrong with her? In the back of her mind, she wondered if Garrett might have sent someone else to do his dirty work. But the cowboy walking in didn't appear threatening. Tara had to get a grip and quit being paranoid.

* * *

Irene's voice buzzed in Joseph's ear, but he couldn't understand her over the loud music.

He jerked back. "What?"

"You'd better call off the drive," she shouted. "I can't get the vaccines for a couple of days. You don't want to chance losing more cattle, do you?"

"Just a minute." Joseph excused himself from the conversation before leading Irene back to the table, where Tara now sat alone. He wondered where his mother and Katelen had disappeared to. As he walked, he said to Irene, "We'll have to risk it. As soon as you can buy some, meet us on the mountain near Firebox Summit."

They'd reached the table, and Joseph noticed Tara staring at someone. Before sitting down, he glanced in the direction holding her attention and noticed Allen's profile in the entryway. As soon as Allen saw Joseph, he headed toward them. Joseph placed his hand on Tara's arm to try to reassure her. She jumped a little from his touch, startled to see him but calmed down when Joseph sat beside her. "Where's Mom and Katelen?"

"In the restroom." Tara kept a wary eye on Allen, who was now standing beside Irene.

Joseph took Tara's hand. "Sweetheart." Joseph thought he'd better address Tara with an endearment to put on a good show. "This is Allen Kendal, my good friend and ranch foreman."

Tara didn't say anything.

Allen reached to shake her hand, and Tara reciprocated but quickly withdrew, grabbing Joseph's again.

"Pleasure to meet you, ma'am. Irene told me about your engagement. Never thought I'd see the day when this one"—he pointed to Joseph—

"would take the plunge again. Irene told me you and Joseph were neighbors in LA. Funny we never met while I was on the force with Joseph." Allen slung his arm around Irene's waist.

"Since when did you meet *any* of my neighbors?" Joseph knew Allen was prying, the detective in his friend still resonating.

Allen shrugged. "You got me there."

Dodging that bullet, Joseph looked at his friend's arm around Irene. Allen had always had a thing for Irene, though he'd never acted on it. With Joseph out of the picture, he must have thought now was the time to make his move. Joseph wouldn't fault him for that. Irene was a good woman, but she might be too much for Allen to handle. The man would find out soon enough.

"You two came to Qualey's together?" Joseph asked.

"I stopped by the ranch to tell you about the vaccines just as Allen rode in." Irene glowed as she looked at the man standing beside her. "Oh, which reminds me, I have something in the truck for Katelen." She hurried away, and the men's eyes followed her.

Allen shrugged. "Irene told me about the trouble you've been having. Wish I'd been there to help."

"Nothing you could have done," Joseph reassured him.

"By the way, a bear got into the shack up on Timber Grove. Made a mess, but I set it right. And I'll have you know all the enclosures are good to go. Denver Harris has no leg to stand on if he accuses our cattle of getting in the stream."

Irene returned and gave Joseph a photograph. "I took that of Katelen on Oreo when we went out to check your horses. Thought she'd like a printed copy." She looped her arm in the crook of Allen's. "Enough ranch talk. Care to hoof it around the dance floor?" She led Allen away. He looked to Joseph like he had no choice but to follow the drop-dead gorgeous woman.

Joseph waved him off. Carefully putting the photo in his shirt pocket, where it would be less likely to bend, he turned to Tara. Her grip had nearly made his fingers numb.

"Can we leave?" she blurted.

"Sure." He knew she was upset and tired. Tomorrow would be a tough day. He forced a yawn. "I'm beat anyway. Mom will bring Katelen home with her."

Tara shot to her feet, ready to go. She'd hardly looked at him, and he could tell something was really bothering her.

* * *

As soon as they stepped out of the café, Tara felt greatly relieved. Allen Kendal appeared friendly enough, and so did Irene, but something was off.

She followed Joseph to his truck and wished she could transport back to the ranch instead of having to endure a long ride. Earlier in the day, Joseph had said he wanted to talk to her about last night, but now he'd probably want to know why she was acting all nervous around Allen. And she didn't know what to say. She felt foolish and overly sensitive.

Joseph pulled onto the road and said nothing. Instead, he turned on some country music that filled the silence, for which she was grateful, and they rode for quite a while with neither of them saying a word.

Eventually, Joseph cleared his throat. "I wanted to talk to you about your finding me praying down by the lake last night."

"I should never have intruded on such a private moment. I'm so sorry." She was relieved he didn't bring up her odd reaction to meeting his foreman.

"Actually, I'm glad you were there. As you can probably tell, religion means a lot to me. I'm not a fanatic who prays if someone swears or the truck won't start, but I do pray every day for guidance. I don't usually go down to the lake. I only go there when I need to feel close to God. There's something about being out in nature. It's probably my Nez Perce heritage."

"Joseph, you really don't need to explain to me. Everyone has their own beliefs." She nervously brushed her bangs away from her eyes.

"What do you believe?" Joseph took his gaze off the road for a second to look at her.

She had never put her belief into words. "I'd like to think there is a God watching over us, but if He's there, why did He take my parents? Why did Grandpa Kelly have to die? And now Rosalie? So, no, I really don't believe in a God who would be so heartless." She wished she could tell him differently, but she couldn't lie.

Joseph didn't look at her but kept his eyes on the road ahead. "I understand your feelings. I sort of felt the same way after Jenny died. But I realized I don't have all the answers like God does. He knows what's best for us. And maybe when people's lives are cut short, there is something more important for them to do on the other side." He shifted down a gear.

Wondering why, Tara gazed ahead at a bend in the road. "More important than being here with you and her daughter?"

"That doesn't seem right, does it? I don't have an answer. I do know I feel more at peace believing in God than not. And I have seen and have felt His guidance. I know He answers prayers. We may not always like the answer, but—"

Tara watched as he geared down and pressed on the brake. His foot hit the floor. No resistance. He jammed on the parking break. Nothing. Joseph's forehead furrowed deeply.

They were going too fast to stay on the road as it curved. Fear welled up in Tara, and she clutched the door handle and bit her lip. Goose flesh prickled her skin.

Joseph frantically pumped the brake pedal as if willing it to catch. The truck slowed a little but not much. "Hang on!"

With white knuckles, he turned the wheel, trying his best not to roll the vehicle. Tires squealed as the truck fishtailed around the bend, going over into the oncoming lane. Fortunately, no other car was there. He righted the wheel, and the truck straightened. Catching his breath, he looked at her as if he could hardly believe what was happening.

She gulped, still clutching the door handle.

He let the truck coast for a while. "Don't worry. We're not far from home. We'll make it without trouble."

She bit her lower lip, trying to keep her nerves in check.

"We'll be all right. I'll take it easy the rest of the way."

"Does this happen a lot?" She squirmed in her seat and clasped her hands together.

"Nope. Can't say it has *ever* happened before."

Remembering what they had been talking about, Tara said, "Were you praying when we rounded the bend?" She raised her brows, waiting for his answer.

"You better believe it. And see? We're fine." He thought for a moment. "Though I am awfully glad I shifted down a gear before we came to the turn. If I'd been going faster, like I usually do, well . . ." He didn't need to finish his sentence. She knew they would have crashed.

"Do you think someone did something to the truck?" She remembered Allen coming in after Irene and that Irene had gone out without anyone with her. Either one had had the opportunity to do something.

"It's possible. But doubtful. There's probably a leak in the brake line. When we get home where there's light, I'll check it over."

Her thoughts went to the feeling she'd had when she'd first seen Allen in the café. Joseph trusted him, and the man had been his good friend for years, but Tara couldn't shake the thought that something about the guy bothered her. She had to say something. "Allen is your foreman, right?"

"Yep. Why?"

"This is going to sound crazy." The words pinged around the cab and settled on her shoulder as if to say "crazy sits here."

Joseph took his eyes off the road for a minute, looking at her as though waiting for her to finish.

"When I first saw him, for a moment, I wondered if Garrett had hired someone to kill me." She gave a nervous chuckle. "Did Allen know Garrett?"

Joseph scoffed. "I've known Allen for years. He was my partner when I was a cop. He'd had enough of California, like me, and decided he wanted a more simple life. Like I said, there's probably a leak in the brake line. Let's not jump to conclusions." He turned his attention back to the road, a scowl on his face.

"You're probably right, though he did come in alone. For that matter, Irene was alone outside too. Either one of them could have done something to the brakes." As the words left, she wished she could retrieve them.

"There were scores of other people coming and going and even driving by who could have done something. Let's wait until we have evidence before pointing a finger." Joseph's hand rubbed over the steering wheel.

He was right, but still, Tara couldn't help but wonder.

CHAPTER FIFTEEN
A More Watchful Eye

Once they reached the ranch, the truck barely rolled into the barnyard. Joseph applied the parking brake, and what little was left of it brought them to a complete stop. He leaned over and grabbed a flashlight from the glove box as they got out.

He crawled under the truck expecting to find a leak, but instead, the main brake lines near the front wheels had been cut in two; however, the rear ones were fine. If someone had meant for him to crash, why hadn't they cut those too? Maybe they had been interrupted and couldn't finish what they'd started. A definite possibility. He knew Tara was nervously waiting.

Crawling out from under the truck, he stood up beside her and brushed the dirt off his legs.

"What's the verdict?" She had been extremely patient.

"The front lines were cut."

She groaned and leaned against the truck. "Now we can point fingers, right?"

"No, I want to check the brakes again in the morning when there's more light. But *now* we can ask questions."

"Who do we ask?"

"No, by asking questions, I mean something like, how could they have been cut? Or who drove the truck last? And where did they go? The terrain around here is pretty rugged. I could have driven over rocks and broken the line or something like that."

Tara took a deep, fortifying breath. "Don't you think we should call Sheriff Conrad? It's too big a coincidence that we've been shot at and the brake line has been cut or broken." She pushed a lock of hair behind her ear.

Joseph put his arm around her, guiding her as they walked toward the house. "There is no solid evidence that someone did this deliberately, so there's not much he can do. I'll call the sheriff and report this though, and then tomorrow morning, we're going on the cattle drive like nothing happened. We'll be safe in the mountains."

As they reached the kitchen door, Digger met them. "What's going on? I was packin' supplies and saw you crawling around under the truck. Don't tell me we're gonna have to fire up your father's old bucket of bolts."

"Well, we're going to need another truck. Brakes are out in mine." Joseph started telling Digger about what had happened, leaving out that the brake line might have been cut. As he spoke, he watched Tara leave them and go into the house. The evening had not gone at all the way Joseph had hoped it would, but they were safe. And what Tara had said made sense, though he wouldn't admit it to her. This was too much of a coincidence, but he had no answers as to what it all meant . . .

Or who was behind it.

* * *

Tara tossed and turned in her bed. Fluffing the goose-down pillow under her head, she settled down and closed her eyes. The puzzle over who cut the brakes needled her. She should have taken a sleeping pill, but after the nightmare she'd had on her first night here, she didn't want to risk another. Determined to stick it out, she thought about what Joseph had told her before they'd learned the brakes didn't work.

He believed in a higher being. God. And Joseph had said he'd been praying through their near-death experience. He really believed God had helped them to not crash, which was more than a little interesting since he'd said that after Jenny had died, for a while he too hadn't understood why God would take her from him. In other words, he didn't understand why God hadn't saved her.

Hmm . . . As Tara thought about it, she realized in Jenny's case that God hadn't taken her, but whoever had killed her had stolen her life. What had happened to Tara's parents and grandfather was different. No one murdered them.

No, God had stolen them from her. She turned on her side, fluffed the pillow again, and closed her eyes. If there was a God, He could have stopped the boating accident that took her parents, couldn't He? She'd been so young when they'd died. She really didn't know the particulars, only that they'd gone sailing and had had an accident.

And Grandpa Kelly's dying was an accident as well. God could have kept him safe and made it so he didn't slip on the loose boards on the dock and drown in the lake. Accidents happened all the time.

Maybe God didn't step in to prevent accidents like He didn't step in to stop a murderer.

Yet Joseph believed God had saved them tonight.

Why save us and not them? Maybe it had something to do with human freewill. She rolled onto her back. Rosalie was murdered like Jenny. Why did either of them have to die? Why would God let that happen? The answers had to be somewhere. Surely if Rosalie's dying had something to do with what Tara had done . . .

If she'd shot the gun . . .

She had stolen Rosalie's life.

Overwhelming sorrow possessed her. If only she could remember and know for certain if that was true or not!

A wild idea came to her. Maybe she needed to pray to remember. She thought of Joseph on his knees by the lake.

Tara crawled from beneath the covers and knelt at the side of the bed. How did she start? Dear God? Or hello, is anybody home? No, she'd pray like she was having a conversation. "God, if I shot Rosalie, please help me remember. Please give me peace. And please, God, help me know what to do." She stayed on her knees, waiting and waiting and waiting.

She stared up at the ceiling. What did she expect? A booming voice? The ceiling to open up to a heavenly choir? *I should have known that if there were a God, He wouldn't talk to me.* Feeling like a fool, she crawled into bed, rolled onto her stomach, and cried herself to sleep.

The smell of bacon awakened her the next morning. She scrambled to the side of the bed and stared at the alarm clock. 7:30. Digger would need her in the kitchen. And she hadn't packed for the cattle drive yet. They were to be gone several days.

Throwing on clothes, she washed her face and put on her makeup, applying concealer to the dark circles under her eyes. Tying her hair at the nape of her neck, she heard people in the hallway, heading to breakfast. She had to hurry and pack.

Quickly gathering some clothes for the trip, she opted to take an oversized T-shirt to sleep in rather than of one of Jenny's nightgowns. She stuffed the clothes in a small overnight bag she found in the closet and shoved her makeup in too. She rolled up the sketches of the picture book and grabbed pencils and put them in. If she had a chance, she'd work on them some more. Then she remembered what Joseph had said about wearing a hat.

After what had happened to them last night and her reaction to meeting his ranch foreman, she felt she needed to do something to make Joseph think she was fitting in. She pulled the hatbox down, opened the lid, and took out the Stetson.

Setting the hat on her head and grabbing her bag, Tara headed out.

* * *

The bellowing Hereford cattle moved like a great armada through the sagebrush. Joseph watched the snorting bulls guarding their harems, keeping their mates in line, all the while on the alert for poaching young upstarts wanting to add to their own harems. He'd brought along a few unsaddled horses, and they were among the herd. He always took extra horses just in case.

Joseph and Tara rode on horseback along the north ridge, watching for strays. Joseph hadn't spoken to her about the truck's brakes except to say he'd reported the incident to the sheriff. While Joseph had saddled their horses, Tara had remained silent, watching everyone and staying far away from Allen. Joseph hoped Tara would soon realize his foreman and friend was a nice guy.

Scrap and the other dogs that had come with their masters to help followed the cattle, nipping at their heels and prodding them along when they went astray.

Tara looked at home on Shotgun. Though the short ride she'd had a couple of days ago had been interrupted, there must have been some kind of bond made between horse and rider because they acted as if they'd been a team for years.

After an hour or so in the saddle, Joseph knew Tara was struggling because she shifted her weight from one side to the other. Most greenhorns went through some soreness until they were broken in. He liked that she'd worn Jenny's hat. Since he took the paper out of the band, it fit her better than it ever had his late wife.

Copper stopped abruptly and reared up on his hind legs, and Joseph heard the familiar rattle of a snake. "Whoa. It's okay." He stroked his horse's neck and guided him away from the trail, then yelled to Tara, "Stay there!"

She pulled back on the reins, and Shotgun halted.

Joseph rode over to her. "Did you hear that?"

"Hear what?"

"That rattling."

"What rattling?" She started to reposition herself to listen better, but her foot slipped through the stirrup. Trying to pull it back, her boot stuck.

Joseph chuckled, leaned over, and righted Tara's boot. "Better?"

"Yes. Thank you."

"Back to the rattling." He settled in his saddle, and the leather creaked from his weight. "That was a rattlesnake."

"Rattlesnake?" Her eyes grew as large as watering buckets. She glanced around, examining each bush and clump of grass. "Do you mean the kind that bite and kill?"

Joseph patted her hand, drawing her attention to him. "Calm down. There's a few of them out here. We haven't had a rattlesnake roundup for some time."

"A rattlesnake roundup?" Her fine eyebrows peaked to exclamation points.

Joseph knew he shouldn't have teased her, especially after last night. He had hoped to lighten her mood. "I'm sorry. There's no such thing as a rattlesnake roundup. I just wanted to see that pretty smile of yours. I didn't mean any harm."

"I have been a bit uptight, haven't I?" she said as though disgusted with her own naiveté.

"Well, yeah, but it's understandable. The reason Copper reared up was because we got close to a rattler. See this?" Joseph turned and pointed to the cantle of his saddle. The rim was covered with snakeskin. "I shot that last year. We were driving the herd near the summit when this long guy slithered out from behind a big rock. Nearly bit me."

Tara's eyes locked onto the snakeskin, and she blinked a couple of times but kept her gaze on it. Her cheeks turned pale. He had to make her understand she was in no danger if she did what he told her. "If you stay on Shotgun and follow me, you'll be okay."

Deciding he'd said enough, he clicked his tongue, and his horse took the lead. The mountain loomed ahead like a towering giant waiting for them to enter its domain.

Minutes trickled by like hours in the hot sun. Pungent sagebrush grew hardy on the desert floor and scented the air as the cattles' hooves crushed it in their trek. "Yeps" and "Getups" came from the drovers sprinkled among the herd.

Joseph noticed a cow wandering off to a copse of junipers. Glancing at Tara, he said, "See that cow?"

She looked in the direction he pointed.

"She's a bit ornery. I'm going to circle behind her. Just keep moving with the herd, and I'll catch up."

"Okay." She was covered with a film of grit. Several strands of her hair had escaped the band and graced her neck. Dark lines underscored her eyes, and she looked bone tired. The same haunted expression that creased her brow this morning framed her face. He hated that she was worried. He couldn't blame her though.

Copper's ears pricked forward, and the horse pranced, wanting to go after the wayward heifer. "I'll be right back."

Tara shot him a you'd-better look of concern.

"I promise," he added, hoping that would help.

He tapped his knees to Copper, and his horse leaped into action. They moved nearly parallel to the cow yet behind, and the horse seemed to mesmerize the animal, heading it toward the herd.

Passing the junipers, Joseph saw a flash. He pulled back on the reins and surveyed the area. Tara had ridden to the lava rise ahead. The cattle were still slowly moving toward the mountain. Bear and some of the drovers were working drag. There was another flash, but it came from behind the junipers this time. After the other day when he'd ignored the flash of light while riding with Tara and then getting shot at, he wasn't about to make the same mistake. Coaxing his horse forward to investigate, he rode into the trees.

Not far from him, Lester Fimble sat astride a four-wheeler, talking with Allen, who was on his horse. Joseph didn't even know they knew each other, but they appeared deep in conversation. What was the old man up to?

And Allen? Joseph had trusted him and told him about the brakes. Allen had told Joseph he hadn't noticed anything out of the ordinary when he and Irene had arrived at Qualey's. All the while, Joseph had watched him, checking to see if he could detect a lie. But Allen was Allen, his good friend. And he'd seemed genuinely concerned.

Staring at the two men talking, Joseph's first inclination was to ride over and find out what was going on. Maybe Tara had seen something in Allen that Joseph couldn't because he was too close to him. The last time Joseph had been too stubborn and ignored a woman's intuition, it had cost his wife her life. He decided to circle around to try to get as close as he could to hear what they were saying.

He nudged Copper forward, going around the fragrant cedars, edging as close as he dared.

"Do what I say." That was Lester. Joseph would recognize his braying voice anywhere.

"Listen to me, old man. You can't stop me. I've waited long enough." Allen kicked his horse and rode away.

Lester started the four-wheeler and peeled out, flipping dust high in the air.

Joseph didn't know what to think. The abrupt end to their conversation didn't make sense. But he did know he was going to keep a more watchful eye on his friend from here on out.

CHAPTER SIXTEEN
BAD BLOOD

Tara followed Joseph as he led the cattle up the mountain trail through pines, quaking aspens, cottonwoods, and scrub oak. Most of the cows followed the trail, but some would head off down a ravine or into the trees. The drovers would have to get off their horses and chase the cattle by foot because the trees grew too thick or the incline was too steep.

Bear and Joseph traveled on foot for a lot of the day, and Tara marveled at their stamina. The herd came to a small clearing, and she found Digger in the truck, waiting for them. He was delivering lunch. He told Tara that during the cattle drive, he'd handle the meals. The Chief needed every hand he could get herding the cattle. Even Katelen was helping with the animals. She rode on her black-and-white pinto, Oreo. Tara had never seen a seven-year-old work so hard chasing one cow and then another, and she felt a new respect for the child take root.

Grateful for a chance to get off her horse and eat lunch, Tara climbed down. Her knees felt like they'd collapse, and her backside ached in spots she didn't even know she had.

"How are you doing?" Joseph had come to stand beside her.

"Tired," she said.

He'd kept close tabs on her most of the day, except when he had flushed the stray cow from the junipers just before the cattle had headed up the mountain. But it hadn't taken him long to find her afterward. And Tara was glad. This way she could defer to Joseph if Bear or Katelen or Allen wanted to talk. Tara knew she needed to be more social, but worry over the cut brake line wouldn't let her.

"You didn't sleep well last night, did you?" Joseph tipped his hat back.

"I never sleep well before a trip." Grateful she'd come up with a good answer, she followed him to Digger. They collected their lunches, and

Joseph guided her to the shade and a tree stump so big they could both sit on it.

"You're doing great." He took a bite of his sandwich.

"For a rookie, you mean." She managed a smile as she unwrapped her sandwich.

He chuckled. "We should reach the top by five. We'll bed the cattle down in the meadow there. Digger's already set up his camp trailer, and Wes is going to drive Bear's trailer up after he takes care of Shamrock and the horses. So it should be there as well. Bear won't sleep in it. She prefers to sleep under the stars, but I thought you and Katelen could. I asked Wes to stop and take our things out of the truck and put them in the trailer."

This was the first Tara had heard of the arrangement. She wondered if Katelen knew. "Are you sure that's a good idea for Katelen and me to be together?"

"Don't worry. By the end of the day, you'll both be so tired, you'll fall asleep."

Tara hoped he was right.

* * *

When they finally reached the mountaintop and the cattle were settled in the meadow, they were able to climb off their horses for the day.

Joseph took the reins of Tara's horse. "You go on into camp. I'll take care of the horses."

Tara wanted to stay and help, but every joint in her body ached. And her knees felt like rubber. All she wanted to do was grab a bite to eat and go to bed. Unless she was too tired and couldn't sleep. That happened sometimes, and when it did, she always took a pill. Tonight the need to sleep would outweigh her worry over another nightmare.

In the camp, two trailers sat one in front of the other, and Digger was busily working at a table. The ranch hands were gathered around a campfire, where several logs lay for people to rest on. Allen Kendal was with the group of men. When the others went back to talking, she felt his gaze on her as she made her way over to Digger.

What was the man's problem anyway? Tara was tempted to ask but abandoned the idea. She hated making a scene. And right now, she was tired and starving, so let him stare all he wanted.

She hurried her step, and as she neared Digger, he was mumbling colorful curses—something about Bear hiding the tomato juice so he couldn't make snakebite kidney bean stew. He nearly growled when he saw Tara. "Would have had supper ready hours before, but I had to make chicken and dumplings instead of what I was planning."

"Can I help?" She leaned against a picnic table.

He studied her more closely. "You look like you've been wrestling steers all day."

"It's good to see you too." She eased down on the picnic table bench.

"I don't mean nothin' except you seem tired, lassie." He grabbed a tin pie plate and went to one of the dutch ovens in his cook fire. Grabbing a T-shaped hook, he pulled up the lid and set it on a three-legged rack on the ground next to the fire. Fetching a large spoon, he lifted a good helping of chicken and dumplings into the pie plate and set it in front of Tara on the table. She was a little embarrassed she'd been served first and glanced back at the others.

The ranch hands began lining up, pie plates and utensils in hand, yet they stood respectively back, waiting for Digger to give them the signal. He winked at Tara, wiped his hand on the dish towel slung over his shoulder, and said to the rest of the crew, "All right. Y'all can come and get it."

In an orderly manner, they held out their plates for Digger to fill. Each and every one thanked him. Bear, Katelen, and Joseph were last in line, which Tara thought odd, but she realized that was the kind of people they were. They made sure others were taken care of before themselves.

Once he collected his food, Joseph came to sit beside her. Bear and Katelen followed him.

"How are you feeling?" Bear asked Tara as she and Katelen sat across the table from them.

"Fine." Tara couldn't tell her about the last time she'd felt so sore and tired; it had been when she'd tried to run a marathon. She'd done it only as a favor to her publisher, who had asked all their authors and artists to participate in the fund-raising event. Sadly, Tara had not earned much for the cause, so she'd donated her own money to ease her conscience.

"She did really well for a city slicker." Joseph nudged Tara's arm and winked.

"Thanks, I think." She wasn't certain if he'd paid her a compliment or not.

"Well, if you didn't get the hang of it today, you get to do it all over again come morning. At least now we're on top of the first range of mountains, and the riding won't be as tough." Bear started eating.

Katelen had been silent the entire time, keeping her eyes on the contents of her plate as she ate. The little girl wolfed down her supper and asked her father and grandmother if she could be excused so she could go to bed.

"Don't you want to sit around the campfire for while?" Joseph appeared surprised that his daughter wanted to leave.

She shook her head, her braids bouncing about her shoulders.

"Okay. I'll be by later to tuck you in." Joseph watched her walk away and step up into the trailer.

Tara was so tired she wanted to follow but knew it would probably be best for both her and Katelen if she waited a while. She stood and started stacking Katelen's plate on hers. She could at least help Digger with the dishes.

"You've put in a long hard day, lass. I'll clean up. You and the Chief go sit by the fire for a while." Digger motioned for them to join the others.

Bear had already gone over. She lit a cigarette and was listening to some of the boys talk about other drives and the good old days.

"Thanks," Tara said to Digger.

She and Joseph sat on a log near the others. The sun was setting, and brilliant pink and orange clouds fanned across the sky.

"Hey, Joseph." Allen added another log to the campfire. "Tell us the story about how your mother earned the nickname Bear again."

"You don't want to hear that," Bear scoffed.

"Sure they do," Joseph said, overriding her objection. "My father always felt Mother was a bear whisperer, especially after they went camping near the summit. This old, ornery black bear sauntered into camp early one morning, and Mom had just cooked a mouthwatering lumberjack breakfast: bacon, sausage, eggs, and flapjacks. She had it on the table ready for us to eat. That old bear thought it smelled real good, so he climbed up on the bench of the picnic table and stared right at her."

"Did she put him under a spell or whisper to him?" one of the cowboys asked.

"Sort of." Joseph had a glint in his eyes. "She politely asked him to leave, and when he didn't, Mom took her big fry pan and knocked him over the head."

"Did he attack her?" Tara asked, caught up in the story.

"Funny thing, that bear shook his head, backed up, and left camp." Joseph chuckled and glanced over at his mother.

"I've always been told to speak softly but carry a big frying pan." Bear took a drag on her cigarette, and everyone laughed.

"And from that time on, people started calling her Bear." Joseph tugged off his hat and ran his fingers through his black hair, then tugged the hat back on, all the while smiling at his mother.

Tara loved to watch Joseph with his mom. They had a special bond she envied.

"Which reminds me." Joseph quit laughing. "I understand a mama bear and her cubs have been causing some trouble near here, so keep your eyes peeled. And don't—under any circumstance—try to do *what my mother did.*" Joseph emphasized his last few words.

The air quickly grew chilly as the sun set. Tara hadn't even thought about bringing a coat, and she hugged her arms to her body.

"I have some extra jackets in the trailer. You're welcome to wear one." Bear had noticed. "They're in the closet near the door. Katelen can show you."

"Thanks." Grateful for something to do, Tara walked away from the small warmth of the fire.

Approaching the trailer, she noticed a tarp had been laid down and several cots with sleeping bags rolled out on top of them were ready for the night. A light shone inside the trailer, which probably meant Katelen was still awake. Tara was hopeful she could merely open the door, see the closet, and take a coat without saying anything. But Katelen was wide awake sitting at the small dinette, and Tara's sketches were spread out before her. She glanced up, a sheepish smile slanting her big, round, penny-colored eyes. "There was a bag in here. I thought Grandma had packed my things in it, but I found these pretty pictures instead. Do you know whose they are?"

"Yes, they're mine. But I drew them for you."

Katelen's mouth dropped open, and she blinked with disbelief. "For me? But . . ." For some reason, she nervously glanced past the doorway of another sleeping area.

"Yes. Just for you." Tara slid into the seat across from Katelen. The girl gazed down at the sketch of the angel casting star beams on the eagle. Tara wondered if Katelen recognized her mother. Curious about the guilty look on Katelen's face, Tara peered at the bed in the other sleeping area but could see nothing unusual, though she could almost bet her next royalty check a surprise was waiting between the sheets.

Joseph must have told Katelen they'd be sharing the living space on the drive, so, of course, the girl had decided to create some mischief.

"Why?" The child nervously bit at her lower lip. "Why would you be nice to me and draw these? I don't want you to be my mom. I don't want you here."

"I would never want to replace your mother. That's why I drew the pictures. I wanted to give you something to always remind you of her, something you could touch and hold." Tara went over to the bed.

There was movement beneath the blanket. Tara choked back the urge to scream and, instead, returned to the child and squatted so she could look directly at Katelen. "I know you don't like me. In fact, I'll bet you don't like me so much you might have even put something in my bed." The child gulped. Her bottom lip began to protrude, and tears gathered at the corners of her eyes. Tara stood. "If you want me to leave, I will. But, Katelen, the drawings are yours."

The little girl wrapped her arms around Tara's legs. "I'm sorry. Please don't go. I didn't know you were nice."

Tara patted the top of Katelen's head and brushed the girl's long black braids over her small shoulders. "It's okay, sweetie. Really, it is." Tara knelt beside the child, hugging her back. "There's one thing I want you to do for me though."

"Yeah?"

"Please take whatever you put in my bed outside." Tara shuddered.

"Sure." Katelen rushed to the bed and pulled the quilts back, revealing a coiled snake. "He won't hurt you none." Katelen scooped it up and went out.

Not wanting to sleep on sheets the snake had touched, Tara searched the closet for other sheets but came up empty.

Katelen tromped back in. "Let's show Daddy and Grandma Bear the pictures." The child grabbed the illustrations, tugging Tara out the door to the campfire.

As Katelen showed everyone what Tara had made her, Tara caught Joseph's eye. Pride and gratitude filled his gaze . . . and something more.

"You've got a real talent. Ever think of doing this for a living?" Bear studied each page before passing it on for others to get a closer look.

"The thought has crossed my mind." Tara glanced at Joseph. A smile pulled at his lips. The chill of the coming night reminded Tara she still needed a jacket. She'd been so involved with Katelen she'd forgotten to grab one. "Excuse me a minute."

A couple of vehicles drove into camp as she headed toward the trailer—Irene's Chevy truck with a camper and a sleek, new GMC truck, also with a camper. They stopped next to Tara and Katelen's trailer. Of course, Irene would arrive as Tara was making progress with Katelen. What would the child do with her here? And then Tara thought about Joseph.

Tara would be stepping out of Joseph's and Katelen's lives soon. He'd hinted that he was drawn to Tara, but she was damaged goods. He deserved someone better, someone who could help him on the ranch and someone everyone in his family admired. Katelen already loved Irene, and she was a perfect fit for both of them.

"Hey, Sarah," Irene called to her as she slammed her truck door. A man got out of the GMC, but Tara didn't recognize him.

"Irene, can I talk with you?" Tara asked, wanting some privacy.

"Sure." She motioned for the man to go ahead to the campfire, where everyone else was gathered.

The ever-confident Irene pushed her hands into the pockets of her suede-fringed jacket, and as if a little impatient, she shifted from leg to leg waiting for Tara to speak.

"Irene, I'm sorry we got off on the wrong foot. I'd really like to be your friend." Tara hoped the woman would accept the olive branch she offered.

"You, my friend? Look, I was semi-nice to you at Qualey's for Joseph's sake. But you're bad news, lady. I've known it ever since I first laid eyes on you, and it's not because Joseph chose you instead of me." Irene shrugged. "I've kinda turned my attentions to greener pasture, so to speak." She looked toward the tall stranger by the campfire.

Tara didn't know what to say. Here she thought Irene had true feelings for Joseph. Obviously she didn't. Silence fell between them.

Irene cleared her throat. "But, hey, we can be nice to one another. Just because Joseph is marrying you, it's not going to stop me from being a part of Katelen's life. I love that little girl." Her face softened as she smiled at Tara. "Let's talk about this later. Come meet Joseph's replacement."

Tara felt like she'd made progress, so she followed Irene, even though she had no desire to meet this man who had caught Irene's attention. The campfire glowed over the pencil-thin stranger's tanned face, accentuating his finely trimmed goatee. He still wore dark sunglasses even though the sun had set, and his pressed Eddie Bauer jeans and long-sleeved T-shirt with "Save the Wilderness" on the chest made him look out of place among the cowboys.

Joseph had stood. So had Bear, and they both appeared caught off guard by this man's presence.

Irene ignored them, leading Tara to him. "Sarah Smith, this is Denver Harris."

Harris took Tara's hand in his and kissed it. "Pleased to meet you."

The saccharine tone of his voice and the way he'd addressed her sent a chill streaking over Tara's skin. Wanting to appear courteous, she asked, "Are you a rancher?"

"No, he isn't." Joseph clenched his jaw, and the scar on his right cheek twitched.

Harris took off his sunglasses and met Joseph's stare, then he turned to Tara. "I'm merely a friend of Irene's. I came up to the mountains to do what I love most—fish."

Looking at the two men, Tara knew they had bad blood between them, but she had no idea why. She glanced around at the other ranch hands. Almost all of them appeared to have the same trepidation Joseph had about the man's presence—everyone except Allen Kendal, and he grinned at Tara like he knew something she didn't.

CHAPTER SEVENTEEN
THE DEVIL HIMSELF

JOSEPH COULDN'T BELIEVE THE NERVE of Harris, showing up in his camp and pretending he was merely here to fish—as if his legal fight to keep cattle off of BLM land wasn't happening. The pure gall of the man set Joseph's nerves on edge. Harris had done nothing but make every rancher's life miserable since he'd moved to Idaho.

The forest service may have to put up with the idiot, but Joseph didn't have to abide his presence in his own camp. And that Irene had brought him here knowing full well how Joseph felt only showed him how vengeful she really was.

With their entire camp surrounding them, Bear reached out a hand to Harris. "I must say I'm surprised to see you."

Harris returned the handshake.

"Being as you believe all cattlemen are only self-serving, I'm more than surprised," Joseph added to his mother's comment. "I'm amazed you'd set foot among us heathens."

Harris shrugged. "Let's just say Irene can be very persuasive." He held his hand out for Joseph to shake.

Joseph had no intention of welcoming him and left him hanging.

Ignoring the snub, Harris turned to Tara. "I understand you and Mr. White Eagle are engaged to be married."

"Yes, we are." Tara looped her arm in Joseph's, and he took great comfort in her small gesture.

Katelen carried the sketches over to Irene. "Look what Sarah gave me. She drew them herself."

Irene studied each page. She looked up at Tara, then back to the pictures. "These are good."

"Very good." Harris added as he glanced at them over Irene's shoulder.

"I bought a picture book for Katelen, and I swear that illustrator has the same style," Irene said. "Can't remember the name though." She stared at the sketch of the mother angel. "Have you done other work?"

Joseph knew they were in dangerous territory, and Tara must have sensed it too because she took the sketches from Irene. "A little." She gave them to Katelen. "Why don't you put them away for now?"

Grateful for Tara's foresight, Joseph said to his daughter, "Besides, you were heading to bed a while ago. We need to rise and shine before the sun. We still have a ways to go yet."

Oblivious to the tension around her, Katelen protectively held the drawings under one arm and, with the other, hugged her father and Grandmother before heading back to the camp trailer.

"I'll go with her," Tara piped up. "I'm really tired." She paused a moment, glancing around at all the eyes watching her.

Joseph realized they expected him to kiss her good night. He leaned over and gave her a quick kiss, then he winked, which made her smile. "Good night," he said. Tara hurried to catch up with Katelen.

Irene stood with a dumbfounded expression on her face, like she couldn't believe he'd kissed Tara or that Katelen hadn't said good night to her. She usually did. For a second, Joseph felt sorry for Irene, but it quickly faded when he once again laid eyes on Harris. Joseph didn't wait to get to the bottom of what was going on with him. "Why are you really here?"

Irene stepped in. "I ran into Denver at Qualey's. I stopped there for lunch on my way. Since I was able to find some cattle vaccines, I thought I'd better head up here." Irene gave Joseph a look he couldn't quite read, as if she were saying listen and learn. "By the way, you're welcome."

"Thanks," Joseph uttered, waiting for more explanation.

"Denver told me he has been up here fishing over the last week. I told him I was meeting you on the drive, and one thing led to another, and here we are." A strained smile came to her lips, her eyebrows raised.

Although Joseph first thought Irene was bringing Harris here out of revenge, he now wondered. Irene might be upset with him, but she generally had his best interest at heart. She must have a reason for bringing Harris to camp. Joseph would have to be patient until he could find out.

"Well, boys, pardon an old lady, but I'm heading to bed." Bear started toward the trailer where her sleeping bag waited outside on a cot. Digger had already set Bear and Joseph's cots up for the night. The others were heading for their bags as well.

"Don't mind if I park my camper here for the night, do you?" Harris asked Joseph.

Yes, he did mind, but as Joseph thought about it, he'd rather have the man where he could see him. Maybe that was why Irene had brought him. What was the saying? "Keep your friends close and your enemies closer." But Joseph couldn't help wondering if the man's true purpose had been to find out exactly where Joseph's cattle grazed so he could pick them off one at a time. It was entirely possible, but there wasn't a thing Joseph could do about it. He shrugged. "It's a free country."

Irene took Harris's hand but said to Joseph, "Tomorrow I'll give the cattle what vaccines I can along the trail. 'Night, Joseph. We'll talk more in the morning." The two left, heading for their campers.

"You all right?" Allen had stayed behind, even though the other workers had turned in for the night, some in tents, others choosing to sleep under the stars. Allen probably wanted to talk about what Joseph planned for tomorrow and how hard they should push the cattle.

"Been better." Joseph had wanted to speak with Allen ever since he'd seen the man talking with Lester Fimble earlier in the day. He'd ease into the subject. "How about you? You were with Irene last night. You can't be very happy about Harris moving into your spot."

"Yeah, well, good luck to whoever she settles down with. You won't believe this, but her father chased me down on the drive. Did you see him?"

Joseph took a toothpick from his shirt pocket, clenched it between his teeth, and nodded.

"He's crazy. Told me to stop seeing Irene. Shoot, I only went out with her once, and that was last night." Allen scoffed and shook his head.

Joseph knew all too well how irrational Lester could be. Joseph had a flat tire to prove it. "He's been a bit upset about Irene and me breaking up. His bark is worse than his bite, though he does seem to have sharp teeth."

"Think he's the one who's been behind all this trouble plaguing us?" Allen's concern sounded sincere.

"Truth be told, I don't know. Which reminds me." Joseph hated to bring this up but had to. "I'm worried about Sarah. She's been under a great deal of stress. Could you and the other guys give her some space?"

"Sure. I haven't spoken to her since last night." Allen seemed confused.

Joseph couldn't blame him with the way she'd reacted to Allen when she'd first met him at Qualey's, but Joseph thought it best to keep the two apart. "I know. Just humor me on this."

Allen agreed and proceeded to ask more questions about the drive. He was acting perfectly normal. Why Tara distrusted the man was a complete puzzle. Joseph and Allen parted ways, and Allen headed off to his sleeping bag.

Joseph sat on a log. He wanted to make sure the campfire was out before going to bed, and as he watched the dwindling flames and red embers, he couldn't help but wonder what else was going to happen on this drive.

He was grateful Katelen and Tara were on better terms, thanks to the sketches Tara had drawn. Irene seemed to recognize Tara's work, though she couldn't place it. If she did figure out Tara was *the* Tara Kelly, he'd have a problem, but he'd worry about that when it happened. He turned his thoughts to Harris. So he'd been in the area all week. He could have shot the cattle and cut the brake line in Joseph's truck. Lester could have as well.

The campfire flames blinked out, and Joseph stirred the embers until they quit glowing. Satisfied it was safe enough for him to retire, he glanced around the sleeping camp, where he could hear occasional snores. He looked up at the starry night, grateful he could gaze at such a sight and know God watched over him.

All at once a bloodcurdling scream wrenched the air. It had come from Katelen and Tara's camp trailer, and Joseph's heart jackknifed into his throat. He jumped over several logs in his path as he raced across the distance. The screaming never quit as Joseph tore open the door, flipped on the light, and entered the camp trailer.

Katelen was sitting up in her bed, rubbing her eyes, but she wasn't screaming, though she looked absolutely terrified.

Joseph rushed to the small bedroom at the back of the trailer. Tara stood on her bed, dressed in only a T-shirt. Her eyes were wide with terror, her long hair in disarray as she stared at the ceiling and continued to scream like she'd seen the devil himself. Joseph leaped up and tried to take her in his arms, but she fought him off.

They fell to the mattress. Grabbing her, Joseph shook her hard. "It's me, Joseph."

She stopped fighting and stared at him. Sweat dampened her skin. She took several deep breaths, and blinked back tears, then finally crumpled into sobs and trembled uncontrollably. "Joseph, I did it."

He noticed movement at the doorway, and Katelen stood barefooted in her pajamas beside Bear. He motioned for his mother to leave.

"Come on, sweetie. Come get in Grandma's bed and look at the stars with me." Bear took Katelen's hand and left.

With them gone, Joseph focused solely on Tara. "What did you do?" He cradled her to him, rubbing her arms in an effort to calm and warm her.

She reared back and looked him squarely in the eyes. "I killed Rosalie."

CHAPTER EIGHTEEN

CHASING COURAGE

TARA SAW THE SHOCK OF her words in Joseph's eyes.

He shook his head. "You had a bad dream is all."

Tara didn't know whether she was relieved or not. Again she had dreamed of Rosalie. Again her aunt had appeared and asked why while gray, gauzy images chanted in the background.

As the nightmare had progressed, Tara had once again been at the dolmen in Poulnabrone, white limestone at her feet. The dark entrance between the portal stones and beneath the capstone had beckoned her. Tara knew she had to go, had to enter the Land of the Dead. Only there could she find answers.

She stepped into the portal, and the earth gave way. Tara free fell into a sea of darkness and crashed abruptly to the ground. She was no longer in Ireland but in Rosalie's house, in suffocating blackness, with two figures fighting. One fell to the ground, and something slid across the wood floor to her feet.

A gun.

The man was beating Rosalie, hitting her with a club. She would die if Tara didn't do something to stop him. She picked up the weapon but became dizzy.

Rosalie cried out. And Tara aimed. As she squeezed the trigger, the figures moved again. A white flash nearly blinded Tara, and the weapon's recoil knocked her to the ground.

Someone ran away.

Rosalie hovered, floating like a cloud over Tara, her eyes turning to flames, her hair tangling with matted blood.

"Why," she'd asked. "Why did you do it?"

A hand stroked Tara's cheek. "Tara, it's me, Joseph. You had a bad dream. That's all." He cradled her to him. She leaned her head against his chest, hearing his heartbeat. Joseph was a good man, a caring man, a man who believed her innocent because he was falling in love with her like she was falling in love with him.

But Tara knew the undeniable truth.

* * *

Tara cried herself to sleep in Joseph's arms. Something besides PTSD was causing her to have ghastly nightmares so lifelike she now believed she'd killed her own aunt. Joseph knew she couldn't have done it. Mac had told him he'd seen Garrett flee the scene and that Tara had been in the garden.

But Joseph could not deny the terror he'd seen in her eyes, and in that moment, he knew he'd never let her go. The powerful feeling he'd had the other night by the lake that she was meant to be with him pulsed once again in his veins. Heaven help him, he loved this woman, this poor, mixed up, troubled woman, who needed someone to love her and someone to believe in her even though she couldn't believe in herself.

Shifting her to the bed, he eased her head on the pillow and tucked her in. He brushed a stray lock of hair away from her face. He could not leave her side, not tonight, not after what she had said and how scared she had been. She needed him here.

He knew Katelen would sleep with Bear, so he decided to sleep near Tara. He reached across and grabbed the other pillow on the bed. As quietly as he could, he took a blanket from the closet, turned off the light, and settled down on the floor.

* * *

The sun shone through the curtains, waking Tara. Sitting up, she felt like a boa constrictor had squeezed her brain. Her muscles were stiff as she moved to the side of the bed. She was late getting up. Joseph had said they would be leaving at sunrise. She put her feet down and stepped on a blanket and pillow. Had someone slept there? A memory flash reminded her of the horrible nightmare and how she'd told Joseph her deepest fear. He'd held her in his arms until she'd fallen asleep. He'd probably slept on the floor.

He must think I'm ready for Twin Pines, and maybe I am. She rubbed her aching forehead and noticed her bottle of sleeping pills on the nightstand. She'd taken one before getting in bed last night. She realized that the night she'd had the nightmare on the ranch, she'd also taken a pill. The pills were supposed to help her sleep not give her horrible dreams. What was the deal?

Grabbing the bottle, she dumped a couple of blue tablets into her hand. Engraved on them was *Halcion 250*. Tara could have sworn the doctor had prescribed Ambien. Maybe the pharmacy had substituted a generic brand, or maybe they'd made a mistake and had given her the wrong meds. Irene might know what Halcion was.

Tara got up and dressed as quickly as she could, putting a pill in her jeans pocket, then she left the trailer, determined to find Joseph and talk to him about last night. The campsite was pretty much deserted, except for movement near Digger's camp trailer. At least he was still here. He'd know where Joseph was.

Why hadn't someone awakened her? As the question formed in her mind, so did the answer. No one would have bothered her after the way she'd screamed like a banshee. With all the work they had to do today, they were probably glad to leave her behind. Her resolve to talk to Joseph diminished. Didn't he have enough worries without her adding to them? It would be better to let things settle. Be calm and collected. Help where she could. And then when the time was right and she could act like a woman who had her life under control, she'd talk things over with Joseph.

She hurried over to Digger. He was loading his gear in his cook trailer when he saw her. "There you are. The Chief said to let you sleep as long as you could."

"Has everyone left except you and me?"

"Yep. Wes should arrive anytime to pull Bear's trailer to the next campsite. Chief thought you might like to help me today, so he gave you a break from the saddle."

The old man steered clear of questions, for which she was grateful, but she had to get what happened last night out in the open. "I made quite a fool of myself, didn't I?"

"Everyone has a bad dream now and again." He pulled a dutch oven out of the dying embers of the fire. "Saved you some breakfast if you're feeling up to it."

Inside were scrambled eggs and two sausage links. Digger grabbed a bottle of ketchup, a plate, and utensils and placed them on the table in front of her. "While you're eatin', I'll finish loadin' up. Like I said, Wes should be here anytime."

Tara ate despite her upset stomach, and with each mouthful, she felt stronger. A slight breeze graced her skin, a bird high in a pine tree sang a cheerful song, and for a moment, Tara could almost put the horror of the haunting nightmare out of her mind.

Yet she knew when she saw Joseph again, he'd have questions she'd have to answer.

After breakfast, Tara kept busy helping Digger. In the back of her mind, she repeated the dream over and over. Did she really kill Rosalie? And if she did, Garrett had been unfairly accused. Many times Digger asked her if she was all right, and she nodded her head and got back to work each time.

When Wes arrived, they moved to the new campsite, which took most of the morning. Irene's truck was already there, but she was gone. She must have parked and ridden out to meet the herd so she could give the cattle the vaccines. Tara wondered where Denver was and remembered he'd said he'd come to the mountains to do some fishing.

Digger had his own rig so Wes didn't have to move the cook trailer. First he towed Bear's camp trailer. Next was Joseph's horse trailer, and Tara drove him back and forth so he could drive the other drovers' rigs to the new site.

As Wes prepared to return to the ranch, Tara was tempted to beg him to take her. She felt once again that she needed to return to LA to talk to Mac as soon as she possibly could. She couldn't put it off. She had to tell him about her dream and let him decide what to do from there.

But even if she convinced Wes to take her to the ranch, she'd have to plead with him to drive her to Idaho Falls, and she knew he'd never do that. Besides, in all good conscience, she couldn't leave without first seeing Joseph. She owed him an explanation of some sort. How she was going to convince him to let her go home was the question. However, after last night's drama, he might be more willing to let her go.

Trying to forget her troubles, she helped Digger with the sack lunches. When it came time to deliver them, he told her he thought it best if she stayed in camp. Wes had brought Digger the stew ingredients that had mysteriously been left behind, and Digger gave Tara his treasured recipe and wanted her to stir it together, claiming he could add his secret spices when he returned.

Left alone in camp, Tara had plenty of time to think as she worked. She couldn't imagine what Katelen thought of her now. She vaguely remembered seeing the frightened child standing in the doorway with Bear and after making such good progress by giving her the sketches too.

Opening seven cans of kidney beans, she dumped them into the giant dutch oven Digger had instructed her to use. The cast iron was as heavy as an anvil. She would not be able to move the thing once she added the ingredients. Next she opened the cans of tomato sauce, and as she poured them, juice splashed onto her hand and looked like blood.

Haunting memories threatened to break free. She held them at bay, thinking of good times she'd had with her beloved grandpa Kelly. That's what the doctors at Twelve Pines had told her to do. Whenever she felt the darkness begin, she was to think of pleasant memories.

Grandpa Kelly.

She pictured him walking down the lane, cane in hand. He'd called it a shillelagh because it was made from blackthorn wood and had been smeared with butter and placed in the chimney to cure. The wood was shiny black and knotty, with a large knob at the top. The knob was a golden ball, and if Tara remembered right, the ball looked like some type of gem.

Rosalie had insisted he be buried with it. Oh, what Tara would give to see Grandfather walking across the field, shillelagh in hand, pointing out this and that. And to hear his magical voice and the way he would roll his r's—that, indeed, would ease her mind. She yearned to be a little girl and sit once again on his lap. She had always felt safe when he'd held her.

Tara remembered how Joseph had held her, cradled her, really. She'd felt safe, like she had as a child with Grandpa. She'd felt like she was home.

Home. Just where was her home now? With Rosalie gone, she had no ties to LA. She could live anywhere she wanted. Tara thought of Joseph's beautiful ranch. A nice idea but out of her reach.

She grabbed several green peppers, sliced them in half, and pulled the stems and seeds out, dropping those in the garbage bag. Before dicing the peppers, she realized all of her life she'd been taken care of by other people. She was tired of wallowing in depressing thoughts; since Rosalie's death, she'd been plagued with the knowledge that she'd been stripped of family, but she'd never thoroughly understood how she'd relied on others until now. She knew she was weak and needed courage but had never finished the thought as to why. She needed courage to be strong enough for someone else to rely on her in return.

Joseph came to mind. He was willing to be her port in a storm. And she wanted to let him, but was that fair to him or his family or her if she wasn't strong enough to be there for them in return? No. What she needed to do was become more prepared for the unexpected. But how? What did soldiers do when under fire? How did they control fear and stay on task? Many of them suffered from post-traumatic stress, which Tara figured might be what she had.

She wished she could think of an answer, but for the first time in a long time, Tara felt she was on the right path.

When Digger returned, he kept her busy making salads and even apple pie. She'd never made a pie before and found it fascinating that she could bake it in a dutch oven. Digger had quite an assortment of the heavy cast-iron pots.

Near four thirty, the sound of mooing cattle sounded in the distance.

"That's them," Digger said as he added more wood to the cook fire. "Dinner should be ready just in time."

Searching the horizon, Tara saw Joseph riding his horse, working the cattle. From this distance, she also picked out Bear and even Irene and Allen. Irene was on a horse Tara hadn't seen before. Joseph had brought extra horses, so her mount had to be one of them.

Tara wondered where Shotgun was but figured he must be with the herd. The drovers were scattered, but they would be here soon and would be looking for food.

Tara helped Digger set out the bowls, utensils, and paper cups for the crew. After the cattle had been settled, Bear, Irene, and Allen rode up. Joseph followed, leading Shotgun. They tied the horses to a cable Wes had drawn between two pine trees before he'd left, and Joseph walked right up to Tara and, in front of everyone, gave her a hug and kiss on the cheek. "Have a good day?"

"Yes. Digger took care of me."

"I hoped you'd say that." He turned to Digger. "Something smells delicious."

The old man's whiskery face smiled. "My stew."

Bear moaned.

Irene and Allen chuckled.

"And for dessert"—Digger paused a moment for emphasis—"Katelen's favorite: dutch oven apple pie."

Joseph looked around the camp. "There's a thundercloud on the horizon. Best we hurry up and eat. Where is Katelen? An hour ago she wanted to ride ahead to camp. Said she was tired."

"I haven't seen her, Chief." Digger's craggy face paled.

A sinking feeling came to the pit of Tara's stomach.

Concern creased Joseph's brow as he searched the campsite as though he'd catch a glimpse of his child.

"I don't see Oreo." Bear's gravelly voice held a tone of panic.

"She probably took a different trail." Though Irene tried to comfort Bear and Joseph, she too had a frightened edginess about her.

Allen stared at Joseph. "I'll tell the guys. We'll fan out and search. I'll head north in case she missed camp and kept going."

"No. Don't head north." Joseph shook his head. "Katelen's been coming to this campsite every year since she was four. There's no way she'd miss it. Take the men south."

"Whatever you want." Allen hurried to the others to spread the word.

Irene strode with determination to the horses tied to the line, and Joseph and Bear followed closely behind.

Tara kept pace beside Joseph. "I want to help."

"I don't have time to saddle your horse," he said over his shoulder.

"I can do it." Tara had watched him before. She could suck it up and do it on her own.

Joseph paused and looked at her. "Chances are we'll ride out a little ways and find her." Bear and Irene had already mounted and rode away, and Joseph grabbed his reins. "No one will blame you if you want to stay in camp."

"I know, but I'm worried too. I want to help."

He gave her a quick kiss on the lips. "I know, but be careful." Sticking his boot in the stirrup and grabbing the saddle horn, he mounted his horse and left.

No one had been there to see that kiss. He'd done it like it was second nature, like she really was his fiancée. The thought spurred her on.

The hackamore had been left on Shotgun, and the horse trailer was conveniently parked only a few feet away. She opened the saddle compartment, and her hands fumbled over ropes, curry combs, and horse blankets. Finally, she touched the hard, leather-covered saddle horn and tugged. It barely moved. Bracing herself with her foot, she jerked with all her might. The large saddle fell onto the ground, and she dragged it to the horse's side. Tara placed the blanket on the mare's back. "It's all right, Shotgun. I'm not going to hurt you."

She hefted the saddle to her knee; took a deep, fortifying breath; and heaved the bulk onto the horse's back.

The animal stepped sideways and whinnied.

Tara rubbed Shotgun's neck. "It's okay, girl. We've got to find Katelen."

Working as fast as she could, Tara hooked the stirrup on the saddle horn and threaded the leather through the cinch buckle. Dropping the stirrup back in place, she untied the horse. Tara stroked Shotgun's forehead and leaned close to the mare's ear, whispering, "May God be with thee and me." Without a thought, she'd said a prayer and meant it.

Tara summoned her courage, mounted the horse, and rode out, determined to find Katelen.

CHAPTER NINETEEN
A PRAYER ON HIS LIPS

JOSEPH HAD HIS CREW SPREAD out to comb the mountain. With his ever-present helper, Scrap, Joseph backtracked where they'd been.

Where could Katelen have gone?

What if whoever had killed his cattle and shot at him and Tara had taken Katelen? The horrible thought chilled him to the very core.

No! Katelen had probably become sidetracked by something and was exploring. That was all.

Nothing more.

Still, the worry needled him.

As he searched behind trees and brush, he thought about earlier that morning when Bear had ridden out with him. His mother had been concerned about Tara and the bad dream that had awakened her in the night.

He had told his mother what he could and admitted he was worried too. He still concealed Tara's true identity, but since his mother knew much of the reason for Tara's being here, sharing his concerns made him feel less alone and more like he had someone else to back him up should the need arise.

Bear counseled him to help Tara face her fears so she could get past the nightmares that haunted her. Bear even told him she believed a shadow was dogging Sarah, but Bear couldn't explain why she felt that way.

He'd ridden quite a ways with no sign of Katelen. His daughter was an experienced rider and knew this mountain better than most men. Where could she have gone? Again the thought he'd tried to push away—that someone had taken her—found him.

Panic streaked through him. Fear was one thing; it was controllable. But panic wasn't. Mac had drilled the concept into him when they'd served together on the force. Panic wouldn't help him find Katelen, and he *was* going to find her if he had to search the entire mountain range till he dropped.

Since his wife's death, Joseph had clung to his daughter. She was his world. He closed his eyes and rubbed his finger and thumb over his eyelids. Tears escaped down his cheeks, and he swatted them away.

Please, God, help me find my little girl.

The mantra tumbled over and over in his mind as he continued searching. A new thought came to him: maybe Katelen had gone over to another canyon for some reason. It didn't make sense, but he had to check it out.

Glancing down at Scrap, he said, "Come on, boy." Leaning forward in his saddle and pulling his hat low over his forehead, he guided his horse up a draw to the next canyon. Scrap kept up, dodging tree roots and bushes. Joseph heard every little noise in the forest, but none held the lilting tone of his daughter's voice. He was a fool to have let her go on to camp alone. She was only seven. What had he been thinking?

But that was how it was on most ranches. As soon as the kids could sit in the saddle, they were put to work, especially when it came to roundup and the cattle drive. And most of the time, Katelen loved it. She was a good kid and loved anything that had to do with ranching, until Tara'd shown up.

But Katelen's attitude toward her had changed last night. Things were better between them, and now this had to happen.

Someone was coming. Irene and several of his men came into view.

"We've already searched the far side of this canyon. Bear has her group up ahead," Irene said. "Maybe we should double back, see if somehow we missed her and she's in camp." Irene motioned for the others to start back.

Joseph wasn't so sure. "Maybe I'll head over to where Ma and her group are."

"Katelen is going to be fine," Irene said, but Joseph could see by the wrinkle lines at the sides of her eyes and the nervous twitch of her hand that even she didn't believe what she'd said.

"I hope so." He kneed Copper, and the horse automatically turned in the direction Irene had indicated Bear had gone.

Riding through the thick-growing pines, Joseph noticed the early stages of twilight. It would be dark soon. Plus, with the increasing thunderclouds, a storm was brewing. The forest was fast filling with shadows. Not far ahead, he noticed what looked like a bundle of clothes lying on a patch of grass.

Katelen?

He leaped off his horse and crossed the distance in record time. Scrap had reached the person before him, but Joseph recognized the large ten-gallon hat on the ground before he recognized the person. It wasn't Katelen; it was his mother.

"Ma!" He scooped her limp body into his arms. She was unconscious and pale. He checked to see if she was bleeding but couldn't find anything. How had she become separated from the others? And where was her horse? It didn't matter because right now, he had to take her back to camp. Filled with a surge of adrenaline, Joseph hefted Bear onto his saddle and climbed on behind her. Holding his mother, he kicked the horse into a run and charged through the trees as fast as he could.

Dodging low-hanging branches, he held her close while guiding his horse out of the forest to the dirt road leading to camp. As Copper charged up the road, Joseph wondered what was going on. Everyone around him was in a free fall: Tara and her troubles, Katelen disappearing, and now his mother unconscious in his arms. How could he stop the whirlwind? He was caught in a maze, and no matter what he did, he couldn't find his way out.

* * *

Tara started to follow the others but then pulled back on the reins. Remembering what Allen had said, that Katelen could have missed camp and headed north, she decided to ride farther up the mountain since everyone else had gone down.

Tara rode quite a ways with no luck and decided to turn the horse around and head back. The problem was she could swear with each step that instead of going down to camp, they were still climbing.

She knew that since she had started out on the lower fork in the road, it only made sense it would be the one to lead to camp, unless she'd become confused. Sadly, that was very possible.

Shotgun kept plodding along like a tank over ruts and rocks. As it grew dark, Tara became anxious. *Poor little Katelen is out here all alone.* She couldn't imagine the fear the child was going through, because Tara's own fear was bad enough. At least they both had horses. And a sure-footed horse generally knew how to return home. That's what Joseph had told her.

Tara let the animal go whichever way it wanted. Her mind went to Grandpa Kelly and when he had nailed a horseshoe over their door. He'd said they could never touch it or take it down and that it would always bring good luck to the family. They'd had it for many years. Only after Grandfather died and Rosalie and Tara had moved to their own places had it come down.

If one horseshoe over a door was lucky, four horseshoes on a horse had to be luckier still.

Shotgun came to a large mountain meadow, and the silvery moon shone on the summit, which appeared too close. They *had* taken a wrong turn. So much for letting the horse find the way back.

What could she do? She glanced behind her down the darkened road. Chances were Katelen had been found long ago and was all right and now people were worried about Tara. *Great.* The citified woman who had awakened the camp with night terrors was now lost on the mountain.

Sheesh!

She turned the horse around and headed the other way just as the wind picked up. Dust filled the air along with occasional leaves and small twigs. Storm clouds were moving in fast.

She was going to have to find some type of shelter on the mountain. She scanned her surroundings. Dark, gnarled trees and reaching bushes flailed about in the wind. Shotgun plodded on. Ahead was an old shack. Joseph had mentioned something about line shacks. Maybe this was one of them. If she tied Shotgun in the pines, where there was a lot of grass, Tara could wait out the storm in the shack. The windows were boarded up, and it looked like a hangout for Stephen King, but it was better than staying outside.

Tara found a stand of trees that would give shelter for the horse, and she dismounted and tied the animal so it could feed on the grass but not tangle its legs in the reins. Remembering what Joseph had told her about loosening the saddle cinch, she fumbled around in the dark until she felt the buckle and loosened it. The task completed, she started for the shack.

She noticed again how the windows were boarded, and though she didn't think anyone was inside, she stepped up on the wooden porch and knocked on the door. "Is anyone in there?"

There was a thud and a moan.

What was that? Was it really a moan?

She held still, listening, but the wind was blowing so fiercely she could hardly hear anything else. Thunder boomed, making Tara jump, and the wind wildly blew strands of her hair into her face.

Big raindrops began falling, and then she heard what was definitely a moan. Someone *was* in there, and it sounded like the person was injured. Tara had to go in.

Pushing the squeaky-hinged door open, she peered into the inky darkness. Her eyes adjusted so she could see the shadow of a kerosene lamp on a table. Grandfather had had a kerosene lamp. Many times he'd lit it to show her what it was like in old Ireland a century ago. With shaking hands and fumbling fingers, she felt around the base of the lamp and found a small matchbox. She drew out a match and lit it.

Once the flame burned on the match, she glanced around the one-room shack at the potbellied stove in the center, a huge water barrel on a rickety workbench, and an old cot against one wall.

And then she saw arms and legs tied together and a gunny sack over the person's head.

The match burned her fingertips, making her drop it. The room snuffed to black. If she was going to help whoever was on the cot, she had to light the lamp. Once again, she lit a match and tugged the chimney off the lamp to light the wick. Replacing the chimney, she picked up the lamp and rushed to the cot.

Tara set the lamp on a wooden crate and pulled the gunny sack away.

Though duct tape covered her mouth, Katelen's large coppery eyes filled with tears at the sight of Tara.

* * *

Charging into camp with his mother in his arms, Joseph reined his horse to a stop. Against the wind, he yelled, "Digger, get your first-aid kit!"

Everyone who had been trying to tie down the camp stopped in midmotion, frozen with shock and disbelief. Carefully dismounting, Joseph growled, "Digger, the kit!" His words slapped people back into action.

In a heartbeat, Irene was by his side. "What happened?"

Joseph eased Bear onto the grass and knelt beside her.

Scrap licked Bear's cheek.

Irene pushed him back. "Get some light over here."

Allen sprinted to the camper.

"She was unconscious on the ground. No one in sight. Where did Mom's crew go?" Joseph stared at Irene.

One of the men who had been with his mother stepped forward. "When it started to get dark, she sent us back to camp and promised she'd be along shortly."

It took all his strength not to haul off and punch the guy, but it wasn't his fault Bear was bullheaded and thought she could do anything she wanted. Joseph scanned the camp, hoping to see Katelen, but he didn't. If they'd found her, someone would have said.

Holding a Coleman camp light high in the air, Allen trotted back to stand over Irene.

"Look at her clothes." Irene loosened Bear's shirt. "She's been dragged across the ground, and there's a bump on the side of her head." Irene examined the injury.

A moan escaped Bear, and she blinked, then opened her eyes. "Joseph." Her voice was weak but urgent.

"Ma, what happened?"

Bear licked her lips and furrowed her brows as she grabbed Joseph's shirt, pulling him close to her. "Someone came at me from behind and knocked me over the head."

"Who?" Joseph clutched her wrinkled hand in his as if he could give her strength.

Bear gasped for breath and began to rise.

"Hold on, Bear. You can't get up until I check you over." Irene pushed her down.

"I thought I saw Harris's truck." Bear stared at Irene.

"Where?" Joseph scanned the trucks and trailers.

Bear moaned. "He's not here. He's camping somewhere else." Irene checked Bear's pulse and studied her eyes.

A sick feeling roiled in Joseph's gut. "He very well could have done this. And if he's taken Katelen . . ."

"Let's not make wild accusations." Irene kept her hand on Bear while looking at Joseph.

Of course she'd defend the man. Just like Joseph would defend Tara. Tara! Joseph glanced at those gathered around them. "Has anyone seen Tara?"

They looked confused.

"You mean Sarah?" Irene asked as she studied the bump on Bear's head.

"Yes." Joseph couldn't believe he'd had a slip of the tongue now of all times.

Digger ran up with his first-aid kit and dropped to his knees beside Bear and Irene. "Had a devil of a time mining this out of the cook trailer. Is she going to be all right?" The tender way the old man brushed a stray hair from Bear's forehead showed how much he cared. Rarely did Digger wear his soft old heart on his sleeve, but the tremble of his chin spoke volumes.

Irene rummaged through the kit. "If we can get her to lie still, I think so. What kind of medicine is in here anyway?" In Irene's desperate search, she held each bottle up to the light. "Feverfew, horsetail, horehound, nettles. Crimeny, Digger! I can't do anything with this stuff!" She looked up at Joseph. "My guess is Bear has a concussion. We need a human doctor to check her over, and the sooner, the better. We've got to get her to the hospital."

With great effort, Bear grabbed Joseph's hand, pulling him down. "Sarah's missing as well as Katelen. Quit worrying about me, and get going! You've got to find them."

He kissed the back of her hand. "I will, Ma. You do what Irene tells you." Joseph looked at Digger's troubled face. "And Digger as well." As tough as Bear was, it would take more than a knock on the head to slow her down.

Digger hefted Bear in his arms to follow Irene.

"Digger," Joseph called to him. "When you get to the hospital, call Sheriff Conrad. Tell him what's happened to Ma and that we need search and rescue up here."

"With night pressing and this storm bearing down on us, I don't think they'll risk sending choppers," Allen said.

"They can get their teams ready." Joseph nodded to Digger to go ahead with what he'd asked. Joseph turned to Allen and the rest of his men. "I know it's going to be dangerous, but there's a huge bonus for anyone who finds Katelen or Sarah or both. Take your flashlights and scour the area. Go all the way down the mountain if you have to."

He turned to Allen. "Look, I don't want anyone to get hurt, so watch over the crew." Joseph strode to his horse and tried to think of everything he might need. He had a rain slicker in his saddlebags, a good flashlight with long-lasting batteries, a Winchester rifle strapped to his saddle, and plenty of ammo.

Joseph leaped onto his horse and headed out into the night, a prayer on his lips and his dog close behind.

CHAPTER TWENTY
A SHIVER OF FEAR

THUNDER RUMBLED, AND THE WIND howled, but for Tara, nature's dazzling show took a backseat as the light of the kerosene lamp flickered over Katelen lying on the cot. Flyaway strands of her black hair had escaped her long braids, and her body shuddered as tears leaked from her eyes. Tara wanted to take Katelen in her arms and tell the girl everything would be all right, but she had to untie her first. She carefully peeled the duct tape off Katelen's mouth, then proceeded to untie her. As Tara touched the child's right arm, Katelen screamed in pain.

"Oh, sweetie. What happened?"

"Someone knocked me off my horse," she said between sobs. "I landed on my arm. It hurts really bad. I can't move it."

There was an unusual bulge on Katelen's shoulder. It could be dislocated or even broken. Tara didn't know, and she was afraid that moving Katelen would do permanent damage. "I think you may have dislocated it, but I'm not sure." Compassion and empathy swelled within Tara's chest.

Katelen bit her lips together as tears trailed down the sides of her face and disappeared in her hair. Tara stroked Katelen's forehead. "It's all right. I'm here now. And I won't let anything happen to you. Did you see who hit you?"

Katelen shook her head and sobbed.

Lightning flashed and thunder exploded like a bomb above them. A wind burst hit the shack so hard Tara wondered if the structure would topple over. Katelen couldn't move without pain, so there was no way they could travel, and with the storm and the fact that Tara didn't know where they were, it would be best to stay put until help arrived. In the meantime, Tara would have to come up with a plan in case the kidnapper returned.

"Where's my daddy?" Katelen cried.

"He's looking for you. He has the entire camp searching the mountain right this very minute. Can you tell me who took you?"

The child peered at her through pools of tears in her brown eyes. Her bottom lip trembled. "I don't know." Her sobs grew louder, and her nose dripped. Tara mined a tissue from her pocket and gave it to her. Katelen would have to calm down before she could give any kind of details. But details were what Tara desperately needed. She had to know what they were up against.

Again lightning flashed and thunder rumbled, fueling Katelen's sobs. Despite wanting to sooth her, Tara needed to find something to defend them with just in case. "I'm going over by the cabinet for a second."

Tara went to the plywood cupboards and rummaged in a drawer to find a weapon. What she needed was a gun. A gun. A shudder went through her as she remembered holding one. No. No gun. Besides, she was sure she wouldn't find one here. She'd settle for a lethal-looking butcher knife, but the only knife she found was one with a dull four-inch blade. It was better than nothing. She slipped the weapon into her waistband. Glancing at the door, she knew she had to barricade it. She scanned the one-room shack again. The furnishings were dismal—no chairs and only one table. She scooted the table to the door, turned it on its side, and wedged it under the doorknob.

Brushing her hands off, she tried to think of something else in case the table didn't hold and the kidnapper got in. Wood. Grabbing a good thick chunk from the wood bin, she returned to Katelen. The child's crying had subsided a little as she watched Tara's every move.

Thunder and wind rattled the shack again. Tara set the wood near her feet, where she could easily grab it, then sat beside Katelen on the cot. The seven-year-old grabbed Tara's hand and held on for dear life. The need to protect and calm Katelen was uppermost in Tara's mind.

Katelen shivered, and though Tara knew the girl's nerves were frayed, the room was also growing cold. Darn cold. "We'll be here until the storm passes. Why don't I build a fire in the stove?"

"Don't leave me again." Katelen wouldn't let go of her hand.

"Honey, I'll be right here. Really." Tara looked down at the child and stroked her head. Although the main question on her mind was who could have kidnapped Katelen and left her here, Tara had to get her to relax. Once the child felt safe and warm, she might more easily remember what had happened. Tara thought of what her grandfather used to do to calm her. He'd tell a story. "Did you know a long time ago in Ireland the people believed fire was a sacred symbol?"

Katelen's waif-like eyes stared up at her.

"They believed spirits lived in the wind." As she spoke, Tara slid her hand from Katelen's hold and went to the wood bin. Paper and kindling lay stuffed next to the wood. Thank goodness the line shacks had been stocked. Crumpling up the paper, she continued. "They even believed spirits lived in the waves of the sea and the swaying branches of the forest."

"That's kinda like the Indians," Katelen said, sniffing.

"Really?" Tara stuffed the crumpled paper, kindling, and wood in the small opening of the potbellied stove, then struck a match to light the fire. She went back to Katelen, and the child grabbed her hand immediately. Warmth filled Tara from the inside out. She'd never had someone need her like this before. Of course, she hadn't been around many children, which was ironic since she wrote and illustrated children's picture books, but she now had an inkling of how a parent must feel, how they wanted to protect their children and loved them so much that they'd sacrifice anything and everything for them. Even though she barely knew Katelen, she suddenly felt that kind of bond between them. It might have started last night when Katelen had been awestruck by Tara's sketches, or it could have happened when Tara had taken the gunny sack off the child's head; whatever the case, it had been cemented when the child had taken hold of Tara's hand.

"Even though Daddy and I are Mormons—" Thunder interrupted Katelen and shook the shack.

Once again, fear that the kidnapper could burst in at any moment flickered in Tara's mind. She felt the knife in her waistband and glanced at the chunk of wood near her feet to make sure it was still within easy reach.

Katelen sniffed again, drawing Tara's attention again. "Grandma tells me about Grandpa's people and what they believe," Katelen said, finishing her sentence. Despite the pain in her shoulder, she had relaxed a little.

"What do they believe?" Tara encouraged Katelen to keep talking, hopeful that she would eventually tell her how she had been kidnapped.

"That Coyote created everything when he captured a monster from the other side of the river. From the monster, Coyote created all the tribes of the world except the Nez Perce." She fell silent.

"Where did the Nez Perce come from?" Tara prodded.

"When Coyote washed his hands, the monster's blood mixed with the water. Coyote sprinkled the drops on the ground, and they became the

Nez Perce, my grandpa's people." Katelen wiped her nose with the back of her hand. Her bottom lip trembled. "Today the monster got me."

Tara stroked the child's cheek.

Katelen swallowed hard. "I was riding Oreo—" Her eyes grew large. "What happened to my horse?"

Tara patted her hand. "I'm sure she's all right. She probably went back to camp, or maybe she went all the way to the ranch. You know how smart horses are. They know how to go home."

The thought appeared to comfort Katelen, which was good since Tara didn't believe it was really true. When she'd let Shotgun go where the horse wanted, they'd ended up here instead of camp. "Did you get a look at who took you?"

Katelen shook her head. "I was riding to camp like Daddy told me to do. I heard someone coming, and I thought it was Daddy or Grandma. They threw a sack over my head, and I fell off Oreo. I tried to fight like Daddy taught me, but my arm hurt so bad. The person grabbed me around my neck, and I couldn't breathe. Everything went dark." Her eyes glazed over as she was caught in the horror of memory.

Tara smoothed a few flyaway hairs away from Katelen's face. The little girl continued. "I woke up, and the bag was still on me. I couldn't move because of the pain, and I was so afraid. I'm glad you came. I knew someone good would come."

"How did you know?" Tara asked, leaning her head next to Katelen's.

"I prayed Heavenly Father would send someone, and here you are."

Tara didn't want to tell her that she'd gotten lost and due to dumb luck and the storm she'd stumbled upon the child. But who was she to say God didn't have a hand in it? Stranger things had happened.

Katelen's tummy growled.

"You're hungry."

Katelen winced. "Guess so."

Fixing something to eat would distract them both from the danger. Plus, something in their stomachs would be good. Tara was determined to act as normal as she could. "I'll see if there's food here." She went to the rickety cupboards and peered inside the upper one.

Chili and stew—can after can of it. Grabbing a can of chili, she searched the drawers until she found a can opener, a pot to cook with, and a bowl to eat out of, but there was only one. She'd let Katelen use it, and she would eat out of the pot. She got the chili ready and placed it on the stove to heat, then she went back to Katelen and took her hand. They watched the flames in the stove's belly.

Tara's stomach growled, making Katelen smile. "You're hungry too."

Tara chuckled. To take their minds off their hunger and their situation, she said, "My grandfather believed in God. He was Catholic, but he loved the legends and myths of his homeland and was always telling me stories of Ireland and how God watched over the Emerald Isle and even the wee folk."

"Wee folk?"

"Fairies or, rather, deenee shee. They were fallen angels who were not good enough to be saved or bad enough to be lost. It is said that the Tuatha Dé Danann, which was also a name for them, were worshipped in ancient times, but as people stopped believing, they began to shrink until they became so small you could hardly see them. They live in the forest."

Steam rose from the pot. She left Katelen to check on the chili but continued talking. "There was a poem written about the fairies. Something like, 'Up the airy mountain, down the rushing glen, we dare not go a-hunting for fear of little men.'" She stirred the chili and poured some into the bowl. Katelen was nervously gazing around as if trying to see a fairy. Tara had meant to give her something fun to think about, not something to fear. "You do know fairies don't really exist, don't you?" Tara said, taking her the bowl.

"Yeah. I have a picture book at home that has fairies in it." Katelen tried to sit up, but grimaced in pain and lay back down.

"Let me help you eat." She spooned up some chili and blew on it before giving it to Katelen.

Tara remembered catching a glimpse of her book on Katelen's nightstand the night she'd overheard Joseph telling his daughter about the white eagle. "Do you like to read?" Tara blew on another spoonful before feeding it to Katelen.

"Yeah, but I like books with lots of pictures," Katelen said between mouthfuls.

They heard Shotgun whinny and another horse answer. Fear swelled within Tara. Someone was out there.

The wind and rain continued to pummel the shack, and Katelen's eyes grew large. "He's back!"

Tara placed her index finger to her lips, set the chili down, grabbed the hunk of wood from the floor, and pulled the knife from her waistband.

She positioned herself between Katelen and the door. If whoever was coming managed to get inside, he'd have to go through Tara before laying a hand on the child.

Someone stomped on the small wooden porch. Then the knob turned, and the door banged against the table. He stopped for only a second before slamming against the door, shoving the table aside.

Tara's heart triple-timed against her ribs. Her mind spun, trying to jump-start her body into movement, but her legs and arms had shut down, and she dropped the knife.

CHAPTER TWENTY-ONE

A FALSE MEMORY

KEEPING AN EYE ON THE imposing figure in the doorway, Tara took control of her panic and scrambled to retrieve the weapon, but the knife skittered out of reach. She bolted for Katelen to shield her with her body.

"Tara!" It took a moment for her to register that the voice was familiar, someone she knew. Whirling around, she saw the intruder's face.

"Joseph?"

He set his rifle on the floor and rushed to them as Scrap bounced in behind him.

* * *

Joseph stared at Tara in the light of the kerosene lamp and the fire in the stove. Behind her on a cot was his precious Katelen. His heart swelled in his chest. The weight and fear of finding his little girl dead on the trail vanished in a flash of relief.

"Daddy!" Katelen winced with pain as she tried to sit up.

"What's the matter?" He knew something was seriously wrong when she laid back down.

"I found her tied up in here. She said someone put a bag over her head and shoved her off her horse. I think her shoulder is dislocated or broken." Tara shut the door.

Joseph shed his rain poncho and knelt beside the cot, studying his daughter. With tender care, he felt her shoulder. Katelen moaned and closed her eyes while he assessed the damage, and then Joseph looked up at Tara's grim face. "I think it's dislocated."

He gazed down at his little girl fighting the pain. "Well, Katydid." He hadn't used her nickname in a long time. He hoped it would calm her. She stared at him with worry and fear. "I can fix this, and you'll be right as rain, but it's going to hurt when I do it."

Fear welled up in her eyes again. As though sensing Katelen's need for comfort, Tara took her hand.

He hadn't meant to scare Katelen, but she had to know what was coming. "Remember when your tooth ached and you had to go to the dentist?"

Katelen stared at him.

Joseph moved the cot so he could get on the other side and have the space he needed to relocate the shoulder. "Well, after the dentist finished, you felt better, right?"

She stared at him, saying nothing, waiting.

"Believe me. You're going to feel better real soon." He gently took hold of her arm. She winced. Tara still held her other hand and stroked her forehead. With a firm grip, Joseph pulled on the arm. Katelen moaned and moved toward him.

"Tara, hold her still."

Tara placed her hand on Katelen's cheek. "Look at me, sweetie." Katelen did as she was asked. "Hold on to my hand and don't move no matter what."

Joseph pulled on Katelen's arm slowly and steadily, easing the arm away from his daughter's body with constant tension. Katelen moaned and whimpered, trying to be brave through the pain. As soon as Joseph felt the joint pop into place, he eased the arm to Katelen's side.

She stared at her father as if he were a miracle worker. "It doesn't hurt near as much now."

Joseph gave her a gentle hug and kiss. "We need something to hold the arm in place." He rummaged in the cupboards, knowing dish towels were stocked in each line shack. When he found one, he made a sling. "You'll need to wear that for a while. And don't use your arm until Irene can look at it." He sat on the cot and scooped Katelen up into his arms, finally able to hold her close, finally able to feel a true wave of gratitude that he'd found her.

He marveled that she was really here. He stroked her head and hugged her again and again, careful of her shoulder, kissing her in between hugs. He checked her over, looking for other injuries. No bump on the head. No cuts. Only welts on her wrists and ankles. Once satisfied she was in one piece, his gaze glided to Tara, who now petted Scrap's wet head. He motioned for her to come join them.

Joseph pulled Tara into their embrace and whispered, "Thank you."

She hugged him briefly and pulled back. "When I came in here and saw Katelen with that gunny sack over her head, I . . ."

Maybe it was seeing her father and having him near, or maybe Tara's words made her relive what had happened, but Katelen started to cry.

Joseph held her close. "What's wrong, Katydid?"

She buried her face in his chest.

He was grateful his child had been found, but now he was worried that the attacker had hurt her in other ways that she hadn't told him about yet. Questions flew through Joseph's mind. Why? Why take a child, tie her up, and leave her? "Katelen, did this person who took you hurt you somewhere else?"

She sniffed. "No."

She said it so innocently he believed her.

"She didn't see who did it." Tara added like she knew what he was thinking.

Whoever had done this had probably planned on returning until the storm hit. He could show up at any moment. Joseph wished he would. He'd give the coward a fight he'd long remember.

What he needed to do was take Katelen and Tara out of here, but not now with the storm raging. He'd heard many stories about how even seasoned mountain men could get lost during a storm on the mountain. Only a fool would take his injured and frightened daughter out in weather like this. They had to stay put. Setting Katelen on the cot for a minute, he picked up the long pry bar they used to move large logs or rocks and barred the door.

"How'd I miss that?" Tara chided herself aloud.

"I'm glad you did, or I wouldn't have gotten in." He went back and took Katelen in his arms again.

Placing his index finger beneath Katelen's chin, he tilted her head so he could look into her eyes. "Whoever did this will never hurt you again. Is there anything you remember? Did you hear a voice?"

"A grunt when I kicked him."

"That's my girl." Joseph was relieved. She'd done what he'd taught her. "Did the voice sound familiar? Young? Old?"

She shook her head. "It happened fast. And he was so strong."

To a seven-year-old, any man would be strong. It could have been Lester or Harris or even Irene, for that matter. Why did he think that? Irene had been with him most of the day.

"Are you hungry?" Tara asked, making her way to the cupboard. "There's a ton of chili and stew here." Scrap followed her, eager to make his needs known.

There was a bowl on the crate beside the couch and a pot on the stove. "Food sounds great. I'll have what you two were having." Still rocking Katelen in his arms, he watched as Tara opened a can and added the contents to the pot.

"I'm glad you're safe," he said. "I should never have left you to go out on your own." He hoped Tara understood.

"Well, I have to be honest. I got a little lost, but luckily, I ran into this shack." She looked at Katelen and pointed at her.

She had fallen asleep. He eased her onto the cot and covered her with an old army blanket from the wood shelf above the bed. Most of the ranch hands used sleeping bags, but he liked to keep blankets handy for the cold nights that haunted the middle of the summer.

Tara brought the heated chili over. Joseph glanced around for a chair, but there wasn't one. He should have remembered his line shacks were bare bones—a place to sleep, stir up some grub, and get to work. He eased down on the floor near the cot in front of the flickering fire. Tara did too. There were two spoons in the pan. Tara poured some chili into the bowl one of them had used and set it in front of the dog, who happily lapped it up.

"Hope you don't mind, but I added yours to the chili I was already eating. I ordinarily wouldn't do such a thing, but we're roughing it here." She spooned up some for herself, then gave him his.

He chuckled. "Don't mind a bit." The warm food slid down his throat and warmed his gut.

"I'm so relieved you found us." Tara gave a sigh and took another spoonful. "I hope Bear's not too worried."

"Oh, that's another story." He explained his mother's situation.

Worry wrinkles furrowed Tara's brow. "Who do you think is doing all this?"

"It's not Garrett. Could be Lester, Irene's father. But I don't think he'd do such a thing. He may be upset with me, but he wouldn't take it out on my mother or daughter."

"So who?"

He nearly said Irene but thought better of it. At this moment, she was trying to save Bear's life. "My vote goes to Denver Harris."

"I haven't seen his truck all day. Wasn't he going fishing?"

Joseph finished off the chili. "That's what he wanted everyone to believe. Bear said she saw his truck. You have to understand how much he hates ranchers and especially me."

"Why especially you?"

"I don't know. Might be because I'm half Nez Perce. Might be because I raise cattle. And it might be all the above." He drove his fingers through his hair and leaned back against the cot. "He hides behind saving the bull trout and the streams, but I know his main goal is to keep the forest as wilderness. Every time he whines, bit by bit, the government gives in. I know what he's up to. So do all the other ranchers."

Tara placed the spoons in the pot and took it all over to the plywood counter. She collected the bowl Scrap had eaten from, filled it with water from the water barrel, and set it down for the dog. "Think we can drink this?" She started back to the cupboard to retrieve some cups.

"Nah, I wouldn't risk it. Scrap's okay. He drinks out of creeks. We only have a water barrel in the shacks to wash with. We stock the shacks with water bottles but haven't gotten around to it as yet. The drive usually happens in June, so I thought we had time, but . . ."

"Isn't there something you can do about Harris?"

"If there's any possible way to prove he is behind these attacks today, I plan to find it. If it wasn't night and storming, I'd be out there right now looking. But we're sort of stuck here until the storm passes." Joseph didn't relish sleeping on the shack's wooden floor, but there was little choice. He rose and tugged the last blanket down. He wrapped it around Tara's shoulders, then settled on the floor beside her. Tara shared the blanket with him, and Scrap came over and curled up on Joseph's other side.

Tara stared at the flickering flames in the stove. "I'm so sorry about your mother."

"She's in good hands with Irene and Digger." He thought about how upset Digger had been over Bear. The old man truly loved her. And despite everything, Joseph smiled over the tender memory.

"Why are you smiling?" Tara looked surprised.

"Oh, it's just life has been full of so many bumps and scrapes and the unexpected." He glanced at Katelen, making sure she was covered and still asleep.

"Irene is coming back, isn't she?" Tara sounded hopeful.

"Probably. Digger and Mom will need her to drive them. I thought you'd be relieved to see her gone."

"I wanted to ask her about something." Her hand went to her pocket as though checking something, but she didn't produce anything from it. Firelight glowed over her, illuminating the sparkle in her eyes, and her thick mahogany hair curled around her shoulders, appearing soft as downy feathers. Tiny lines creased her forehead.

"What are you worried about?" Joseph slid his arm around her, pulling her to him.

She leaned against his shoulder and avoided eye contact. "We never talked about my night terror. You were gone when I awoke."

"I've told you before, nightmares are to be expected." He knew how PTSD worked and that she was suffering from it.

"I know you don't believe me, but dreams also come to people to help them." She took a deep breath, glanced at Katelen as if to make certain she was still sleeping, then said in a low, soft voice, "I remember holding a gun and feeling the recoil when I squeezed the trigger. A dream wouldn't do that, would it?"

Joseph didn't know quite what to say, then thought of something that might help her, but he'd have to start with the truth. "I don't know. But Mac found you in the garden and said nothing about a gun, right?" He waited for her reply, but her silence spoke volumes and meant he was on the right course. "Remember our talk about survivor's guilt?"

She nodded.

"Don't you think guilt is still doing a number on you?"

She raised up and stared at him like she was hopeful he was right but afraid his answer was too simple.

He was making progress. "Hear me out." He didn't know quite how to explain, especially since Tara was sensitive about her breakdown, but he prayed for help and forged ahead. "Did you know studies have been made about the power of our thoughts?"

She gave him a what-does-that-have-to-do-with-anything look.

"Just bear with me. It's true. Take for instance basketball players. Many coaches have them visualize standing at the free-throw line, bouncing the ball, and shooting. And here's the important part, they are supposed to see themselves making a basket."

"What does that have to do with my dreams and remembering I pulled the trigger?"

"The thing is, after several weeks of visualizing, the player creates a false memory. This memory preconditions the player with confidence, and he is able to actually score. I think your dreams are creating a false memory."

Tara appeared to think this through, biting her bottom lip and rubbing the side of her head. "I suppose you could be right, but still, when we return to the ranch, I'd better leave for LA to tell Mac. He needs to know."

"I'll go with you."

"No, you won't. You'll stay here and find out who kidnapped Katelen and attacked your mother."

"Of course, but so will you, right?"

She didn't reply and avoided his gaze.

He couldn't believe she wanted to leave. He knew she felt obligated to help with the investigation of her aunt's murder, even if it meant blaming herself, but he couldn't let her do that. She didn't understand that PTSD could play with her mind. "I want to be with you through this, especially when you tell Mac about these dreams. I have a feeling you're going to draw the wrong conclusions." Her backbone stiffened, and he knew he'd offended her. He needed a different tactic. "Look, I'm also worried about Mac. He's been through a lot, and he's going to need both of us to help him."

She sighed and finally looked up at him. "All right. How long do you think it will take the sheriff to start the investigation here?"

"He'll probably meet us in camp. I asked Digger to phone him and get search and rescue involved." He pulled her close again, wanting her to lean her head on his shoulder like before.

She cozied up to his side, and Joseph felt her body rise and fall with each breath, breath that meant she was alive and well and here with him. Tara was a kind-hearted, good person. He wanted to help her in whatever way he could, and if that meant going to LA, a city filled with bad memories, he would because, in the end, he knew she was meant to be with him.

"I hope the nightmares stop. I didn't have them for a number of years, but when Garrett left and Rosalie insisted I stay with her for a while, they started again . . ."

He didn't want her reliving the pain. "Don't think about it. Just rest. It's going to be all right."

She reached up and lightly traced his scar with the tip of her finger. Touched by her tenderness, he caught her trembling hand and drew it to his lips.

"Thank you for everything," she whispered with tear-filled eyes.

And Joseph knew he'd said all the right things.

CHAPTER TWENTY-TWO
DODGING FLAMES

THE FAINT SMELL OF SMOKE from the stove floated in the air, and morning rays peeked through the cracks of the boarded windows, playing over Tara's oval face. After she'd fallen asleep, Joseph had moved her so she was resting on his lap. He'd leaned his head against the cot and slept too but not for long, wanting to be alert if Katelen awoke or Tara had another nightmare or the man who had brought his daughter here returned. He was glad he'd gotten some sleep, though the crick in his neck and the ache in his back made him regret it just a little.

Watching the morning light stream between the planks on the window, he wondered why Allen hadn't taken them off when he'd prepared the place for the season.

Tara moved. Unable to resist, he lightly touched her silken hair that fanned away from her face, spilling over his pant legs like water. He'd been so very lucky to have found Tara and Katelen.

He wondered if his mother was all right, if Digger had been able to call the sheriff, and if search and rescue was now combing the mountain. He glanced at Katelen still sleeping on the cot, and anger pulsed through him. What kind of jerk could have kidnapped her and brought her here? It didn't make sense. Nothing made sense except it was time to get going and find some answers.

Joseph gently shook Tara. She moaned, wrinkled her delicate nose, and blinked open her bright green eyes. Immediately, she bolted up. "Is Katelen all right?" Her eyes sought the child on the cot.

"She's fine." Joseph stood, stretched, and peered down on the two of them. "We need to get going. I'll go see how the horses fared while you roust Katelen."

Tara rose and gently stroked Katelen's head, waking her.

Before reaching the door, Joseph caught a strong whiff of smoke. Was the wind blowing down the flue of the stove? The smell grew steadily stronger, and he suddenly realized the room was now hazy with smoke.

"What the . . . ?" He rushed to the door. Lifting the iron bar, he opened it a crack. Fire leaped at him. He slammed the door shut. "The shack's on fire. We've got to find a way out!" He scanned the room filling with more smoke while Tara helped Katelen to her feet. The boarded-up window was on a different wall than the door. He checked to see if the boards were loose, but they had been solidly nailed and wouldn't budge.

Smoke grew thicker and thicker as he coughed and searched for any little niche, any little ray of hope.

In the center stood the potbellied stove. No help there, but . . . maybe the wood bin. The wood bin loaded from the outside, and it would be tight, but he knew Tara, Katelen, and Scrap could squeeze through the small passage.

"Help me!" Joseph began throwing logs out of the bin while trying to keep the lid up. "Hold this," he said to Katelen. Using her good arm, she held open the lid.

Tara and Joseph flung one log after another to the other side of the shack. Large pieces of bark broke off, driving small needlelike slivers into Joseph's palms. He ignored them and shoved heavy chunks aside. Finally, there appeared to be enough room. He turned to Katelen and squatted down to eye level with her. "Once you're outside, stay close and wait for Tara and Scrap."

Katelen hugged her good arm around her father's neck, kissed him on the cheek, and climbed into the bin. She hesitated a moment.

"You can make it," Tara coached her. "I'll be right behind you."

Joseph motioned for her to go.

Katelen bent down and tried to open the outside door. Only able to use one arm, she failed. "I can't open it."

"Maybe I should go first, then I'll be there when Katelen comes out."

Knowing Tara was right, Joseph helped his daughter move aside.

Tara crawled to the door and tried to push it open.

No luck.

She tried again. Didn't budge.

Turning so she lay on her back, Tara used her legs to kick the door hard. It gave way, and she immediately scrambled to her hands and knees and disappeared.

Joseph gave Katelen a hug and set her in the bin.

"I'm scared." She looked up at him, coughing.

The dog jumped in with her. "Scrap will help you."

Katelen grabbed hold of the dog's bandana collar.

"Love you, Katydid. Now hurry!"

She and the dog crawled out of his sight.

"Hurry, Joseph!" Tara yelled to him from outside.

"I'm too big. Just get away from the building!"

"Daddy!"

"Tara, please," he yelled. "I'll try something else. Whatever happens, keep Katelen safe."

* * *

Tara had never thought that he wouldn't follow them, couldn't follow them. Filled with dread, she grabbed Katelen's hand and forced her away from the blazing shack. The child screamed for her father, and as soon as they were on a patch of grass away from the fire, Tara knelt down and made Katelen look at her. "You told me you believe in prayer. Let's pray that your dad gets out."

As the child bowed her head, she sobbed as she prayed. When she finished, she stared at the blazing building as if willing her father to appear. Tara feared the boarded-up windows left him no escape, but he had to find a way out. He had to. The blaze had spread to the tops of pines where the horses had been tied. Shotgun and Copper whinnied shrilly, terrified, and tugged and pulled on the reins that held them captive.

Tara could do nothing to help Joseph, but she could help the horses. "Katelen, I need you to keep Scrap here. Don't move!"

Still crying, Katelen managed to take hold of the dog's collar, and Tara dodged the flames as she raced to the animals. The horses' cries and hooves pounding the ground sent a chill down her spine.

Ash rained down as she neared. "It's okay. It's okay." Tara tried to soothe the animals, but all the while, she had to keep her eyes on their hooves as they stomped and kicked.

With each jerk the horses made, the knots tightened. Branches blazing with fire dropped around them, and Tara's eyes stung from the smoke. She scraped her knuckles against the bark but finally managed to untie Copper. He reared back and took off.

Now Shotgun. "It's okay, girl." Tara stroked the horse's neck. Muscles twitched beneath her hand, yet the horse seemed to know she was trying to help. Tara immediately set to work on the knot. As it loosened, she tried to grab hold of the reins so the horse couldn't flee. They would need her to get out of here. Despite Tara's efforts, Shotgun lunged forward. The leather sliced Tara's palms, cutting deeply until she let go. The horse took off. Blood smeared her lacerated palms, but she couldn't dwell on the pain. Smoke coiled around Tara, sucking the air from her lungs. She looked toward the shack.

It was totally engulfed.

CHAPTER TWENTY-THREE
RAIN OF FIRE

THE CRACKLING OF A LARGE timber sent new shivers of fear streaking through Tara. A massive pine tilted as the hungry flames corkscrewed up its trunk, and fire dripped from the boughs like wax from a candle.

Katelen stood staring at the shack, sobbing, the dog by her side. A shower of hot ashes fell from the canopy of flames and peppered her face and arms. Tara raced to the little girl's side and snatched her up in her arms.

A pine slammed to the ground behind them with a mighty swish and rumble that shook the ground. Immediately, hundreds of little fireballs rolled over the forest floor. Trails of flames hungrily licked after them toward a larger, ancient tree, and fire-wind fanned sparks over their heads. The heat was intense, and Tara shielded her face with her arms as she strained to see any sign of life in the burning building.

Part of a wall fell from the structure just as a war cry sounded from within. A human form leaped from the bowels of the fire and dropped to the ground, rolling until the small flames clinging to his body were out.

"Joseph!"

He sprang to his feet, jerking off the soaked blanket that had covered his head and upper body. Water flipped from his clothes and hair and ran down his aquiline nose. He was drenched. His eyes sought his little girl and Tara.

"How did you get so wet?" Tara asked, still holding Katelen.

"The water barrel." He took his daughter, gave her a quick hug, and shifted her around to ride piggyback. "Hang on."

Joseph patted Tara's arm. "Come this way!"

She and Scrap followed him down the burning hillside. He was going in the same direction the horses had gone. The ground was already covered with falling ash, and the forest was a maze of fighting flames dancing in front of them, greedily eating grass and brush. Tara's eyes stung so badly she could hardly keep them open, and she stopped momentarily to rub them. Her lungs burned with each breath. When she opened her eyes again, she couldn't see Joseph. Trying to call out, her throat choked off. Coughing and sputtering, she barely managed to get any sound out. "Joseph!"

* * *

Joseph glanced behind to make sure Tara was following. She was gone. He scanned the billowing flames, trying to see her, and made out her shape near a giant evergreen that was now a towering holocaust three times the size of the other trees. The greedy fire feasted on the wood, and the giant tree teetered. Tara would be smashed if she didn't move. She appeared dazed. Joseph set Katelen on the ground and shouted, "Stay here!"

Joseph sprinted forward, every nerve in his body tingling. *God, help me.* ·

The tree was falling.

With a giant lunge forward, Joseph tackled Tara to the ground and lay on top of her to shield her the best he could.

The thundering crash of the tree shook the earth like an explosion. Fissures of flames swam from the mass, leaving trails of fire.

Joseph felt overwhelmed by how close they'd come to being killed, but he knew he didn't have time to dwell on it. He grabbed her arm and started to run. When they came to Katelen and Scrap, he once again lifted his daughter onto his back, grateful the dog had kept her safe.

Joseph surveyed their surroundings. He turned to Tara. "We've got to keep ahead of the fire. If we can reach the stream below, we'll have a fighting chance."

She nodded that she understood.

With a firm hold on Tara's arm and Katelen on his back, he started down the hill.

Tara tripped, dropping to the ground and out of his hold. She motioned for him to keep going as she slowly rose to her feet.

Skirting around trees yet untouched by the fire, they pressed on, but Joseph was beginning to wonder if they were lost. They should have come to the stream before now.

Peering upward through gathering black smoke, he saw it—a white eagle swooping near them, up and around and back again as if the bird were saying, "Follow me."

Keeping the eagle in sight, Joseph guided Tara down the path. He wondered if Katelen had seen the bird. Her little body pressed against his back, her good arm hugging his neck. Surely she had.

As suddenly as the eagle had appeared, it disappeared. Had he really seen it? Joseph studied their surroundings. They had reached the familiar hill that fell to the creek, and with each step, shale slid beneath their feet, hurrying them along.

Once down the hill, they splashed into the ice-cold water, slipping on mossy-coated rocks and nearly falling. Joseph sat Katelen down in the water, and she gasped.

"You need to be wet." He turned to Tara. "You too."

Tara sat beside Katelen while Joseph splashed water over both of them and Scrap to give them a protective shield. Satisfied they were wet enough, Joseph took Katelen to the creek bank and sat her on a boulder, then turned to Tara. "You okay?" He glanced down at her leg, where he knew she'd injured it when she'd fallen. "The water should help."

She didn't even look down, and he could tell she was choosing to ignore it.

"There are two ways out. I need to go ahead and see which way to go."

"No!" Katelen grabbed for her father.

Tara took her hand. "I'll stay with you. It's all right." She stared at Joseph, and in her gaze, he knew she was saying, "Stay safe and come back to us."

He nodded and, with Scrap at his heels, disappeared into the smoke.

CHAPTER TWENTY-FOUR
WEBBING SMOKE

BECAUSE OF THE WIND, THE fire had crept downhill, heading toward the creek bank and following their path to the water. Tara scanned the blazing countryside, searching for any sign of Joseph. Then she stared into the heavens. It was morning, yet the sky was black, dark as night, from the smoke. Fire charged across the treetops, leaping from limb to limb like a garland draped by the Almighty's hand.

She looked at Katelen. The child peered up at her, and fear creased her soot-covered face. Katelen coughed, hacking up black smoke, and Tara stroked Katelen's back as she searched the hillside for any sign of Joseph. What was taking him so long?

Something moved downstream. Hopeful that Joseph had returned, Tara helped Katelen onto her back for another piggyback ride. Once she had her secure, Tara walked downstream to where she'd seen the movement. She peered through the webbing smoke at two small bear cubs in the water ahead. Baby bears meant a mama was close by.

Tara had to get to shore. As she turned, her foot slipped, and she fell into the water, dousing Katelen with her. She fumbled to check Katelen, worried about her injured arm, but Katelen shot to her feet and pressed her arm in the sling against her as she shivered and blinked. She was all right.

Tara looked to see where the cubs were. They had lumbered downstream, away from them and the flames, and didn't seem concerned that Tara and Katelen were near, which was good. Tara didn't know what to do but figured the best thing would be to stay away from them.

Taking Katelen's hand, she started for the muddy bank. Out of the corner of her eye, she saw a mass of black fur. In the cover of an elderberry bush on the other side of the creek was the mama bear. Tara drew Katelen's attention, put her finger to her lips, and pointed at the monstrous animal.

Katelen's little hand tightened within hers. Tara didn't know a lot about wild animals, but she had heard she should never run from a bear because they could outrun humans, and she'd heard the campfire story about Joseph's mother hitting a bear with a frying pan. She hoped the mama bear would keep on going and pay them no mind.

That was when the bear turned her large head and faced them. Tara held her breath, waiting for the animal to pass judgment. It appeared to take note of them and was sending Tara a message: "You leave my cubs alone, and I'll leave yours alone." Seconds hung suspended. Then the mama bear went back to escorting her cubs away from the fire.

On weak and rubbery legs, Tara guided Katelen to the creek bank and sat down.

"Tara!" Joseph crept down the hill with his dog at his heels, out of the smoke.

Scrap started barking at the bears. "Heel!" Joseph ordered. The border collie whined and looked up at his master.

Joseph gazed back at the trail he had come from. "I just made it down. All the trails are gone. We have to follow the bears."

Tara stared at Joseph's rugged face. Soot and burns pocked his cheeks. A large gash with clumps of drying blood cut across his forehead, and a fresh burn reddened his scar.

He trudged into the water, the dog at his side. Joseph took Katelen on his back, and together he and Tara started to walk, keeping a safe distance from the bears ahead. Scrap kept a wary eye on the creatures. After what seemed forever, the wind shifted directions, blowing the flames away from them and up the mountain.

The bears left the stream with the mama in the lead. She could have easily come after them, but instead, she took her cubs to the opposite side and led them away.

Tara followed Joseph, who had Katelen on his back, out of the water onto dry land. Scrap shook, flipping water all over. Coming upon a fallen quaking aspen, Joseph gently set Katelen down and checked to make sure she was all right. Exhausted, the little girl sat without saying a word, her bottom lip quivering. Scrap jumped up next to her and licked her face.

Tara knew she'd be next for Joseph's examination. Before she could step away, he grabbed her arm and turned her hands so he could see where the reins had sliced her palms. It was amazing they didn't hurt, but fear of the fire had been more important than her pain, and the cold water had helped numb her hands.

While he studied her, she studied him. The ends of his hair were singed as well as his eyebrows and lashes. "You've got a cut on your head, and your cheeks are burned in places."

"I'll be fine." He gazed down at her, then leaned closer and kissed her forehead.

Katelen came to them, and the three hugged. They'd somehow made it through the inferno and knew they were lucky to be alive.

"Well, as much as I hate to break this up, we're not out of the woods yet." Joseph chuckled. Tara and Katelen looked at each other, then laughed at his pun.

It felt good.

It felt normal.

"But seriously, the wind could shift, and the fire would be on us again." His face grew somber.

Tara knew danger still lurked, and they needed to keep moving.

Joseph swept Katelen into his arms. "Once we go up this knoll, we should reach a dirt road that leads down the mountain. It should be a straight shot to camp."

Tara hoped he was right.

* * *

Firefighting planes and helicopters flew overhead as Joseph walked down the dirt road with Tara by his side, Katelen nestled in his arms, and the dog following. Horses with riders appeared over the rise at about the same time, and he recognized his mother's hat and her speckled mare. Digger rode beside her. They were leading Shotgun and Copper, and when Digger saw Joseph and Tara, he let out a loud whoop, and he and Bear galloped to them.

"Mom, why are you out here?" She should be in bed, but she was as stubborn and bullheaded as he was when it came to the safety of her family.

"Chief, I tried to tell her to take it easy." Digger flipped his baseball cap around. "But you know she's as ornery as a pack donkey with a full load when she wants to be. Wasn't listenin' to me for love nor money."

"Do you honestly think I could stay in bed with Katelen, you, and Sarah missing and a fire raging on the mountain?" The shine returned to his mother's smile as she looked down at them from her horse.

"Grandma!" Katelen reached out with her good arm, wanting to go to her, so Joseph hefted her to sit in front of his mother.

"What happened?" Bear studied the sling on her granddaughter's arm and looked at Joseph.

Joseph wanted to tell them everything but didn't want to go over the details with Katelen around, afraid she would relive the nightmare. She'd been through enough. "We'll fill you in when we catch our breath."

Bear hugged Katelen to her. "It's so good to see you all."

His mother's forehead crinkled as she stroked Katelen's back. "We're lucky you guys made it out. I had the fright of my life when they said they'd found Denver Harris's camper up near the line shack. There were several empty gas cans in it. But there was no sign of Harris. Looks like he was behind everything and deliberately started the fire. Makes no sense. I thought environmentalists wanted to preserve the forest, not set it ablaze."

It didn't make sense to Joseph either, but the more he thought about it, if Harris had kidnapped Katelen and hidden her at the shack, he might have been hoping Joseph would find her there, and then he could . . . What?

Kill them both?

But why?

Over bull trout?

Over saving the forests and keeping cattle out?

Nothing made sense.

CHAPTER TWENTY-FIVE

DO THE RIGHT THING

NOT LONG AFTER JOSEPH, KATELEN, and Tara met up with Bear and Digger, Sheriff Conrad and the search and rescue team descended upon them, wrapping Tara's hands and the gash on her leg, giving Katelen a new sling, and tending Joseph's burns.

The sheriff confirmed they'd found Harris's camper but had no idea where he was. It looked like the man had decided to target Joseph and his family, though the sheriff was still investigating. Joseph appeared concerned. Tara was relieved that everything that had happened to them wasn't somehow connected to her.

The paramedics strongly suggested Joseph, Tara, and Katelen go home and recuperate. Of course, Joseph declined but insisted Digger take Tara, Katelen, and his mother to the ranch.

Tara worried about Joseph. He'd already been through so much. She was amazed at his stamina but was learning that he had an endless amount of stick-to-it-iveness. Joseph was staying on the mountain with the rest of his crew, even though Bear told him Allen was taking care of the men and the cattle. The firefighters didn't want the drovers' help, so Allen was keeping them busy rounding up the herd and continuing their trek.

The rapid response of the firefighters and the previous night's rain had helped contain the fire, and it was nearly out. It had mainly burned the west side of the mountain, and thankfully, the cattle were on the east. Still, Joseph appeared worried, but he assured them the drive would probably be over by the end of the day and he'd come home and rest then. Katelen was unusually quiet on the trip home and snuggled up to her grandmother. When they reached the ranch, Digger pulled the truck to a stop next to the trailer Wes had brought back from the drive.

"After you collect your things from the trailer, why don't y'all go in, take a shower, and get some rest? I'm going to unload the supper I planned to prepare on the drive and get it ready to serve here. Once the drive is over, they'll gather at the ranch like hungry, orphaned strays comin' back to the herd." Digger opened his door and got out.

"Want some help?" Tara asked as she dragged herself from the truck.

"Holy Hannah, haven't you been through enough for one day, little lassie?" He pulled the seat forward to let Bear and Katelen climb out.

Bear patted Digger on the back. "This old codger has been rustling up grub for well over twenty years. I think he can manage on his own."

A smile came to his face as he watched Bear walk to the trailer to collect Katelen's things.

Tara climbed into the trailer to grab her stuff, which Digger had gathered into one spot. She peeked inside her bag to make sure her pill bottle was there, then slung the bag over her shoulder and hurried to catch up with Bear as she and Katelen headed for the kitchen door.

"Katelen, do you need help with your bath?" Tara wanted to make sure she knew she could rely on her.

"I'll help her," Bear said. "I may have a good goose egg on my noggin, but I haven't been running for my life through fire. Go. Take a shower, and get some rest."

With great reluctance, Tara left them and went to her room. She didn't normally bathe, preferring a shower instead, but right now, a soak in a hot tub sounded like just the thing to help her sore joints and aching muscles.

Turning on the faucets, she peeled off her clothes and eased into the steaming water, letting it envelop her body in warmth. She took the wrappings from her hands and left them on the lip of the tub. Her thoughts went to her pills. Yesterday she'd planned to ask Irene about them but had never seen her. And Irene had been nowhere in sight today. She was probably pretty upset about Denver's disappearance and his being accused of setting the fire. She had seemed quite taken with the man the night she'd brought him into camp.

Poor thing is probably in shock.

Maybe Irene would show up later today or tomorrow. Tara held her breath and sank into the water, letting it completely cover her head.

After getting out of the tub, she slipped into clean underwear and put fresh bandages on her leg and hands. Her bed called to her. Giving in, she slipped under the clean sheets, nuzzled the soft feather pillow beneath her head, and drifted off, setting aside the haunting images of fire and trees.

* * *

The drovers had already rounded up the herd by the time Joseph rejoined them. As they reached the area he'd leased from the BLM for summer grazing, Allen rode up beside him. "You look pretty beat."

"Being as I narrowly escaped becoming a flaming burrito, I'm not surprised."

"You do look a little crispy around the edges." Allen glanced at Joseph's singed hair and clothes.

Joseph chuckled, hoping he wouldn't have to go into details. "Jumping through a fire will do that. Thanks for keeping the men busy with the herd so they were away from harm. And, by the way, you did a great job stocking the line shacks. If it weren't for the barrel of water, I wouldn't be sitting in this saddle."

Allen shrugged. "Just doing my job. That Harris guy was crazy. He had to be the one behind all this."

"That's what the sheriff believes. Just wished they could find him. I mean, why would the guy go all killer-crazy over bull trout?"

"Hey, people have killed for less, as you well know." Allen leaned back in his saddle.

"Yeah. We saw quite a few nut jobs in LA, didn't we?"

"You, Sarah, and Katelen are alive. Let's be grateful for that." Allen tilted his head like he always did when he made a good point.

Still trying to think of all the possibilities, Joseph couldn't help but wonder about Garrett. Mac said the man was heading to Seattle, but he could have been wrong. Garrett had been two steps ahead of Mac the entire time. What if, for some reason, he knew Tara was coming here? He'd have to be awfully smart and maybe have an accomplice. That accomplice could have been Harris. A bit far-fetched, but anything was possible.

Joseph looked at Allen. Joseph used to bounce murder scenarios off him all the time. Had Allen met Garrett after Joseph left LA? "Do you remember a guy on the force named Garrett Parker?"

"Talk about out of the blue. What made you ask that?" Allen stared at him, concerned.

"Just humor me."

"Geez, it's been so long." Allen thought for a moment. "You know, I think he was starting when I left. He was fresh from the academy and a real brown-nosing rookie. Why?"

"Did he do everything by the book?"

"Yeah. He was a wiz kid on computers. He'd had some legal training and was always quoting the law. Drove Mac nuts."

Joseph didn't know what to think. Mac hadn't told Joseph about Garrett's legal background. The picture he'd painted of the guy made him sound like a man with a short fuse and a bad temper, and those types weren't known for quoting the law. Joseph would have to ask Tara a little more about Garrett. Deciding to change the subject, Joseph said, "By the way, you left the windows boarded up on that shack. Did you take them off the others?"

"Really? Could have sworn I took them all down."

"Maybe Harris put them back on when he left Katelen there."

"Probably. They found his camper not far from the shack. Must have wanted to stick around and see what happened to you but then took off." His serious face suddenly brightened. "I must be looking better to Irene right about now."

"Irene's been through a great deal the last little while. Cut her some slack." Joseph adjusted in his saddle. His muscles had had enough abuse and would definitely make him pay come tomorrow.

"Speaking of Irene." Allen turned serious again. "When she dropped Digger and Bear off this morning and heard that you, Katelen, and your fiancée were missing and a fire was burning out of control on the other side of the mountain, she high-tailed it out of here."

"Some people handle crisis differently than others. She probably thought working would keep her mind off of things she could do nothing about." Joseph was surprised, but he wasn't going to let on to Allen.

"I'll give her a call once we're at the ranch to check on her." Allen noticed a calf straying and reined his horse to go after it.

Joseph couldn't stop thinking about Irene. Where had she gone? To her father's? Even though everyone thought Harris was the one behind everything, Joseph couldn't help the nagging feeling that the nightmare he'd been living was far from over.

* * *

Tara slept for several hours and finally dragged herself out of bed around five thirty. She'd slept much longer than she'd planned. She thought about everything she'd been through in the last twenty-four hours, from riding out alone to search for Katelen to the overwhelming need to protect the child, and she realized she did have courage. Aunt Rosalie would have been proud.

Aunt Rosalie. Tara needed to call Mac again. Fueled with her newfound courage, she knew she could do everything and anything she had to in order to solve Rosalie's murder.

She dressed, then went to the bathroom to put on her makeup. As she finished, she remembered the pills. She still wanted to talk with Irene about Halcion, so she took one pill out and shoved it in her pocket.

She bumped into Bear when she left her room.

"Feeling better?" Bear asked.

"Somewhat. How about you?"

"Somewhat. I wanted to thank you for taking such good care of Katelen. And it was a really nice thing you did giving her those sketches. I just left her in her room. She's taped them up on her walls. They look very professional. You've got real talent."

Tara was flattered. Bear knew she was on the run, but she didn't know she was a famous illustrator. And it would probably be best to keep it that way. "Thanks. Is Joseph back?"

"Don't know, but I do know you're changing the subject off of yourself. While I was in with Katelen, she showed me a picture book. She pointed out how your drawings are like the ones in her book."

Tara gulped.

"You're Tara Kelly." Bear folded her arms.

"I can't talk to you right now. I really need to speak with your son." Tara sidestepped her.

"Hold up there." Bear reached out and grabbed her arm. "Now, Katelen is only seven and she'll never figure out who you really are, but from what Irene said the other night, she might put two and two together. Your story is unraveling, and it might be best for everyone—especially my son and granddaughter—for you to get going if you've got a mind to leave. Katelen is getting attached to you."

All at once, the elderly woman before her reminded Tara of the black bear and her cubs, and like the animal she was nicknamed after, the woman was taking care of her family first. Tara couldn't argue with her. Joseph and Katelen had been through enough. "You're right."

Bear stepped back.

"I'm planning to leave as soon as possible, but I wanted to speak with Joseph first. Is tomorrow morning soon enough?"

Bear thought for a moment. "Yeah. You probably need to call Mac tonight. He'll understand. And when you talk with Joseph, be gentle. He's already had his heart broken once. If anything happened to another woman he loved . . ." Bear's brows pinched together. "See, he loves you, darlin'. I've seen the way he looks at you. And after today and all you've been through, he's going to be more attached to you than ever. You've even won over Katelen. And I can tell in your own way you love them too. But after all they've been through, they deserve someone who doesn't have a threat hanging over her like a thundercloud."

Tara knew in her heart she wasn't the woman for Joseph and could never be a mother to Katelen. She was jinxed. She had been all her life. Everyone close to her ended up dead, and she wasn't about to let that happen to Joseph, Katelen, or even Bear. Tara had already planned to leave, and though Bear was giving her a good shove, she knew she was only protecting her family. Tara could have been offended by the plain-spoken woman, but she wasn't. "Bear, I do love them, and I'll do everything in my power to keep them safe. Don't worry."

Tara turned, leaving the older woman alone in the hallway. She was going to Joseph's den right now to call Mac. Pushing the door open, she quickly crossed to the desk, where the phone waited. She tried Mac's cell, but the operator said it was no longer in service, which seemed odd.

Who could she call to help her? Joannie, of course. Though Garrett was probably watching Joannie's cell, Tara had to chance it. Besides, Joseph thought Garrett was in Canada. If he was there, he probably didn't have access to the equipment he needed to trace a call. Anyway, she wouldn't stay on the line long, just long enough for Joannie, who worked at the station, to tell her where Mac was and what was going on. Tara punched in the numbers, and the call rang through.

"Hello?" Joannie's voice was friendly, familiar, and welcoming.

"Joannie, it's Tara."

"Tara! Oh my gosh! Where have you been, girl?"

"I'm sorry, but with everything going on, I couldn't risk calling you. I didn't want to put you in danger."

"What do you mean? I've called your cell I don't know how many times. We've been looking for you." Joannie's voice turned sharp, even a little testy.

"Looking for me?" Tara didn't understand.

"Garrett's about gone out of his mind, worried sick about you. Would you like to talk to him? He's in his office."

Numbness prickled Tara's skin. Garrett was in his office! "But . . ."

"Hang on. I'll go get him."

Not knowing what to do or say, Tara gave in to her first impulse and hung up.

CHAPTER TWENTY-SIX
A MESSAGE FROM GOD

WHEN JOSEPH PULLED INTO THE barnyard, there were banquet tables set up on the lawn to feed the crew. Digger had been busy. He'd already set out two large trays of fried chicken and several bowls of mashed potatoes, and as Joseph neared the house, he could swear he smelled strawberry pie. He caught up to Digger in the kitchen. "How's everyone?"

"Bear's in with Katelen." Digger had a bag of heavy-duty paper plates and a box of plastic utensils in his arms. On the counter next to him were several pies. "Sarah's been sleeping most of the afternoon." He headed for the door but stopped. "Oh, Irene called and begged off coming to supper."

"Thanks." Joseph couldn't help but wonder why she wasn't coming. Maybe she was too upset over Harris still missing.

He decided he'd take a quick shower before eating to get the smoke and cattle smells off of him. The water revitalized him, but he couldn't shake the anxiety he still felt. He chalked it up to the events of the day and went to find Tara. She didn't answer when he tapped on her door, so he poked his head in to check. There were crumpled pillows, tangled sheets, and blankets, but no Tara. She was probably already outside with the others.

He passed Katelen's room, where she was sitting on the floor, staring up at the sketch of the white eagle Tara had drawn. Katelen had had a bath, and her still-wet hair was in a new braid. Her arm was in the sling the paramedics had given her.

As soon as she realized Joseph was standing in her doorway, she jumped up and hugged him with her good arm. Joseph hugged her back, basking in the joy that his little girl was alive and well. The hours when she'd been missing had been excruciating.

"Did you see it?" Katelen asked.

"What?"

She guided him over to the picture she'd been admiring. "The white eagle. Did you see it when we were running through the fire?" The memory of the bird flying overhead came back to him. It had appeared right when Joseph had become disoriented and didn't know which way to go. "Yes, I did."

"Mama was watching over us, wasn't she?" Katelen's big, brown eyes blinked as she stared at him, awaiting his answer.

He squatted down to her. "I'm sure she was." A warmth of gratitude overcame him and filled his heart.

Katelen looked back at the picture. "That's what I think too. Did Sarah see it?"

He took Katelen's hand. "I don't know. Why don't we ask her?"

They started down the hallway toward the kitchen, but Joseph noticed the door to his den was open. He peered inside to see if Bear was in there looking for something, but it was Tara sitting at his desk instead.

"Here she is." Joseph led Katelen into the den but when Tara didn't seem to notice them, he got worried.

Something was wrong.

Very wrong.

"Did you see the white eagle today?" Katelen asked Tara, not realizing anything was amiss.

Tara didn't reply.

Katelen stroked her arm. "Sarah?"

The touch awakened her, but she still didn't answer. She stared up at Joseph with disbelief and desperation.

Joseph had to get to the bottom of this, but he couldn't with Katelen standing there. He bent over to talk to her. "We need to ask Sarah about the bird later. Why don't you go find Grandma and tell her she needs you?"

Katelen thought about what he'd said for a moment and smiled. Joseph had used this ploy before, and his daughter knew it was code that he needed her to leave him alone for a little while. She quietly left, closing the door behind her.

"What's wrong?" he asked without preamble.

"I wanted to call Mac, but his number was disconnected."

"He had to get a new one. I should have told you, but we've been gone. That shouldn't upset you."

"Since I couldn't call Mac, I called my friend, Joannie. She works for the department too."

"Did she tell you Mac's new number?" Joseph leaned against his desk.

"We didn't get to that. She . . . she said they've been looking for me."

Confused but not wanting to show alarm, Joseph folded his arms and leaned against the desk.

Tara's face paled. She took a deep breath. "She said Garrett's been worried about me. She wanted to know if I wanted to talk to him. He was in his office."

"*What?*" The anxiousness he'd been feeling now threatened to burst.

"I know! I can hardly believe it. Do you suppose Garrett has done something to Mac—somehow gotten the upper hand and is now using the department to find me?"

Joseph reached for the phone and dialed Mac's new cell number. It rang a number of times, then went to voice mail. He hung up. "Maybe. I'm beginning to think more and more that that's a possibility. Mac told me Garrett was heading to Seattle, but Garrett hacked Mac's phone once. Maybe he did it again and found out more than we thought. How well do you know this Joannie person?"

"She's a good friend. My best friend."

"It wouldn't be the first time the boyfriend and best friend had an affair."

Tara adamantly shook her head. "If that were the case, why did Garrett come after me and kill Aunt Rosalie?"

Joseph knew she had a point and didn't know what to say.

"I need to go back, find the chief captain over the division, and tell him everything."

Joseph couldn't stand the thought of her going alone. "Once your friend Joannie tells Garrett you called, he'll trace your call and be on the next plane here."

She rubbed her forehead. "This keeps getting worse and worse. I have to go back to make this right or at least to keep your family safe."

"Well, you're not going without me."

"No, Joseph. You need to stay and protect your family." She stood. "You've done enough. I can take it from here."

"Everyone at the ranch except Katelen knows how to handle a gun. I'll tell Bear what's up before we leave. Besides, Allen's here. He's a darn good shot. They'll be all right." He reached to take her hand, but remembering her wound, he took hold of her arm. "You're not an officer or detective. It's too dangerous for you." He jerked open a drawer and pulled out the phone book. He flipped through the pages until he came to the airport number in Idaho Falls. "I'd use the Internet to book a flight, but Mac warned me not to, so I'll do it the old-fashioned way."

Before he could dial, Tara took the receiver from him. "No, Joseph. This is my battle, not yours. I have to do this alone."

"Okay, now you're talking gibberish. There is no way I'm letting the woman I love out of my sight."

"You love me?" The doubt in her voice and worried slant of her brows made him realize she didn't quite believe him.

To prove what he said was true, he placed his hands on her face, drew her close, and kissed her softly. The phone started the annoying left-off-the-hook bleep. Ignoring the racket, he deepened the kiss. Oh, how he loved this woman. He pulled back and found her long-lashed eyes closed, and she swayed toward him.

Her green eyes blinked open as he took the receiver from her. "We're in this together. Only after I know for sure and certain you're no longer in danger will I let you out of my sight." He dialed the first number.

Tara grew quiet and sank into the chair beside him.

As soon as someone answered, he asked for two seats on their next flight to LA, but there wasn't anything going out until tomorrow. He dialed the next number and the next and got the same answer each time. Finally, during the last call, he bought two tickets and set the receiver back in the cradle. "Looks like we're stuck here until tomorrow."

She reached up and took his hand. "You need to speak with your mother."

"Besides telling her what's going on, is there something in particular I need to say?" He lightly rubbed his thumb over the bandage on her hand.

"She knows who I am."

He massaged her shoulders. "She was bound to find out. My mother won't tell anyone."

"I'm not worried about that." She grimaced liked she didn't want to tell him.

"What, then?"

"She's worried the others will find out, but mainly, she's worried if something happens to me, you'll—"

"What? Fall to pieces?"

"Yes."

Joseph huffed.

Tara stood and gently took both of his hands in hers, despite her bandages. "She's your mother, and she saw how Jenny's death affected you, and she doesn't want a repeat."

"Neither do I. Remember the night you found me at the lake?"

Tara nodded.

"I'd been praying for guidance, and you appeared. For a brief moment, the way the firelight reflected off of you . . . Well, I thought you had angel wings. As I watched you walk away, the most profound feeling that we were meant to be together overcame me."

She smiled weakly, though he could see the denial in her eyes.

"There was a time when I would have been skeptical too, but not now. I know God watches over us. I know He loves us and wants to see us succeed. I know if we put our faith in Him and follow His promptings, miracles can happen. Think about it, Tara. The last few days, one miracle after another has happened."

The skepticism slowly left her face.

"When you first arrived, I thought you looked like my wife, which was really odd. After looking at Jenny's photograph, I realized you didn't, but for the first several hours, I could have sworn she was your twin. Some may say that was because I'd been lonely for her or because I found you attractive from the first time I laid eyes on you or my mind was playing tricks on me, but I don't think so."

Tara leaned toward him. "That makes sense, doesn't it?"

"I think something more was going on. I think it was a message from God. He wanted me to know I needed to take care of you and love you. The Spirit bore witness to me that night at the lake as you walked away. And that's why we're in this together." He pulled her into his arms and kissed her once again. Here was the woman he loved, the woman who had awakened him from long, lonely years of grief. He was not about to let her go or let anyone hurt her in any way.

She broke the kiss. "I have leaned on someone all my life—my parents, my grandfather, and my aunt. I'm touched. I love you. But, Joseph, I have to have the courage to stand on my own."

"No one is ever alone, Tara. God is always with you if you just give Him a chance."

"Well, I have to find Him in my own way. You can't do it for me."

Joseph rubbed his hand over her back. "Nothing says I can't stand by your side during the journey. Everyone needs a little help every once in a while. We can help each other."

"When Rosalie died, I was lost. But you came along. I don't believe in coincidences. So in a way, I do believe as you do: that we are meant to be together. Yet, I feel I'm lacking."

Joseph took her hand in his. "The only thing you're lacking is confidence. Tomorrow you and I can go to LA and get to the bottom of all this. But even the bravest person needs back up. And, sweetheart, I'm yours."

CHAPTER TWENTY-SEVEN

DECEIVED

JOSEPH KEPT TARA BY HIS side as they met the crew outside for dinner. They acted as if nothing was wrong. As everyone dished up their food, the conversation centered on the fire and how lucky Joseph and Tara had been to find Katelen and get out alive. Then the topic turned to Harris and how everyone believed he was behind the fire, kidnapping, and shootings. They wondered what could have happened to him. Some thought he had an accomplice; others believed he was lost in the fire.

In his peripheral vision, Joseph watched Tara to make sure she was all right. She was holding up pretty well considering the news she'd received about Garrett being at the police station in LA.

Eventually, the evening wound down, and the hired hands said their good-byes and left. Wes and Allen disappeared to the bunkhouse, and Joseph asked Digger to put Katelen to bed while he and Tara spoke with Bear in the kitchen.

After they'd all sat down, his mother stared at him. He knew this was going to be hard. "Ma, Tara and I need to go to LA. We've got some things that need to be looked into there."

Bear rubbed her chin, then turned to Tara. "You didn't listen to me."

Tara gave her an I-tried-but-couldn't look.

"Yes, she did, Mom." Joseph took Tara's hand in his. "She doesn't want me to go with her. But I have to. If you were in my place, you'd do the same thing."

"I hate it when you say that." His mother felt her shirt pocket. Joseph knew she was looking for her cigarettes but couldn't find them. "So these 'things' you need to take care of in LA, do they have anything to do with Mac and this Garrett fellow?"

"Yeah. We can't get ahold of Mac, and Garrett's been at the station."

"Holy mackinaw." Bear patted down the pockets of her pants. "Where's my smokes?"

"So we've got to go." Joseph retrieved his mother's cigarettes from her coat hanging on the peg near the kitchen door and handed them to her. "Maybe now would be a good time for you to take Katelen through Yellowstone. Take Digger. I want you to be safe. There's a chance Garrett might turn up here."

She tapped the cigarette box on the back of her hand to shake one out. "What about Wes and Allen?"

"He won't bother them; they're not family. And someone needs to stay at the ranch. Besides, they can take care of themselves."

Bear shrugged. "I suppose you're right. Guess you want us to leave first thing in the morning?"

"That would be best." Joseph pulled out his lighter and held it up for his mother to light the cigarette between her fingers.

Bear lifted the cigarette until it was nearly to her mouth, then hesitated and suddenly crumpled it. "In the past few days, I've seen you change for the better son. It's time I did the same." She looked at Tara. "Remember what I said to you this afternoon when we got back?"

Tara nodded.

"Well, it pains me something awful to admit it, but I was wrong." She peered at Joseph, then back at Tara. "You two need each other. Be careful and come back to us."

* * *

Tara woke at eight the next morning. The flight Joseph had booked them on was scheduled to leave Idaho Falls at two, so after making herself presentable, Tara went to the kitchen, hopeful she wasn't too late to say good-bye to Bear, Katelen, and Digger before they left for Yellowstone.

No one was about. *They must have left already.*

She poured a glass of water and sipped it while she peered out the window to see where Joseph might be. A Lincoln Town Car with a rental sticker on the tinted windows pulled to a stop in the barnyard.

She watched in disbelief as Mac got out. His graying hair looked nearly white in the sun. Dressed in a suit as usual, he reminded Tara of an aging George Clooney. He must have been on his way here last night to tell her what was going on, and that was why he hadn't answered his cell phone. He straightened his suit jacket and tucked in his tie as he walked the path to the house.

Relieved and eager to welcome him, she opened the door. "I'm so glad you're okay."

"Why wouldn't I be?" Mac gave her a welcoming hug. "It's good to see you. Where's Joseph?" He looked past her into the kitchen. "He's supposed to be watching over you."

"I'm sure he's around here somewhere." She had to tell him about Garrett. "I have something important to tell you." She didn't know how he was going to take the news, but she was ready to burst wanting to tell him. "I tried to call you last night but couldn't reach you, so I called Joannie. She told me Garrett was in his office. Do you believe it? He must have gone in as soon as you left."

Mac scanned the barnyard. He was first and always a cop, always watchful and wary.

But Mac wasn't reacting like she thought he would about her news. "Did you know he was there?"

Mac gave a heavy sigh. "That's why I've come. I need to talk to you somewhere private to explain. Come for a ride with me."

They had plenty of privacy here, but there was a chance Wes or Allen could walk in. She also realized that in the last few days of investigating Rosalie's murder, the most privacy Mac had known was probably in a car, so she relented. "All right."

Mac guided her to the Lincoln, but instead of taking her to the passenger side for her to get in, he opened the back door. She tried to peer into the tinted windows to see why she wasn't riding up front with him, but she could see nothing except her own reflection.

As she bent to step in, Mac nudged her completely inside and slammed the door. She turned to ask what he was doing but stopped when she realized someone else was in the back seat.

Their eyes locked.

"Rosalie!" Tara's hand trembled as she reached to make contact. She had to see if her mind was playing tricks on her again. Tara touched her aunt's arm. Flesh and bone! She was real, not a dream. Aunt Rosalie sat dressed in slacks and a tailored shirt like it was her day off or something. Goose bumps prickled Tara's skin. Shock squeezed off her voice, her lungs. Still, she couldn't believe what her eyes were telling her.

Tears slipped down her cheeks as she hugged Rosalie. "You're alive! Where have you been? In the hospital? Why didn't anyone tell me you were all right? I don't understand."

Rosalie hugged Tara back. "I'm so sorry we had to deceive you, but it was necessary." Rosalie smoothed a lock of hair out of Tara's eyes like she had so many times when Tara was young. Her hair was never as well mannered as her aunt's shoulder-length hair that was as unnaturally red as it had been in Tara's nightmares.

"Why was it necessary?" Tara moved to the edge of her seat, anxious to hear the answer.

Mac started the car and spun out of the graveled drive, making Tara fall to the floor. Crawling back up, she glanced out the window. They were headed toward the mountain. "Wait! We need to tell Joseph that Rosalie is still alive."

Rosalie pulled her close. "Don't worry about Joseph. I'm more concerned about you. We know you've been having nightmares and hallucinations again. We're here to take care of you."

"What? I'm fine." Tara felt the car accelerating. "What is the matter with you two?" She looked to Rosalie, who gave her a parental grin like Tara was a naïve adolescent. Tara glanced at the rearview mirror, but Mac was concentrating on the road up the mountain. Panic swelled within her. "Stop the car!" Tara yelled. She grabbed for the door handle, but Mac had turned on the child locks. She couldn't get out.

Rosalie clasped her hands together, and her brow rose like it always did when she had to explain something Tara didn't understand. "Tara, you don't need to worry. I'll take care of you like I always have."

"But . . ."

Rosalie patted Tara's leg. "It's going to be all right."

"Look, I'm not a child. I can take care of myself." Why were they treating her like this? Something was really wrong. Tara thought of Garrett and realized Mac hadn't answered her about why he was at the station. She grabbed the back of the driver's seat and nudged Mac's shoulder. "Why was Garrett at the station last night?"

"He's a man dedicated to his work." Mac looked at her in the rearview mirror.

That didn't make any sense at all. Full-fledged panic flooded through Tara.

"I'll make sure you're okay." Rosalie patted her arm. "Father always said your needs come first."

Rosalie was treating Tara like she had ten years ago when she'd admitted her to Twin Pines.

Rosalie tisked and smoothed a hair from Tara's face. "You're confused. But not to worry. I won't let you kill yourself in an asylum like my mother did."

A chill skeetered up Tara's spine. *My grandmother killed herself?* That was wrong. "Grandpa never said Grandma was in an asylum or that she killed herself."

Rosalie had a gleam in her eye that Tara had never seen before. "He kept things from you for your own protection." Rosalie pulled rubber gloves out of her pants pocket and started to tug them on.

Tara's thoughts twisted in a whirlwind: Rosalie was alive, Garrett was in the office, Grandmother had committed suicide. This was too much new information to comprehend, too much to digest. She had to get away. She grabbed the door handle and pulled on it. She even kicked at the door. There had to be some way out.

"You're getting yourself all worked up. You don't want your grandpa to think the Evil Eye has found his precious little artist, do you?" Rosalie snapped her rubber gloves in place. "He was more proud of you and your drawings than he was of his own police-officer daughter."

Tara remembered the fight Rosalie and Grandfather had had on the night he died. The sight of Grandfather floating in the water near the dock flashed in Tara's mind, and her mouth grew instantly dry.

"Said the Evil Eye resided in me because I was living in sin," Rosalie said. "Threatened to take me out of his will." Her eyes glazed with madness. "You never met his attorney, did you?"

"No."

"You didn't have a grip on reality then either. I had to admit you to Twin Pines the day after the funeral."

Tara felt like she was in the throes of another nightmare. This couldn't really be happening. This was not the aunt who had taken care of her, the aunt who was more like a sister.

But Tara knew she was not dreaming. Staring at Rosalie, Tara thought of the nightmare that had started it all. "I saw Garrett beating you. I heard a gun go off."

"There, there. It was only a bad dream. I'm going to take care of you." Rosalie smoothed Tara's hair behind her ear.

Nausea roiled in Tara's stomach. Rosalie was completely ignoring her.

Mac stopped at a lookout point on the mountain, and Rosalie pulled a hypodermic from her purse. She really thought Tara was having another breakdown. Tara was not a depressed teenager, and she wasn't going back to an asylum. She had to get away.

Mac unlocked the doors and got out of the car. Tara frantically grabbed the handle and flung the door open, but Mac was standing there ready. She lunged at him, scratching and kicking, but he easily deflected her, pinning her to the backseat.

Rosalie stroked Tara's forehead. "Don't worry, honey. You'll only feel a little prick."

"Please listen to me!" Tara yelled. "You can't do this. Go talk with Joseph. He'll vouch for me."

Mac chuckled. "Cousin Joseph has trouble of his own right now."

What was that supposed to mean? Tara turned to her aunt, hoping she would explain. Rosalie merely gave her a sickly sweet smile. A maleficent smile. A smile Tara had never seen before. Revulsion churned in her stomach. Her aunt was a stranger to her. Something horrible, something terribly wrong was going on here, and after what Mac had said, it didn't just involve Tara. It involved Joseph too. Realization dawned on her. All of Joseph's troubles at the ranch had not happened at the hands of disgruntled ranchers, Irene's irate father, or Denver Harris. For some perverted reason she couldn't fathom, Mac had caused Joseph's troubles. But Mac and Rosalie had been in LA; they couldn't have done it alone. "Who's been helping you?"

It had to be someone who had been here since Tara had arrived. Someone close to Joseph. Someone who would know the comings and goings of the ranch.

"Give her the shot!" Mac yelled.

Rosalie jammed the needle into Tara's arm and pushed in the prong. A burning pain stabbed Tara's muscle as the drug entered her system.

Her aunt pulled the needle out. "There, there."

Tara's vision blurred.

Mac's face hovered over her, and then she was being lifted and carried.

Rosalie's voice wafted into her thoughts. "Tara, you've been very depressed about my death, so much so that you can't go on without me. And now you're going to jump."

CHAPTER TWENTY-EIGHT
A WHITE EAGLE

JOSEPH STOPPED THE TRUCK. FIRST thing this morning, Allen had told him a ranger had called and said they'd found something suspicious at the burned-out line shack and wanted him to take a look at it. Joseph figured he and Allen could probably drive up and get back before eleven, which would give Tara and him time to catch their plane.

He wasn't prepared for the sight before him. Charred and blackened trees littered the scorched earth. He was grateful the wind had taken the fire down the side of the mountain away from the main road. He'd packed a shovel and pickaxe in case they'd need them, but there was nothing left except the potbellied stove. Drawn to where the shack had been, Joseph stooped down and stroked Scrap, who had followed him. "We were lucky, weren't we, boy?" Scrap's brown eyes seemed to empathize.

The site sickened Joseph and made him realize how truly blessed he'd been to have gotten Tara and Katelen out alive. Tears threatened to gather in his eyes. He didn't want to look at it anymore yet was unable to turn away. He heard Allen walk up to the edge of the shack behind him. Joseph stood and said, "Can't believe we got out." Taking a deep breath, Joseph added, "I thought you said the ranger was going to meet us."

"That's what he said."

Scrap growled. Joseph turned to find Allen aiming his Winchester at him.

"What the . . . ?"

Allen shrugged. "Sorry it's come to this."

Scrap's hackles rose as the animal bared his teeth.

"What do you mean?" Joseph could hardly wrap his mind around the fact that one of his closest friends, the guy he'd trusted his life to so many times was now pointing a weapon at him.

"Look, man, they threatened to blame everything on me."

"They?" Of course Allen wouldn't have done this on his own. Joseph stared at his friend. "Lester and Irene? Tell me the real reason you met Lester on the drive, and don't give me the excuse that he was upset that you were seeing Irene." Joseph caught sight of the pry bar from the shack. If he could somehow get his hands on that, he could knock the rifle away from Allen and try to talk some sense into him.

"Honest! That's why Lester was there." Allen stepped back.

Lying had been Allen's expertise on the force. The lies he'd told gang bangers and crazed meth heads had saved them many times. But Joseph never thought he'd lie to him. His mind ran through a million scenarios in LA and everything that had happened the last couple of days.

Scrap crouched, ready to attack as the animal inched toward Allen, issuing warning growls.

"Call off your dog, or I'll kill him first."

Joseph stared at Allen, not saying anything to the animal. If Allen aimed the weapon at Scrap, Joseph would tackle him. "Katelen . . . You took her, didn't you?"

"Look, you know I'd never hurt her. I love Katelen like she's my own." Allen's face contorted in anguish as he shook his head.

"You knocked her out, dislocated her shoulder, put a bag over her head, and left her alone in the shack for hours." Joseph had to keep his temper in check or he'd beat his friend senseless for what he did to his daughter. Again, Joseph took another step. The pry bar was near his foot. If he could work the toe of his boot beneath, he could kick it up.

Allen's teeth worried his lower lip. "When I put the bag over her head, she struggled and fell off the horse. She was only bait to lure you and Tara." He glanced at Scrap, whose growls were growing more threatening by the second.

"So you planned it all?"

"You have to believe me; I had no choice. I was following orders."

"Orders?" Realization hit as the words left Joseph's mouth. Allen had been the one who had shot the cattle, cut the brakes, and left the windows boarded up on the shack. "Why, Allen? Tell me why. I deserve to know."

Allen's finger slid to the trigger as he prepared to shoot. Sweat beaded across his forehead. The man's face turned gray with profound grief, and for a moment, Joseph thought he'd drop the gun, that maybe all their years together on the force did mean something. But then Allen shook his head and refocused.

Joseph had seen that steely look in Allen's eyes before, and Joseph knew he had to act. In one fluid motion, Joseph shoved his foot under the pry bar, kicked it high enough to grab, and knocked the rifle out of Allen's hands. Scrap attacked him, biting at his leg. He backed up to get away and tripped and fell over a burnt stump.

Joseph scooped up the rifle and rushed to Allen, who was sprawled on the ground and not moving. Joseph pushed Scrap aside to get a better look. Allen had knocked his head against a large rock. His jaw was slack, and he didn't look like he was breathing. Joseph placed his finger on Allen's neck and felt a pulse. Relieved, he stared at the unconscious man as questions tumbled through Joseph's mind.

Why had Allen turned on him?

Who had given him orders?

And why?

* * *

Blotchy images clouded her vision, and Tara struggled to keep conscious. They'd left her standing alone. Why? Where did they go? Were they ahead? Behind?

Rosalie is here. She's alive.

And she wants me dead!

Stay awake!

Focus.

A trembling grew from deep inside her.

A breeze brushed against her cheeks. The sun shone on her face. And then a bird screeched overhead.

Was it the white eagle? Was it guiding her home?

Straining to see, Tara's eyes finally focused. Straight ahead was sky, white wispy clouds against blue.

She peered down. She was on the edge of a very tall cliff. Giant slabs of granite pulled her, wanted her to come to them. Haunting voices from the Land of the Dead called from the Hole of Sorrows. "Come . . . come . . . come."

Her skin prickled, and her heart fluttered against her chest, her pulse thunder-clapping in her ears.

"Step forward. Just one step," someone said from behind.

Rosalie?

Was she here at the dolmen at Poulnabrone?

Looking behind, Tara saw her aunt, though the woman's features were distorted.

When she looked back in front of her, there was no dolmen.

Wait, where am I?

The drug.

The injection.

Yes, the injection Rosalie had given her. Tara wasn't dreaming. Rosalie was real. But the voices?

Tara had heard the eagle, had felt the sunshine and the breeze—all real.

Tara turned to look at Rosalie as Rosalie walked toward her.

"For some stupid reason, I can't seem to push you over myself," Rosalie said. "So, Tara, you're going to have to find the courage to do this alone. Just take a step forward."

Alone. Joseph had told her she was never alone. God was always with her. Was He with her now?

A motion behind Rosalie caught Tara's attention. Mac leaned against the fender of the car, staring at Tara. *Mac?* What had he done? Rosalie loved him, but had she let him turn her into someone else? Had Grandpa seen the change? Had Tara missed it until now?

Rosalie was all she had left.

No parents. No Grandfather. No one.

Except God . . . He would always be with her.

And then Tara thought of Joseph . . . Katelen . . . and Bear.

They were her family now.

* * *

Joseph found rope behind the bench seat of his truck and tied Allen's hands behind him. He loaded the unconscious man in the cab.

Scrap jumped inside as Joseph got in and settled on the seat with his muzzle on Joseph's lap. Allen was leaning on the passenger door, unconscious. Stroking his dog, Joseph said, "He was my best friend. Why did he try to kill us? What happened to turn him?" Joseph couldn't imagine. Unable to think of an answer, he turned on the engine and pressed the gas pedal to the floorboard. Something more was going on, and he knew he had to get back to the ranch in record time.

Lester had been a prime suspect in Joseph's mind, but Allen had said "They," so if Lester was involved, maybe Irene was too.

Irene could have shot the cow and could have shot at Tara and him. She'd put on a very good show of jealousy when she met Tara, but she could have been acting. And she and Allen had been pretty cozy the other night. But that didn't seem right.

The road switched back just as an odd feeling overcame him, prompting him to look up at the edge of the cliff. He didn't have time. He had to get to the ranch. Again the feeling came. Was he being stubborn to not look? His muleheadedness had led to Jenny's death and caused him so much pain. What would it hurt to look?

He slowed down and looked up. For a moment he wasn't certain, but it looked as though someone was up there on the edge! He zeroed in on the image and made out a woman in jeans and a long-sleeved shirt.

Tara!

Joseph stomped on the brakes. The truck swerved and slid over the dirt road until it came to a halt, and he jumped out.

Why was she so close to the edge?

Someone moved behind her.

"Tara, get back!" he shouted.

She didn't seem to hear him but was staring up at the sky as if she didn't see the cliff.

Someone grabbed Tara from behind, and for a moment, Joseph thought she was saved. Then a shot rang out. The bullet zipped past and hit the cottonwood tree beside him. He dropped to the ground next to Scrap. Who had Tara, and what were they doing up there? "Come on, boy." Joseph crawled behind the truck, the dog following. He had to get to her. It would take too long to drive. No, the only way was to scale the cliff. There was a shortcut to the ledge, but he would have to leave the truck and Allen behind.

Careful not to draw fire, Joseph eased the passenger door open and checked on Allen. He was still out cold. Joseph grabbed the Winchester and closed the door. Getting on his hands and knees, he crawled over to the cottonwood and took off on foot with Scrap close behind.

Reaching the shortcut, Joseph shimmied between two giant lava boulders and levered himself against the rocks so he could slowly crawl up their porous surfaces until his head hit the familiar overhanging ledge. He managed to shove the rifle on top. Scrap yipped below. "Sorry, boy. Can't take you."

Now all he had to do was get his body on top of the ledge.

Back when he was nimble and thinner, it would have been no problem, but now, hampered with adult weight, his fingers were slipping from their holds.

Joseph swung his leg up, and the heel of his boot caught on the rocky ledge but suddenly dropped back down. Small pebbles and bits of dirt rained over him.

"Come on," he said under his breath, trying to rally his strength. Again he swung his leg wide, missing the ledge. His grip slipped.

Joseph thought of Tara; she needed him. Demanding strength in his hands and limbs, he tried again. This time, when he swung his heavy leg up, his boot caught on the ledge's lip. With sheer willpower and determination, Joseph pulled himself over, scraping his shins on the jagged black rocks.

The sound of a rifle cocking stopped him, and Joseph turned to find Mac pointing the Winchester at his head.

* * *

"Mac won't be long. He'll bring his cousin back and then you can both die together, and all our problems will be solved." Rosalie pointed her 45 mm Glock at Tara.

The fog in Tara's mind was lifting. "How can you do this? We're family."

Rosalie's eyes glowed with interest, but then, in Tara's hazy mind, they became flames of amber. A wave of pain and regret washed over her. All the time she had been basking in her grandfather's love, Rosalie must have felt left out. But she was wrong. "Grandpa loved you. He worried about you. He told me how devastated you were when my mother died." Tara fought a sudden wave of dizziness. Trying to hang on, she continued. "He told me how he tried so hard to give you the love you deserved even though he was grieving too."

Rosalie's interest morphed into anger. "Liar!" And then she laughed.

"It's not funny." Tara had to get through to her.

"Yes, it is. The Evil Eye he was so afraid would get you got him. I loosened the dock boards."

Tara nearly collapsed.

* * *

"I knew you'd backtrack up this rise." Mac motioned with the rifle for Joseph to begin walking.

"*Mac?*" Joseph's cousin was holding a gun on him. "What's going on?"

He didn't lower the weapon. "I remember coming here with you when we were kids. But you never could mind your own business."

Staring at the barrel of the gun the man he thought would always have his back was aiming at him, Joseph momentarily felt betrayal, sorrow, and grief pulse through his veins, but they were quickly replaced with anger. From the time he'd called and asked Joseph to hide Tara until this very moment, Mac had been calling the shots—and using Joseph's best friend. "You have something on Allen, don't you?"

Mac nudged him with the rifle barrel. "Keep walking."

What had made Mac such a two-faced liar? As Joseph started up the rise, his mind reeled through scenes from the past: the information he'd found about a bad cop helping the Martinez gang, Mac trying to steer him away from the investigation. He stopped and whirled around. "You must have been getting some pretty good payoffs from the gang, weren't you?" Joseph hoped he was wrong but, at the same time, knew he wasn't.

"For what it's worth, I am sorry Jenny got caught in the crosshairs. But it was your own stupid fault. Couldn't leave well enough alone, could you?" He motioned for Joseph to walk.

They'd come to the car. Beyond, Joseph saw Tara. She looked pale, as if she were in shock. The woman with a gun had nearly the same nose and mouth as Tara. She had to be her aunt.

Joseph locked eyes with Tara.

Mac rammed the barrel of the Winchester between Joseph's shoulder blades. "Go stand by her."

Joseph wanted to take Tara in his arms and never let her go, shield her from whatever was going to happen. He was going to lose the woman he loved again because someone was after him.

She took his hand. He squeezed her cold fingers, trying to give her comfort in the only way he could.

Rosalie motioned with her gun for them to turn around. "I couldn't push my niece over before, but now, with the two of you, I'm forced to do what I didn't want to. But I can't bear to look at your faces."

As he turned, Joseph looked down the jagged cliff face, and Tara gasped. She wasn't peering downward; she was looking up into the sky.

She stood transfixed. "It's coming, Rosalie." Tara's eyes and head moved like she was watching something circle above them.

"What are you talking about?" Rosalie stepped closer.

Tara fixed her gaze to the heavens. "Dullahan, king of the Land of the Dead; his death coach is almost here."

"If he's coming, he's coming for you. Let me help you on your way." She reached to shove Tara over.

At that moment, a dog growled, and Scrap came out of the brush, teeth bared. The border collie's ears were pinned back, his hackles raised. The faithful animal snarled and snapped as he slowly crouched, ready to attack Rosalie.

Joseph knew this was his opportunity and that Mac wouldn't shoot him if he went after Rosalie. He spun around and tackled her, knocking the gun out of her hand. Her weapon soared through the air, and Tara reached out to catch it, but it went over her head and skittered down the face of the cliff. Joseph put a hammer lock on Rosalie and turned to see where Mac was.

Scrap had gone after Mac, biting his arm. In the tussle to get away from the animal, Mac squeezed the trigger. The dog gave a pain-filled yelp and fled into the bushes. Rage tore through Joseph, but before he could move, Tara leaped on Mac's back and knocked him away from the ravine onto the ground. He dropped the rifle as they fought.

It wouldn't take Mac long to gain the upper hand. Joseph had to get the rifle. He dragged the struggling woman near the weapon, but he couldn't grab it and risk Rosalie breaking free, so he kicked the gun and sent it skittering over the dirt until it came to rest at Allen's feet.

Allen?

How in the world had he freed himself?

Joseph locked eyes with his former partner. Would he complete the job Mac had hired him to do? Would he sacrifice his honor and all he'd pledged when he had been an officer years ago to save his own hide? They'd been through so much on the force. They'd seen the ugliness of society, and never once had Joseph doubted Allen's trust until today.

"I've got this." Allen pointed the weapon at Joseph.

With all hope lost, Joseph released Rosalie.

"It's about time you showed up." Rosalie started over to Allen to take the weapon from him, but he skirted her and gave the rifle to Joseph, then grabbed Rosalie from behind, pulling her arms in back of her. She tried to kick Allen but missed.

"Not so fast," Mac's voice stopped them. In the ruckus with Rosalie and Allen, Joseph had lost track of him. Mac pressed the barrel of his service weapon to Tara's temple while he held one of her arms behind her. They were near the cliff's edge.

Joseph's heart thudded in his throat. He aimed the rifle at his cousin, but if he took the shot, Mac would kill Tara. Her eyes were wide with fear. Joseph had to do something.

Allen maneuvered the struggling Rosalie to the cliff. "Drop the weapon, Mac, and let Tara go, or I'll throw her over."

Mac stared at Allen. "You're giving everything up, even your own mother's well-being?"

Allen repositioned his hold on Rosalie, grabbing her arm and wrenching it behind her. She yelped and gasped. Allen stepped so close to the edge that small rocks spilled down the rock face. "If my mother survives the shame I've brought her, she'll manage."

Rosalie glared at Mac in a gesture for him to do something.

Reluctantly, he dropped his gun and released Tara. She crumpled to her knees.

Allen let Rosalie go.

Joseph started toward Tara to pull her away, but Mac drew a gun from his waistband and aimed it at Allen. Of course he always carried two guns on his person. Joseph pointed the rifle at Mac once again. He had a clear shot. He had to stop him from killing Allen. The air exploded with gunfire as both his and Mac's weapons discharged.

Joseph's bullet hit Rosalie, who had jumped up to protect Mac, and she collided with Mac, forcing them both over the cliff. Allen turned to Joseph, shock in his eyes as blood began to saturate the front of his shirt. He looked down at his wound, then looked back at Joseph like he had so many times when they'd been on the force, like he was about to say something witty or clever, and then . . . he collapsed, falling over the side of the cliff too.

The edge was eerily empty.

Vacant.

One moment they were there, and the next . . .

"No!" Tara yelled.

Joseph dropped his weapon and held Tara. She clung to him, trembling. There was nothing they could do. Poor Tara had reunited with her aunt and then lost her again almost as quickly.

And Joseph . . . He'd lost a cousin and a good friend.

Deep gratitude and humbling grief folded over Joseph. He stared at Tara. Although tears stained her cheeks, she had stopped crying, and her trembling had ceased. Despite the sorrow and treachery, despite losing people he cared for, at this moment, he saw love . . . eternal love in Tara's eyes.

Joseph took her hand. "Let's go find Scrap. If he's alive, Irene will fix him up."

CHAPTER TWENTY-NINE
PUTTING PIECES TOGETHER

JOSEPH WATCHED THE SHERIFF'S CAR drive away and took hold of Tara's hand. She'd been by his side throughout the day: rushing Scrap to the ranch so Wes could take care of him, notifying the authorities and taking them to the bodies, and answering the sheriff's endless questions.

Joseph kissed Tara's hand. "You've been amazing."

"So have you." She leaned into him.

"Are you ready to set the record straight, and tell everyone who you really are? Bear, Digger, and Katelen are back. The sheriff was able to track them down just outside of Island Park, and they turned around as soon as they heard everything was okay. It would be good to let them know the truth about you." He wouldn't blame her if she was too tired and said no, after all she'd been through she had the right to go to bed and rest.

"Setting the record straight with your family and friends will be a piece of Irish Johnny cake compared to what we've been through." Tara sighed as she looked toward the house. "Irene's in there too."

"I think this entire experience has mellowed her quite a bit. She had a hard time believing that Allen had roughed Harris up like he did and framed him for the fire. I'm glad the firefighters found Harris and got him help." Joseph started walking, leading Tara. "When Irene told me she hadn't stuck around because she was afraid, I felt pretty bad for her. I had no idea she was that scared of fire. I told her she didn't need to come out to the ranch, but she wanted to check on Scrap."

"I hope she feels at peace knowing Mr. Harris is okay. That night at the camp when they arrived together, I could tell she had feelings for him." Tara smiled and Joseph knew by her calm demeanor that she would be all right.

As they entered through the kitchen door, they found everyone crowded around the dining room table with their eyes focused on Joseph and Tara.

Katelen ran to her father. Joseph picked her up and hugged her. Setting her down, he pulled out chairs for both Tara and him. Katelen crawled onto his lap, and Joseph cleared his throat. Looking at his mother, Digger, Wes, and Irene, he said, "I know you're anxious to learn exactly what happened today. But before I explain how Allen and Mac died, I need to set the record straight. See—"

"Let me." Tara interrupted. She took a deep breath and then started. "There was a woman who died with Allen and Mac today. She was Rosalie Kelly, my aunt. I'm not Sarah Smith, and I've never been Joseph and Jenny's neighbor. My name is Tara Kelly."

The room was quiet. No one moved. No one said a word until Irene got up and disappeared down the hallway. Joseph wasn't sure if she was angry or what, but his main concern at this moment was Tara.

Tara nervously smoothed a hair away from her face as if she didn't know whether to continue talking without Irene there or not. Joseph nodded that she should go ahead. "Joseph told you I was his fiancée to protect me and all of you. If you had known who I really was, your lives could have been in danger. My aunt was trying to kill me."

Katelen crawled from her father's lap over to Tara and gave her a hug. "It's all right. Daddy will keep you safe."

"I know he will." Tara hugged her back, closing her eyes like she was drinking in the moment.

Irene returned, drawing everyone's attention. She had one of Tara's Irish picture books. "*The* Tara Kelly?" She pointed to the author/illustrator name.

Joseph answered for Tara. "Yes, *the* Tara Kelly."

Irene rolled her eyes like she should have known all along but then smiled and nodded at Joseph as if to say, "After what you've been through, it's okay. I'm with Harris and you're lucky to have Tara." Joseph knew all the hurt was forgiven.

Katelen hugged Tara again. Wes and Digger were all smiles.

Bear leaned over and touched Joseph's hand. "I'm relieved the truth has finally come out. Now tell us what happened to you and Tara on that mountain and what Mac had to do with it."

Joseph told them everything he knew, but there were still blank spots that only a trip to LA could fill in.

* * *

Tara and Joseph escorted the bodies to LA. Dressed in plain clothes, Garrett and Joannie met them at LAX. Joannie spotted Tara and Joseph first, and with a warm smile, she hugged Tara. "I can't believe it. Can you?"

Tara shook her head. The last twenty-four hours had been mind-numbing as she'd tried to piece together what had happened and why.

"Nobody can," Joseph answered for her. Instead of wearing his usual cowboy clothes, Joseph was in dress slacks and a polo shirt, his usual California attire. He shook Garrett's hand, who had been standing behind Joannie. Garrett wore a dark suit and a white shirt that made his tan look even darker. His short blond hair had grown a little since the last time Tara had seen him and was feathering the top of his ears.

Garrett turned to Joseph. "I've heard a lot about you."

"I've heard a lot about you too; however, most were lies." Joseph gave him a friendly smile. "Want to help me with the luggage?"

"Just a second." Garrett awkwardly gazed at Tara. "I'm so sorry. That night when I stopped to see you, I should have known something was wrong. And the next day, Rosalie said you'd taken off and she didn't know where you were. I . . . I just . . ."

Tara patted his arm. "It's all right. You couldn't have known."

Garrett gave her a grateful nod. "I have so much I want to tell you. Since Joseph called, I've been putting the pieces together."

People crowded around them on their way to retrieve their luggage. "We'll talk later." He left to help Joseph collect what little luggage Joseph and Tara had brought.

Tara walked beside Joannie toward the exit. "I had no idea Aunt Rosalie was so unstable. I can't believe all those years I didn't have a clue."

"Rosalie fooled everyone. So did Mac. I tried to call you back the night you called me, but when I pressed redial, it came up unlisted. I called your grandfather's lawyer. He said he'd meet with you the day after the funerals. I hope that's okay." Joannie had been so helpful, even insisting Tara and Joseph stay with her while they were in town.

"That's probably for the best. There's so much to do. Joseph wants to visit Allen's mother and let her know her son died a noble death. We have the funerals to plan. Just what kind of funerals do you have for cops who were criminals?"

"The chief will take care of things. He wants you and Joseph to stop by the station so he can help you." Joannie patted her arm. "Don't worry."

Tara had once thought she was all alone in the world with everyone in her family dead. She knew better now. God was her anchor, Joseph was her family, and she had good friends.

* * *

Joseph and Tara sat across from Chief Randall Johnson at his mahogany desk, along with Garrett and Joannie. The chief was a formidable man in his officer's uniform, even though he had a freckled complexion and bald head. He helped Tara and Joseph decide what to do for the funerals, and then he turned to Garrett. "Officer Parker has done a good job of sorting out why Mac and Rosalie did all of this."

Garrett scooted to the edge of his seat and turned so he could see both Tara and Joseph at the same time. "After talking with Joseph, I was able to backtrack. When Rosalie admitted you into Twin Pines Psychiatric Hospital all those years ago, she became the executor of your grandfather's estate. In his will, he stipulated that if you were mentally unstable, she would be in charge of your money. Your grandfather left the bulk of his estate to you. Mr. Cranksaw, the lawyer, was pretty tight lipped about how much money was involved. He wants to tell you the particulars, but when I told him what Rosalie had done, he was a little more forthcoming with other information. Rosalie would have remained the executor until you turned thirty. Your birthday is in July, isn't it?"

"Yes." Tara could hardly believe what he was saying.

"If you were still mentally unstable, she would remain in charge of the money. So that explains why she switched your sleeping pills with Halcion. If I hadn't come over that night, she would have probably checked you into Twin Pines again. I still need to do a little more research into Doctor Faris, who runs the place, but I wouldn't doubt if Rosalie bribed him so he'd keep you there."

Tara put her elbow on the arm of her chair and held her head. She remembered how Rosalie admitted to loosening the boards on the dock so Grandpa Kelly would fall into the lake and drown. The way she'd calculated and planned Grandfather's murder only stood to reason that she was capable of manipulating a doctor to do what she wanted.

Still, Tara remembered how Rosalie had come to visit her when she was in the hospital. She'd been kind and attentive and had brought her ice cream and her favorite magazines and books. And when Tara had been released, Rosalie had helped her go to college. She'd been her biggest fan when it had come to Tara's artwork. And she'd seemed thrilled when Tara's picture books were published. Rosalie's voice came to Tara. *He was more proud of you and your drawings than he was of his police-officer daughter.*

Even though Rosalie had tried to kill her, Tara felt sorry for her aunt. Tara had every right to hate her, but she didn't, couldn't. Hate and revenge had consumed her aunt, making her become someone Tara didn't recognize. Tara wanted to remember the good things Rosalie had done, not the sorrow and pain she'd caused. But she couldn't do that either. Rosalie had killed her own father, and that knowledge would always overshadow the good she'd done. Always.

Joseph touched her arm. "You okay?"

"Yeah. It's just a lot to take in."

"I have information for you as well." Garrett now directed his words to Joseph. "That night when I went over to see Tara, I also talked with Mac. I'd been working on a cold case—your wife's death, in fact."

"I already know Mac was behind Jenny's death."

"But here's the thing." Garrett paused a moment, as if collecting himself. "I told him I thought you were onto something with your research, and I wanted to get in touch with you. I thought it was a courtesy to check with Mac first, since he was in charge of the case five years ago. That must have spooked him into thinking he'd get caught, so that's what made him put pressure on Allen to kill you. He instigated the shooting of the cattle so people would think it had to do with the ranch. Anyway, I feel responsible."

Joseph swiped his hand over his face. "Well, don't. Allen came through in the end. If it weren't for him, Tara and I would be dead."

A tap came at the door. Chief Johnson's secretary poked her head in. "You have a meeting in five minutes."

"Thanks," Chief Johnson said.

Johnson stood and reached across his desk to shake Joseph's hand. "Any possibility we could talk you into coming back and working on the force?"

"Tempting as that is"—Joseph looked at Tara, then back to the chief—"I have other plans for my future." He stood and took Tara's hand, helping her up.

She glanced at Garrett. A month ago, she thought her future was with him. He looked at her as if he understood.

Garrett and Joannie followed them out of the chief's office. As they walked to the elevators, Joseph took Tara's hand. Tara looked at Garrett. "I hope you don't mind."

Garrett smiled. "I think you two being together is great."

EPILOGUE

TARA CHECKED HER VEIL IN the bathroom mirror one more time. She wanted this day to be perfect.

Over the last month, so much had happened. After the funerals, Tara and Joseph had cleaned up Rosalie's house and sold it. They'd helped the police with the investigation of Rosalie, Mac, and Allen. Joseph had visited Allen's mother, which had been hard on both of them but had to be done. The woman was gracious in her grief and thanked Joseph for telling her what actually happened.

And the meeting with Grandpa Kelly's attorney, Brandon Cranksaw, was quite a surprise.

Tara had no idea Grandpa was a millionaire. Cranksaw apologized profusely, saying he met with Rosalie only because of Tara's mental state. He'd checked with the hospital and they'd confirmed Tara had been a patient, so he'd talked with Rosalie about money matters. However, several months ago, he told Rosalie that with Tara's thirtieth birthday coming up, he wanted to meet with Tara personally. Rosalie promised a meeting, but it never happened. Cranksaw was horrified by Rosalie's deceptions. Tara felt the man was sincere and had no idea he was being duped. With the funerals and everything taken care of in LA, Joseph and Tara decided it was time to focus on their family in Idaho.

And that meant a wedding.

A knock came at her bedroom door. Tara opened it to find Bear. Her hair was curled, and she wore a new sky-blue pant suit. "You know, I knew from the first day I saw you that you would be the one."

Tara smoothed the wrinkles in the bodice of her white, lace dress, remembering that first day and how intimidating Bear had appeared. Once she'd had the opportunity to get to know Bear, Tara knew the woman's only faults were loving her family too much and smoking. The first one really wasn't a fault, and the second one Digger was helping her leave behind. Tara had grown to respect and admire Bear. "I know you did. You turned a city apple into a home-grown one, despite my bruises and scrapes."

Bear's eyes reddened as tears threatened. Unable to look at Tara, she brushed lint from her pants. She pulled her emotions together and buttoned the matching jacket. "A strong, courageous woman such as yourself, who puts her own life at risk for her man and his daughter, is of high worth. Joseph's father would approve of your joining our family."

She hugged Tara tightly. "Now, don't keep my son waitin'."

Tara followed Bear out the french doors and down to the lake—the lake where Joseph had prayed, the lake that had given them peace.

Dressed in a western-cut tux, Digger held his arm out to Bear. She pulled a hanky from her jacket and dabbed her eyes before slinging her arm in his.

Katelen stood beside her father as his "best man." She was in a pretty pink chiffon dress, her hair in springy ringlets.

Joseph's onyx eyes that had frightened Tara when they'd first met now glanced over her with love. He was dressed in the white ceremonial deerskin robes his father wore for his own wedding. His shaggy black hair accentuated his chiseled features. Only his black Stetson looked out of place.

As Tara approached, Joseph took off his hat and winked at her as if to say, "And this is another reason I take off my hat." He reached out for her.

Bishop Jeffery stood in front of them. Tara had met him at the wedding rehearsal, and he now cleared his throat to begin the ceremony. Tara and Joseph locked eyes.

When the bishop asked for the rings, Joseph turned around. Coming down the path to them was Scrap. He still limped where the bullet had wounded him, but Irene said the animal would fully recover with time.

Attached to the dog's back was a fancy lace pillow with two rings tied to it. Joseph patted the dog's head and untied the rings. He slipped Tara's on her finger, and she slipped his on him.

A loud screech sounded from above, and everyone looked up. A bald eagle gracefully glided just above their heads.

A joyous shiver raced over Tara's skin.

"Daddy!" Katelen tugged on her father's arm. "Did you see it? It's not white. Maybe now the eagle isn't sick anymore."

Joseph took her in his arms, holding her up so she could better see the bird. It soared in one elegant circle and spiraled up to the distant white clouds, disappearing in the puffy mists. He hugged his child to him and then let her down.

Katelen gazed up at Tara, beaming with joy.

Joseph took Tara's hand and pressed it to his lips, then whispered in her ear. "I love you."

Tara knew she was home. No more would she believe herself a jinx or that death followed her because she knew God was watching over them.

ABOUT THE AUTHOR

AFTER TAKING A TRIP TO picturesque Little Lost River, Idaho, Kathi Oram Peterson wanted to make it the setting for one of her novels. She also wanted to people the story with unforgettable characters. Researching the Nez Perce and their legends and then visiting Ireland and learning about their folklore, she found the roots for two very strong main characters and created magical myths that added to both. With the combination of the setting and characters, this book about faith and rising above challenges came to life, and she is happy to share it with her fans.

When her children finished school, Kathi earned her English degree at the University of Utah. She worked for several years writing and editing children's books for a curriculum publisher. Upon leaving the workforce, she turned her attention to writing novels. She currently resides in Salt Lake City. You can contact Kathi through her website, www. kathiorampeterson.com, and her blog, www.kathiswritingnook.com.